THE BARD'S BALLAD

Praise for C.T. Carey

<u>For The Bard's Ballad</u>
"… mix of everything that is wonderful… excellent storyline, great characters, and exciting adventure and I recommend that everyone out there grab their copy and get reading."
-Reader Views, *Five Star Review*

<u>For Model Number Unknown</u>
"The suspense, intensity, and complexity of a tangled tale… make for a pleasurable read. Simply written and persuasively told, this is a mystery novel you can't ignore."
-Reader Views, *Five Star Review*

THE BARD'S BALLAD

C.T. CAREY

ISBN: 978-1-962715-35-5

This book is for all the people who told me that I can. You know who you are, and I can't love or appreciate you more.

This is also for Em. You can do great things little girl.

Works by C.T. Carey

<u>Standalone Novels</u>

Model Number Unknown

<u>Series</u>

The Cantatio Tales

The Bard's Ballad

<u>Children's Series</u>

Jack B. Nymble Mysteries

The Mystery of the Missing Shoe

The Mystery of the Salted Tea

The Mystery of the Lost Little Pig

The Mystery of the Stolen Cake

"Music has the power of producing a certain effect on the moral character of the soul, and if it has the power to do this, it is clear that the young must be directed to music and must be educated in it."

-Aristotle

PROLOGUE

istory is what defines us. When we forget our history, we forget a part of who we are. That is why I have begun to record each event that happens to me. Now, I know that no one wants to read the story of someone they haven't met, so I should probably start by introducing myself.

My name is Clef—Clef Cantatio. Many people would consider me to be a minstrel. However, I find the term bard to be more appropriate. Most of the population considers these words to be synonymous, but they could not be more different.

A minstrel is someone that *tells* history through song, while a bard is someone that *makes* history through it. I have spent the better part of my life learning to weave spells and incantations into my words and songs.

You may find it fascinating to learn that it's not actually the words that hold magic. Moreover, I don't have the magic myself either. Rather, the magic comes from a connection that I have with them. If I sing the wrong words or am off-key, nothing will happen. But even if another person sang the song perfectly, they could do nothing unless they were a bard. Bards don't always have to use songs though, we can also use just a single word or command, though these spells are simpler and not nearly as intricate. Songs are where our real power comes from.

It may, in fact, surprise you to know that *most* music has magic in it. Those feelings of joy or sadness you get from hearing a specific song are more than what you may think. Most bards discover their powers by accident. They begin to notice things happen, or people start to behave differently. Or perhaps a kind elder instructs them in their abilities.

On the other hand, wizards and mages have to have some type of focus that allows them to cast their spells. For some, it's a staff or a wand, but others may have more unique items like teeth or cards.

Bards do traditionally have an instrument they use—I personally favor the lute—but this isn't *really* a focus, rather, it enhances our powers. We can still cast our spells without an instrument, it's just *much* harder. Bards are quite unique in the world of magic. Even I don't understand every aspect of our powers yet. But I'm sure you'll come to understand us better shortly.

Bards are also very charismatic. I can oftentimes charm an innkeeper into a free room, or a barmaid into a free drink without any magic at all. Though that may also be due to my extreme good looks or humbleness.

But this isn't the story of bards. It's the story of me.

There are many places our story could begin. Such as the forest I was raised in. The streets I lived on. Or even the cottage I was trained in.

But I think our story shall start in a tavern known as the *Brazen Unicorn*. It's just like any other tavern you would come across in your travels, I suppose. There are a few tables with chairs around them spread out through the main room, with a bar to one side. While this may be just like any other tavern you've seen, it's what's unseen that makes this one special to me. This is because the *Brazen Unicorn* is my home. Well—not actually the tavern itself, but there are three rooms above it, and one of them is mine.

My room isn't anything special. There is an old lumpy bed in one corner. It wasn't comfortable at all when I first came here, but after a few months of sleeping on it, it became comforting and brought the feeling of safety.

On the opposite wall, there is a desk with an old stool. The only light in the room comes from the soothing glow of my hurricane lamp. Next to the desk sits an old wardrobe. This wardrobe is where I keep my few belongings. I could barely fill a quarter of it. On the wall next to the old wardrobe hangs a beautiful lute—*my* beautiful lute.

I work at this tavern as a performer, it doesn't pay well, but I receive room and board. I don't have to work in the morning or early evening, but I perform for the patrons later at night. My small earnings grow primarily from tips. Though I must admit, I sometimes charm the patrons into giving a tad more. Don't judge me. It's not like I'm making them sign their soul over to me. I just convince them to provide me with a few extra coins, which they likely would have spent on mead anyways.

Even though it isn't the most glamorous lifestyle, it is a life of luxury compared to my past. I didn't have what one could call the ideal childhood.

My mother was a human, while my father, an elf, was from a high elven clan. This led to me constantly feeling left out and like I never really belonged anywhere. Humans always thought I had too pointed of ears, and the elves thought they were too round. Neither of the groups would accept me as one of their own. Even my own family abandoned me. It left me feeling like I needed to find a place to fit in. But when I was very young, I decided that I was going to make my own path, my own destiny. I no longer cared about fitting in, I wanted to be my own person.

I wasn't exactly looking for a family, but that was precisely what I found. First, there was *her*. The most important person in my life. It still pains me every day to think about her.

Then there were the others at the *Brazen Unicorn*—the barkeep Brand Brewster and the barmaid Tillie Bennett.

Even though we didn't spend much time together away from the *Brazen Unicorn*, they were still like a family to me.

Most recently, though, there have been the people I work with. No, I don't mean just the people at the *Brazen Unicorn*. I have yet to mention another part of my life that very few people know of. While the *Brazen Unicorn* keeps me sheltered and fed, my other job is a way to push myself to the limits of my strength and endurance.

It allows me to use my talents as a bard for more than a few extra coins each night. Let me fill you in a bit more.

But first, I must warn you, don't go spreading any of this around. This is privileged information about my life. Besides, even if you do speak of it, I could just charm whoever you tell into forgetting.

I work for The Lily, a secret organization that employs teams of fighters. These teams are then hired out to save others in crisis. There are dozens, if not hundreds, of Lily agents. There could be one in your family you don't know about. For all *I* know, you could be one yourself. Even a member such as myself doesn't know everyone.

The Lily places members onto teams with others who will complement their skills. Traditionally, there is at least one magic wielder, another with brute strength, and—when possible—they have a healer.

The team I am a part of is made up of the most well-trained, strongest members. This means we are the most desired team. The Lily sends us on only the most perilous adventures, trying to prevent our death from something simple like a harpy or a drunken satyr.

We are only tasked with the most demanding jobs, with the highest risk of death. It should be noted that while our team has been together for a handful of years, we have had no fatal injuries—knock on wood. This allows us to proudly say that we have the highest rate of survival. Not a single other team can claim that. It is a rarity for a member to last for more than a handful of missions.

My team consists of five members: two magic wielders, a healer, a fighter, and a—well—I don't really know what he is. While all of us love being an agent for the Lily, we all have other jobs as well—similar to my job at the *Brazen Unicorn.* That way we can do what we love, while also having a roof over our heads. While the Lily pays decently, we are more often compensated with items and special perks, rather than gold.

First, there is me, the appointed leader of the group, and I swear to you, there was no magic involved in that decision. Okay—maybe I charmed them a little bit. But in my opinion, I am by far the most qualified of them. And—as I've said— I'm incredibly humble—clearly leadership material.

Anyways, the member of our team that I'm closest to is a woman named Bonneville Arroway. Though most of the people that know her just call her Bon-Bon. But let me tell you, she isn't nearly as dainty as her nickname sounds.

Bonneville is—well—how do I say it. A free spirit. She is tall, nearly as tall as me, and that's surprising given that I tower several inches over six feet.

She has waist-length blonde hair, which she typically ties up when in battle. She appears to be in her thirties, but from the wisdom she gives and the look in her eyes, I really couldn't tell you what her actual age is… and it's not something you ask a lady, and definitely not something you ask a warrior.

Bon-Bon has practically two different personalities. Out of battle, she is one of the most cheerful and personable people you'll ever meet. The moment we enter a town, she immediately becomes friends with at least five people and often finds a stray animal she takes in and cares for, always finding the stray an owner before we leave. She truly tries to avoid conflict as much as possible, but she will not back down when it is unavoidable. But when battle is inevitable, she becomes a very different person.

While she is not a magic wielder, I have seen her accomplish remarkable feats. Once, I saw a spear fly and hit her chest, and—bracing myself for the worst—I was surprised when it bounced off her like a tack. It hit the ground, and I could see that the end of the spear point was broken off.

I asked her how she did this, but she didn't seem to be willing to tell me—or she didn't know. I pity the soul that gets on her bad side. When not defeating her foes in battle, Bonneville works as a guard for a noble family.

The next member of our team is Roscoe Cobbletoss. I speak from experience, Cobbletoss is more than just his last name. I'm telling you, don't mention it to him, or you will find out why people call him that. Roscoe is one of the smallest people I have ever met, barely reaching my waist. Yet he is also the loudest person I have ever met, even louder than a flock of harpies. What he lacks in size, he makes up for in personality and volume.

While Roscoe does pack a strong punch, he is also precious to our team because of his religious background.

Roscoe was raised very strongly in the church, specifically under the goddess Anar. Anar—according to Roscoe—is the goddess of life and nature. Every morning you will find him praying and devoting himself to her in worship. His theological knowledge does not end with Anar. You could ask him about any god, be it dwarven, elven, or fae, and he could tell you just about anything you would like to know. He spends all his time away from the Lily as a cleric in one of Anar's temples.

His devotion to Anar has given him the ability to communicate and pray with her in times of severe distress. She often grants him the ability to rescue and heal other living beings as she so chooses.

The fourth member of our team is Finnon Aleslosh. While he is also a magic wielder, we use magic very differently. He prefers evocations, while I favor charms.

More interestingly than his preferred style of magic is the fact that he and Roscoe are half-brothers. You can find many similarities in them, such as their diminutive stature. Finnon is just as small as Roscoe, and still just as loud.

Like Roscoe, his surname is more than just a name, rather a title he has earned. I have seen him drink more ale than any full-sized man I've ever met, and—working in a tavern—I have seen men who can consume a *lot*.

I may not know much about Finnon and his personal history, other than he is a professor at a college, and he is an impressive mage. He has a few select spells that are very strong, traditionally elemental, working primarily with fire and earth. His choice of magical focus is a bag of small stones, which is quite unorthodox, but they are powerful and have saved us from many dire situations. When he uses them, ancient runes matching the element of choice glow on them. He can manipulate these elements any way that he wants, such as a volcanic explosion from the ground or making a canyon appear where there had been flat ground.

I personally favor my charms and enchantments, I have never been one for large and explosive spells, but Finnon seems to do just fine with them.

The final member of our team is truly a frightening one. He is called Kriv Mystan. Something everyone can plainly see when meeting Kriv is that he isn't quite human. His body is mainly that of a human—his posture, torso, legs, arms. Everything except that he is nearly eight feet tall, he has blue scales, a long tail, and a draconic head. Kriv is part dragon.

Now, you may wonder why and how he looks like this. Well, his father was a human, while his mother was a dragon. Please, don't ask me how. I honestly don't know and am too scared to ask. He mentioned something about a curse, but Kriv doesn't talk much.

Because of his armor-like scales, he doesn't actually need to wear clothing. Fortunately, he traditionally wears a loincloth, which the team is very grateful for.

While having a dragon on the team may sound great, there is a downside. Kriv doesn't always have the highest of morals—as in—he has nearly no standard of right and wrong. Once when we were on a mission, I saw him swindle an old lady out of gold. I tried convincing him to give it back, but he just stared at me. His solid black eyes sent a chill down my spine. I believe his time away from the Lily is filled with thievery and crime.

All in all, we work well as a team. There is a natural brotherly feud between Roscoe and Finnon. And Kriv and I have never really seen eye to eye. But as a whole, the team works very well together. Even when the missions don't go as expected.

CHAPTER ONE

The Message

It was a day just like any other at the *Brazen Unicorn*. I had just finished my performance for the night. It was a slow song, just my lute, no words. I always played this song at the end of the night. The patrons had come to recognize it, and the ones that were still coherent began to grumble. I finished playing an hour or so before the tavern closed, but they still knew they would have to leave.

I let the last note of the song ring out and then stood up from my wooden stool. I now got a chance to look out into the tavern and saw a very familiar scene. There were a half-dozen intoxicated men, barely able to remain seated in their chairs. Seated near them were women who were clearly not at the tavern for the drinks, but for my enchanting songs. The ladies all had piles of uneaten food and mugs of ale left untouched.

I don't know if it's my sandy blonde hair or shockingly blue eyes. Maybe it is my enchanting singing voice or my muscular body. Or better yet, perhaps it was just my dashingly good looks. But whatever it was, something simply made women fawn over me. But I never paid them any attention.

Every night was the same thing. The women would try to flirt with me, and I was just lucky that their husbands were too drunk to realize what was happening, or I would have dealt with many black eyes.

Tonight, there were three women trying particularly hard to gain my attention. I ignored them as I grabbed the tin cup I collected tips in. I shook it, happily realizing that I likely had enough money to replace my tattered clothes.

Typically, my attire consists of a stark white tunic and a leather-laced vest. I had mid-calf brown leather boots matched with black trousers. When it became the colder winter months, I would add a dark-green wool cloak to the attire. As of now, my cloak was torn on the bottom, becoming more and more frayed every day. The boots had holes in the sole, and my blouse was old and stained. In addition, I could no longer lace my vest, as the cord that held it closed had snapped.

Being a performer, the first thing people see is my clothing. I always need to look my best. I had been wanting to replace the clothes for a while, but I hadn't collected enough money. I had another outfit stashed away in my cupboard, but it was even more shredded and stained than my current one, and there was no way that I could ever wear it in public.

I stepped down from the make-shift stage, which was really just some old crates stacked together in a corner. As I began walking through the tavern to the stairs, I felt someone grab my bicep and squeeze. When I turned, I saw it was one of the women who'd been fixated on me.

"That was some great playing tonight, Clef." She had dark hair falling in ringlets around her face, which was caked heavily in rouge. She regularly came to the bar, and—I'll tell you—she wasn't coming for the food or drinks.

I have no idea what her name is, but clearly, she knows mine. Looking over her shoulder, I saw the man she had been with was passed out on the table with food on his face and spilled ale on his shirt.

"Uh, thanks." I gently pulled my arm out of her grip and kept walking to the stairs.

"I'll be here again tomorrow, Clef," she called after me, waving her hand. As she said this, the two other women with her also called after me, trying to gain my attention. I just turned away from them wordlessly.

Brand was just bringing out a tray of food as this happened. I made eye contact with him and smirked, rolling my eyes. He laughed and shrugged his shoulders as if to say, "What can you do?"

Finally, I made it up the stairs to my room without any issues. I took off my boots and threw them in a corner, glad to know I wouldn't need to wear them much longer. Taking my vest off as well, it got hung in the wardrobe. Once that was done, I sat at my desk, counting out the tips. It was more than I usually got, and along with my small stash of money, I would be able to replace my boots, tunic, pants, and vest. I might even be able to get a warmer cloak. I smiled at the thought, it was getting to be the winter months, and it would be nice to spend them warm.

My thoughts of warmth were rudely interrupted by the sound of someone knocking at my door.

Sighing, I responded, "I'm sorry, I'll be performing again tomorrow. We can talk then." I stood to make sure I had locked the door. I could only assume that it was the brunette or one of her friends following me. This wouldn't be the first time I had that happen. I had to ask Brand to add a lock to my door when one woman barged in after my show, trying to kiss me—and that was all without a charming spell.

I told you, wickedly handsome—and humble. I had almost every woman in this town fawning over me on a regular basis. None of them meant anything to me though. There was no one that could compare to *her* beauty. She was the love of my life, but it had been so long since I had seen her.

"It's Tillie," her voice was demure and timid. She was sweet, around eighteen, a couple of years younger than me. She had left home when she was very young. Her mother and father had been drunkards. She was desperate to find a better life. I found it very ironic that she decided to work in a bar to get away from drunks. I don't know if she noticed the irony as well.

"Oh, well, then come in," I replied, unlocking the door, and opening it for her. She stepped through, but stopped, standing awkwardly in the opening, not looking up at me. She had made her affections for me very clear when I first came to the *Brazen Unicorn*. But to me, she was just like a sister and nothing more. Since then, there has been an air of awkwardness between us. I would always have a brotherly love for her though. Since my parents had abandoned me, I treasured these friends that had become my family.

"Come on, sit down," I gestured for her to sit on the one stool in my room. "No need for shyness between us." I sat down on the edge of the bed. It creaked as I sat, and I sunk down farther into the mattress than comfortable. I shifted a foot to the left and found no more comfort available. Finally,

I tried tucking one leg up under the other. It helped a little but not much.

Tillie sat down on the stool, though she still wouldn't look at me. She was petite, with a thin, long face, which was framed by pale brown hair that cascaded past her shoulders. She was wearing her usual barmaid attire—a white blouse with oversized shoulders and a long green skirt. Over this, Tillie wore a brown corset, and around her waist was a white apron. Her clothes were wet in some places, and the white blouse and apron were stained yellow in large splashes. Based on the scent of alcohol, I assumed it was from the beer, ale, and other assortments of liquors that had been spilled on her.

She sat on the stool, twisting the ends of her apron between her fingers mindlessly. I saw a look of nervousness in her eyes, like she had something to say, but she couldn't bring herself to voice it. There were several moments of silence, to the point where it would have been uncomfortable if we didn't know each other so well.

I was about to ask her what she needed to say, but when I opened my mouth, she said, "I'm going to miss you, Clef."

"I'll miss you too, Tillie." Even though I didn't have romantic feelings towards her, she was still very dear to me. Suddenly, I realized what she had said. I wasn't aware Tillie had a trip planned. "Wait, where are you going?"

"I'm not going anywhere. You are," she said with a rolling laugh.

"Huh, am I getting fired? What am I getting fired for? Why am I leaving? It's not like I stole anything. I admit, I did sneak that one glass of mead, but I mean, I can get those for free anyway." Surprisingly, despite my magic coming from words, when I get nervous, I tend to ramble. Fortunately, Tillie cut me off before I revealed any more incriminating evidence against myself.

"No, you're not getting fired," she laughed again. It was a kind laugh. Even though she grew up abused as well, she still had a lovely joy in her laughter. "You'll be back," she pulled a rolled piece of parchment out of her apron. She handed it over to me. I looked down at the scroll and saw it fastened with a thin yellow ribbon. Turning the scroll over, I found that it was sealed with a glob of white wax. On a closer inspection, it revealed the wax seal had a lily emblazoned on it.

"Already?" I said, annoyed. "I had to go take care of that bridge troll only a month ago." Typically, I would get called out by the Lily only every few months. Never this close together. Given my team's experience, we were only used in the direst of situations.

"Please be careful, Clef. I don't want to see you get hurt again." About six months ago—on one of the Lily missions—I wound up with a twisted ankle and broken toe. It was complicated. There was a four-eyed ogre, a centaur, and three turkeys. Long story short, I had a limp for a solid week, and a bruise for a week after that.

"I promise I will," I don't make a habit of lying, only when I need to… and now I needed to. I never really could be careful. The point of the Lily was to take risks and help people. I nearly always came back with some sort of injury. That wasn't something Tillie needed to concern herself with.

Tillie then stood up and walked over to me. She leaned down and kissed me on the cheek. Softly she said, "I know you can't promise that, but try to be safe." She walked to the door and gripped the handle, but stopped before turning it.

"Oh, also, there was a package left for you. Brand will bring it up soon." Tillie then opened the door, but before she left, stopped in the doorway as if she was going to say something, though stayed silent and instead walked out the door with a heavy sigh.

Now that she was gone, I was able to read the parchment. I took a deep breath and then broke the wax seal on it. I unrolled the parchment and found a single word written in a familiar script.

Farhold

After reading it, I realized that I had spoken aloud. This was how the Lily always worked. We would be sent a message with the name of a town on it. Once we arrived there, we would meet with the rest of our team and receive our mission.

We were never told how we would meet the rest of our team. Instead, we had to figure out some sort of clue, typically involving lilies.

I walked over to the dresser in my room and opened it. I then reached down and pulled up the bottom of it. This was something that I had fashioned myself. It's not that I didn't trust Brand and Tillie, but the Lily was very private, and I needed to keep that part of my life secretive. I told Brand and

Tillie as much as I could. But if the Lily knew even some of what I had revealed, they would have my hide.

Out of the hidden compartment I pulled a large sack. Before I opened it though, I locked the door to my room and closed the shutters of my window. Out of a drawer of my desk, I pulled a large map of the region. Laying it out, I searched for Farhold. The *Brazen Unicorn* was in Evenglade, a small town in the forested part of the kingdom.

The kingdom—called Pulchala—was one that many foreigners came to. It was ruled by King Richard, a fair and just ruler, and Queen Rowena, a beautiful, gracious, and compassionate woman. To the north, was the forested region, and to the south, a dry desert.

Finally, I found Farhold. It was nearly three days east of Evenglade. As I finished rolling up the map, I heard another knock on the door, this one much louder and stronger than Tillie's.

"Clef, it's Brand," his voice was deep. If he were a singer, he would surely be a bass. "I know you are probably getting ready right now, so I'll just leave this package here. But make sure to tell me before you leave. I have something else for you… from me." Brand was in his mid-thirties. He had inherited the *Brazen Unicorn* from his father, who had gotten it from his father, and so on. He cared greatly about his work.

I was fortunate that Brand was so understanding of my work with the Lily. He never pried more information out of me than I was willing to give. The most significant benefit was that he would let me leave at a moment's notice, and he even guaranteed me a job upon my return. In fact, Brand was the one who encouraged me to join the Lily.

In addition to that, every time I left, Brand would give me several days' rations. He really was like the brother I never had. I knew that he really cared about me. In just the same way, I cared about him as well. I would do anything to protect him and the *Brazen Unicorn*, and he knew that. A few years ago, there was a group of thieves that tried robbing him. They had grabbed Tillie, holding a knife to her throat, demanding the gold in the till box. I quickly stepped in, and with some well-chosen words, and a few spells, they— well—let's just say those men won't be coming back to this tavern again.

I heard Brand's footsteps retreat down the stairs. Once I had the map put away, I unlocked the door and grabbed the package. It was a small bundle wrapped in brown fabric, tied together with a brown leather cord. I tossed it down on the bed, and began to open it.

The Lily did this occasionally. They would send some random items to us along with the parchment telling us where to go. Each of us would receive something best suited for our skillset. If I received a pan flute, then Bon-Bon would get a glaive. If Roscoe got a battle-axe, then Kriv would get… well, I don't really know what Kriv would get. I rarely saw him with anything other than his loincloth, a sword, and stolen goods.

I finished untying the cord and unfolded the fabric. I discovered that this time they had sent me a new set of clothes. Several missions ago, we encountered a dragon. My clothes had been burned up by its breath. I had suffered second-degree burns over my whole body. Fortunately, after a prayer from Roscoe, and some divine intervention—literally—the burns turned into a lovely tan. Unfortunately, I had to spend the rest of the mission wearing Kriv's spare loincloth. Typically, I prefer much more coverage than a loincloth can provide, but it was better than the alternative.

It seemed that the Lily was trying to make up for this endeavor.

I pulled out the new clothes and inspected them. Style and cut-wise, it matched my current clothes. I was always impressed by how much the Lily knew about our personal lives. Other than color, it was a replica of my current tattered attire. However, these clothes were in better condition, of course.

The cloak was a dark grey with an oversized hood. Along the hem was a string of embroidered yellow lilies. There was a light-yellow tunic with a black vest to go along with it. They sent a new pair of boots, also black. Finally, I found dark grey trousers. I was grateful for the new attire, as it meant the gold I had been saving could go towards other needs. I personally wouldn't have chosen the black and yellow combination, but the thought of dry feet again quickly sent any ungratefulness from my mind.

I was finally able to inspect the items in my personal pack. First, I pulled out a black belt with a loop on the left hip. Into the loop, I would slide a silver rapier. I always prefer to use magic when I can, but strangely there are some creatures that are immune to charms like mine, so I like to prepare for the worst. I always favored this thin-bladed weapon when it did come to combat, though, as it was effective and easy to use. I could quickly parry a swing and then slash back at the attacker in a single stroke.

I had a few other weapons as well that I kept only for emergencies. I have a short sword tucked away on the side of my pack. I also had a dagger that I kept in my boot, in case something extremely unexpected happened. This dagger came in handy when a trio of hags decided Bonneville and I would make an excellent appetizer to a dinner of two small men and a dragon-man.

The final item that I pulled out of the sack was tiny compared to the others. But it was the most essential item a Lily member could have.

It was a brooch, about the length of my thumb, and just as wide. It's in the shape of a lily and painted as such. This was the mark of a Lily agent. Every member received one. It was our sign so that we could receive information when needed. It also ensured that we could find our teammates if one had died and needed to be replaced or if you were being reassigned. Though I've been working with my team for so long, it would be hard to forget them.

I reopened my window and looked out. It was late, likely nearing around one in the morning. I decided that I would get a few hours of sleep and leave early the next day. But first, I went to see what Brand had for me.

CHAPTER TWO

The Brazen Unicorn

The bar closed at midnight, so I was sure he was already in his room. I went out into the hallway. Across from my room was Tillie's, and at the end of the hallway was Brand's. I went down to his room and found that the door was already partially open. As a courtesy, I knocked on the door and—after getting a grunt of approval—pushed it the rest of the way until I could walk in.

Brand was sitting at his desk, staring down at nothing. He was a healthy man. Even through his dark blue tunic and black trousers, you could tell that he had a muscular build. Around his waist was a thick oversized leather belt with a large silver buckle in the front.

I cleared my throat. "Hey Brand, you said you wanted to see me." Lifting his head, he looked at me. He looked tired. He worked himself harder than he should every day to try and keep the tavern running.

"I did. Come with me." Brand led me out the door of his room and down the stairs. It was always strange seeing the tavern without patrons. Even in the morning, there were generally at least a few early-morning drinkers there. But now, it was completely quiet and empty. It gave off almost an eerie feeling, like something was missing.

Brand seemed to be thinking of something else while he did everything, and his eyes seemed out of focus. He went behind the bar and pulled a platter out from under it. I saw a large loaf of dark bread with several pieces of dried meat on it. There were also two waterskins. I knew that one of them would be filled with water, and the other with mead. After laying the tray on the counter, he pulled a leather pouch tied closed with a leather cord from behind the bar, but he kept it in his hand, not putting it down.

He paused for a moment and stared at me with very little emotion on his face. Finally, he said, "I'm worried about the tavern Clef. I'm nearly out of money. I don't know how much longer I can keep the tavern open."

"I should only be gone for about a week, a couple at the most," I said, trying to comfort him. "When I get back, we can figure something out. We always do."

"I don't know if it will even last that long…" He started talking more to himself, "Five generations of Brewsters, and it's under my watch that the Brazen Unicorn closes down." His face scrunched up, and I now realized that the tiredness I thought I had seen on his face earlier had actually been sadness. He had been crying before I went to talk to him. I thought back through my years knowing him and realized I don't think I had ever seen him cry.

This tavern meant a lot to Brand, and seeing him upset like this made me emotional myself. I couldn't imagine what it would be like to come back to not have a job… to not have a home. And I couldn't even imagine how Brand felt. I knew this place meant even more to him than it ever could to me. He had been raised here. His first steps had been right in this bar.

He started talking to me again. "I haven't told Tillie yet, her poor heart couldn't take it, but I thought you should know, especially given there might not be a tavern for you to come back to. I also wanted to give you your next few weeks of pay, just in case you come back to town without a job." He tossed the bag towards me, and I found that it was filled with gold coins. It was more money than I have had in a long time. I had to stop myself from counting out the money right there, with much difficulty, I might add. I also noticed that it was much more than several weeks' pay, just by looking at it.

I pushed the gold back towards him, "Brand, you know I can't take this. If the place is running low on money, you should keep this. I'll take my money when I get back."

"Clef, please," he looked at me, and I could tell from his face that he needed me to take the money, or else I would be taking his pride. "This place means everything to me, and I must not have any other guilt on my mind if this place does close. I hope that none of this is necessary, but if it is, I need to do this."

"I understand, but if I am even going to think of accepting this, then you need to do something for me." He looked at me and nodded his head, telling me to go on. "I want one more drink," I said with a smile.

He looked up from the bar, and I could see a faint smirk on his lips. He nodded to a table in the corner. I walked to it, flipping the chairs off the table and setting them on the floor. Brand picked up two tankards from the bar and filled them with mead. He walked over to the table I was at and sat down, placing one of the tankards in front of me and taking the other for himself. We lifted the cups and tapped them together, and we took a long drink. Brand's mead was the best around. It had a sweet taste with the faintest hint of honey in it. I have traveled all around the kingdom, and I have never tasted mead anywhere as good as his. I guess that's what happens when several generations of brewers work on a recipe

Brand and I didn't say anything to each other, but just being there for each other was more than enough. We sat there for about an hour, even after we had finished our drinks. Eventually, we both got up from the table and went back upstairs. I stopped at the bar on the way to grab the tray of food and pocket the money before going back to my room.

Brand was still in the hall when I got up the stairs. We looked at each other, and I nodded my head at him before we closed our doors.

After closing the door, I cleared off my bed and collapsed on it, so exhausted I didn't even take my clothes off.

CHAPTER THREE

The Last Meal

I woke up early in the morning. The sun had just barely begun to rise. It could be seen as an orange haze on the horizon.

I quickly took off my old clothes, leaving them nicely folded on my desk. I put on the new Lily clothing. Fastening the belt around my waist, I then slid the rapier into its loop. Taking the meat and bread, I wrapped it up in the fabric my clothes had come in, and I slid it into my pack. Grabbing the lily brooch, I fastened it to the lapel of my new vest.

I grabbed my lute from its hook on the wall. The last thing I did was take a simple silver necklace with a blue gem out of a drawer in my desk. I strapped the lute to the side of my pack, then fastened the necklace chain around my throat, tucking the gem into my shirt. The cold blue stone on my chest gave me a sense of ease and comfort. Now that everything was prepared, I was ready to leave for Farhold.

I walked out of the room, wondering when I would see it again and, more importantly—*if* I would. I gave it one more good look around, then closed the door, locking it with my key on the way out.

Before going downstairs, I stopped at Brand's room. I knew that he would already be down in the tavern serving the early morning patrons. Walking to his desk, I took a piece of parchment from it and wrote a note on it.

BRAND,
    THIS MONEY IS MORE IMPORTANT FOR YOU TO HAVE FOR THE BRAZEN UNICORN. THINK OF THIS MONEY, NOT AS THE MONEY YOU GAVE ME, BUT AS AN EXTREMELY EARLY BIRTHDAY GIFT.
    I WILL BE BACK SOON. YOU CAN PAY ME BACK THEN, I WOULD RATHER NOT HAVE MONEY THAN SEE THIS PLACE CLOSE DOWN.
    YOU DO NOT NEED TO TELL TILLIE ABOUT THIS. THIS CAN STAY BETWEEN JUST US.
    SEE YOU SOON,
    — CLEF C.

I took the note and the pouch of gold he had given me last night and placed them on his bed.

I left his room, closed the door as quietly as possible, and headed towards the stairs. I stopped for a moment next to my door. It was always hard going, never knowing what I was in for. As I started walking towards the stairs, Tillie came out of her room. We both stopped and looked at each other. I gestured for her to go first, myself following close behind.

When I got down to the tavern, I saw that only the regulars were there, and they were already drunk. There weren't any women there yet. They wouldn't come until the evening when I was supposed to perform. I wondered how they would react when they discovered I wouldn't be there for them to watch.

I looked over to Brand, who was preparing for the larger number of patrons that would come later in the day.

I saw that he had recovered from last night somewhat, though he was wearing the same tunic and trousers, which were thoroughly wrinkled as if he had slept in them. I went to the bar, sitting on a stool across from Brand.

"Hey, you mind if I get some breakfast before I leave?" I asked, knowing he wouldn't care. He nodded and placed a plate in front of me. It had a hunk of dark bread on it, a fillet of fish, and some cheese. He also set a mug of ale in front of me.

I sat there enjoying the breakfast, not knowing when I would have a full meal again. I was savoring the fish—which was perfectly seasoned—when Tillie walked over and spoke to Brand. "Brand. Can I have that book you borrowed back?"

"Oh, yeah, it's up in my room. I'll go grab it." I looked up quickly, realizing that meant he would find the money and note. I stood up from the stool, almost knocking it over in the process. I blocked Brand from walking out from the bar. He looked at me as though I had lost my mind, but I knew I couldn't let him find the money, at least not before I left, or he would be furious.

"Uh, I can grab that for you. You have all these customers that you need to take care of. You wouldn't want to leave them all for Tillie." He looked around. There were only four customers in the *Brazen Unicorn*, one of which was passed out drunk. There was a silence cut short by a loud snore from the unconscious man. Just the universe trying to prove me wrong.

He replied slowly, sounding confused, "I think Tillie can handle it. And if not, I'm sure you'll chip in." He shouldered past me and went up the stairs. I went back to my stool and continued eating. There was nothing that I could do now. Brand would find the note with the money, and he would be livid about it. Now I just had to sit and wait for the lecture.

Several long moments later, Brand came back down the stairs holding a book in his left hand. He walked over to Tillie and handed it to her. They exchanged a few words, though I couldn't hear what they were saying.

Brand then walked over to me, staring straight into my soul the entire way. He came back to the bar, took my mug, refilling it with more ale. Looking up, he simply said, "Thank you." I could see that what I had done meant a lot to him. Brand doesn't show emotions often, but I had known him long enough to be able to read them when he did.

"You're welcome. This place means almost as much to me as it does to you. This tavern is like a home to me. And you're like a brother, and that really means something."

"I know it does…" He paused as if he wanted to say more, "and by the way, nice outfit. You look like a honey-bee." I saw him laugh under his breath. If something came out of this outfit, at least it was able to bring a bit of joy to Brand.

"Thanks. Not my idea of stylish, just one of the perks of working for the Lily," I replied with a foolish grin. I had to laugh myself. I mean, who thought that pale yellow and black clothing was a good idea. I finished up the rest of my meal and got up to go. I felt bad leaving. I thought that I should stay and help Brand save the tavern, but I also knew I had a duty to the Lily. In the end, I knew I had to leave.

I grabbed my pack from the stool next to me and put it on my back.

Shaking hands with Brand and smiling, I said, "I expect my job when I get back, don't go hiring some new guy." He laughed again. Sometimes humor is the best solution for a bad day. Luckily, comedy has always been one of my talents— or, at least—I like to think it is. My friends may say otherwise.

I walked over to Tillie and gave her a hug, and I said, "I'll see you in a bit." I looked at her and saw a single tear run down her cheek. She wiped it away with her finger and walked away to the bar. I had a feeling Brand hadn't told her the news yet, and I knew that wasn't my place. I left the tavern, hoping that it would still be there when I got back.

Out on the street, I took a final look at the sign hanging out front. It was a simple metal sheet in the shape of a unicorn. There were no words on it, just the outline.

With that, I started walking down the street on my way to Farhold.

CHAPTER FOUR

The Stables

I went about a mile down the road from the tavern. I had traveled this road often, but had never dealt with such conflicting emotions. Fear, regret, excitement, and even hopefulness. I was lost in my thoughts, and it took me a moment to realize how early it still was.

The sun had just barely broken past the horizon. I assumed that it was around six o'clock in the morning.

I realized that I had only gotten a couple of hours of sleep last night, but I didn't feel an ounce of tiredness. Adventure is funny like that. It gives you energy and awareness when you least expect it.

I walked through Evenglade, down the familiar city road, seeing shops opening for the day. Wives were beginning to hang out and beat their laundry for the day, keeping a careful eye on their children who played on the dirt trail. I was nearing the end of the town, but stopped, knowing that I had one more stop I wanted to make.

I came to the local stables. They were run by a man named Langston, who wasn't the kindest of men. He consistently tried to swindle people out of their hard-earned money, making them pay more than they should have to pay for a horse or gear. I had paid exorbitant prices for a steed too many times to count.

I made a habit of renting one of his horses during my more extended travels like this. I had never out-right bought a horse as I didn't have the space or time to care for one.

I went into the stables and found that there were only a few horses there. Most of them seemed to be overworked and tired, much too old to be worth the high prices Langston would charge. I was inspecting the one horse that seemed capable of making the trip I had ahead of me, when one of the stable boys came out. I recognized him as one of the newer workers. He was short and pretty scrawny. His black hair was cut rough and choppy, as if a family member had done it for him. His skin was deeply tanned, given that he worked outside most of the time. He was pretty easy to get along with, though. I knew his mother well. She was a friend of Brand. I knew the boy's name to be Brenner.

"Hey Brenner, where's Langston?"

"He isn't at work yet. He makes us stable boys work the early morning shift. He'll be in later in the afternoon." He was clearly trying to hide his annoyance about Langston, but I noticed a hit of disgust. "What can I get for you today?"

"I've got a pretty long trip ahead of me. I think this one looks up for the journey." The horse was almost entirely white, with some spots of chestnut brown across him. His tail and mane were also a chestnut color. He seemed very active, constantly kicking his legs around and rooting around in his pen. "What's his name?"

"Eques… though not many people can ride him. He is rowdy and uncooperative. Of course, don't tell Langston I told you that," I nodded my head in agreement. "Though if you want to give him a shot, it would be ten gold coins per day or a hundred to buy him." I counted out the money I had. I knew I would have to buy him. It was going to be at least six days of travel, along with several just to do the mission. I shook my head as I counted out the money, the cost of the horse was nearly all of the gold that I had, but I didn't have a choice.

"Alright, I'll buy him, but how about you throw in a bridle and saddle, along with two weeks of feed." I decided not to use any charms this time. I could tell that Brenner just needed to make some money for his poor family.

His mother was a seamstress, working when jobs were available, and trying to raise six children, all below the age of twelve. His father had died in the Ogre Wars, and Brenner was trying to help his family as much as he could, being the eldest.

"Uh, I don't know how much Langston will like that. You know he's a stickler for money. He doesn't like me giving things out for free."

"Yeah, but he's not here, and what he doesn't know won't hurt him." I knew Langston wouldn't actually care if a few items were missing. He was usually drunk and probably wouldn't even notice.

"Yeah, fine, you just have to promise not to tell anyone." He walked to the back of the stables and grabbed a set of gear from the wall. They were simple ones, and they looked well-worn. He went to put them on Eques.

"Are those really the best ones you have?" It's not like I was taking anything from Brenner, just from Langston. And I *hated* Langston with a passion. Along with anyone who abused their position of authority over those below them, for that matter.

"Well, uh yeah, but those are one of the premium sets…" I looked at the kid and raised my eyebrow. He walked back to the wall and got down a different set of gear.

It was beautiful. It consisted of light brown leather that had silver brackets running all along it. Between each bracket, there was a red gem embedded in the leather. I couldn't tell if they were a ruby or a garnet. The skirt of the saddle was a hand-woven red fabric with a black floral pattern embroidered into it. Brenner started fastening the gear onto the horse.

"That one will be perfect," I said brightly. Brenner then went and grabbed a leather pack off the wall. He proceeded to fill it with hay, alfalfa, and an assortment of other plants from a pile in the corner.

I could tell he was cramming as much into the pack as possible. While he was doing that, I began to inspect the horse's saddle. I found that on each side of it, there was a metal hook. I took my pack off my back and hung it from the saddle. Brenner finished packing up the feed and strapped it to the other side of the saddle. The pack was nearly busting at the seams, and straw was sticking out the top.

"Here you go, Clef. And take a few of these too." He handed me half a dozen red apples. "When he gets hard to control, these will typically calm him down." I took them, adding them to my rations.

"Perfect, though while I'm getting all my gear, you wouldn't happen to have some rope I could have, would you?" He went back to the wall and grabbed down a large coil of rope. There had to be at least eighty feet of it.

"Okay, so we decided on ninety gold for everything, right?" I knew it was less than we originally agreed upon, but it was still more than I should have needed to pay.

"Uh, sure. I guess that works." I could tell he was trying to add the numbers up in his head.

I handed over the gold to him, along with the extra ten from the original price, "There, and these, are for you, Brenner." I said, putting the ten gold in his other hand. "Langston doesn't need to know about them." He took the gold pieces, pocketing ten of them, and placing the rest in a wooden box next to the door.

I'm not an absolute monster. I had nothing against Brenner, just Langston. I finished checking the saddle on Eques and led him out of the stable, walking beside him. Once we were on the road, Eques started getting rowdy as Brenner had warned and pulled on his reins. I tried soothing him, but nothing really would work to calm him. I pulled one of the apples out and tried giving it to him. He devoured it greedily, but it still didn't help. He kept pulling on the reins.

I decided to resort to more drastic measures. I began to hum under my breath an old melody. Eques kept fighting on the reins for a couple of moments but then started to calm down slowly. By the end of the tune, he wasn't fighting against me at all.

"Yeah, I think we are going to get along just fine ol' boy. Though I don't love the name Eques." When I said this, he pulled against the reins. "And I don't think you like it either.

Let's give you a more suitable name. Let's see, how about Trooper… or Jasper." He didn't seem to like either of these names. "How about Andante?" He almost seemed to nod his head at this one. "Yeah, you like that? I do, too, Andante."

Once we got to the edge of the town, I pulled him over to the side of the road and hopped up on his back. It was a rough ride for a while, but I started humming the melody again, and he seemed to calm down substantially.

Once we got that all taken care of, the ride was actually very soothing. The saddle was surprisingly comfortable, more excellent than any I had ever used. It took us two nights to get to Farhold. All of it was very uneventful.

Given that I was low on money, and even more so after spending so much to buy Andante, we had to sleep on the side of the trail each night.

The rocky ground wasn't comfortable, but it was better than not being able to sleep at all. It was around noon on the third day of travel that we arrived in Farhold.

CHAPTER FIVE

The Jolly Fairy

Once I got into town, I dismounted Andante and walked, guiding him beside me. The town was small and quaint. It was only about a mile in any direction before you left the city again. I started out by trying to find the tavern. I was hungry and needed a drink. Brand's mead was worth its weight in gold, and I wanted to save it for whatever was to come.

I asked a man on the street how to get there, as I had never been to Farhold before. He pointed to the left, and his eyes seemed to light up when I mentioned the tavern. I thanked him and went on my way. It only took me about a minute to find the place. I looked up and saw the sign. It read *The Jolly Fairy,* and small images of fae and various sprites were painted around the words. Each of them was holding a tankard of ale and had a foolish grin on their face.

I couldn't help but groan in disgust. I hated it when places tried to be cute. A tavern was meant to serve alcohol, give food, and then send you home. It wasn't meant to make you feel like a wizard was attacking you with happiness and sparkles. Which really happened on one of my Lily missions, and it's not as fun as it sounds. I had sparkling dust stuck in my ears for weeks.

I tied Andante to a post outside the tavern, contemplating whether or not the food and drink were worth what I was going to find. It took several minutes before I finally came to my decision. It was a hard one, and I knew that I was going to regret it eventually, but I really was hungry and very thirsty.

I decided to risk it and went into the tavern. When I entered the room, I nearly turned around that second to leave.

Inside was exactly what I was expecting. There was an overly chipper barkeep that was asking everyone how their day was, seeing if they needed directions anywhere, or if there was anything he could do to ease their travels. Then practically bouncing around the room was the barmaid, making sure that no one's cup went below half full. Every wall was covered with tapestries. They depicted scenes with fae and other magical creatures on a woven canvas

I went up to the bar, and the man started talking immediately, "How are you doing on this fine day, sir? My name is Oberon. Is there anything that I can do to ease your travels? We have ma—"

I cut the man off and said, "I'd like food, some drink, and silence." I looked up at him, making sure that my stare was enough to get him to hand me my items without the chipper act.

"I can do that for you, but it will cost you ten gold pieces." I was shocked. A typical meal would cost about two gold, four if it were incredibly delicious. I looked at him, and he kept a solid glare at me.

"Are you sure about that? I think you may be mistaken. I asked simply for some food and a mug of ale. Nothing more.

I believe that should be about three pieces." I reached into my pouch and pulled out the three pieces of gold. I placed them on the bar and slid them over to him.

The man pushed them back towards me and said in a steady tone, "I believe what I meant to say was that it will cost you ten gold for your meal, and another four for your drink." I stared at him slack-jawed. This man was trying to rob his patrons blind.

I looked around the room and saw that all of the customers in the tavern had blank looks on their faces. They seemed to be in some type of charm, like they couldn't control themselves. I took the time while I was looking away to mutter under my breath, "*Detinimo*." It was a charm that was meant to make someone passive and easier to control.

I turned back to look at him and said, "That seems like a very steep price. Is there anything you can do to lower it? I am but a poor traveler trying to make some money with music. I could offer you five gold and a lively tune for your patrons for the whole meal." He continued to stare at me, showing no signs of surrender. "Please, my horse, *Detinimo*," I tried the spell again, "is tired, and I need a place to rest. So I just ask for food and drink." At this point, I didn't as much want the food. I just wanted this man to be somewhat reasonable. This had become a battle of wills.

"I feel that a bard like you should know that your spells wouldn't work on fae creatures. Really, is this your first day around my kind?" He was right. My magic didn't work on magical creatures like fae, though I don't know how that matters now, and had he called me a bard? How did he know that?

Then all the pieces started falling into place. *The Jolly Fairy.* The tapestries of the fae. The mindless patrons. My spells not working. Everything. This man, Oberon, was a fairy.

That's how he was able to get these people to pay so much. He had charmed them into not knowing they were being gouged of their money. That's why that man on the street had seemed so pleased with the mention of the tavern. I was sure Oberon had half of this town charmed.

Fae magic is strange, unlike any other form. They don't use magic or spells per se, but just their presence is intoxicating. They can charm the people around them into a subdued state of mind, making them easier to control.

That's what he had tried doing to me, but it hadn't worked. Along with my training in learning these magic words, I had also gained the ability to not be charmed—at least not easily.

I glared at him furiously. This man had tried taking my money. I stood up from the stool, knocking it over with an echoing thud, and reached across the bar to grab Oberon by the collar of his shirt. I didn't know what I was going to do, but I was angry and not thinking straight.

The man continued showing no emotion on his face and said over my shoulder, "Peablossom, could you please take care of the customers." I let go of him and looked over my shoulder. The barmaid stopped pouring a man's drink and nodded her head to Oberon. Peablossom began to dance around the room, making a circle around each table. The customers got up, all at once, and mindlessly began to walk towards the door of the tavern, leaving in a single file line.

"Please, come back tomorrow. We'll be waiting for you." Her voice was high and squeaky. She waved at the customers as they left, fulfilling the typical image of the fae, being kind and sweet, yet when the last customer walked out the door— she changed.

There was a shimmering over her whole body. Her rags of clothing disappeared and were replaced by a thin blue satin dress that draped all the way to the ground. She shook her body once, and suddenly a set of nearly translucent blue wings sprung out from behind her back. I looked back at Oberon and saw that he was now shirtless, wearing just light-pink loose trousers. He also had wings coming out of his back, light pink ones to match his pants.

For a fae, he was very muscular, more muscular than most men I know. I felt that he could do some damage by hitting me just once. I heard a sound from behind me, and when I turned, Peablossom was walking slowly towards me. Though I can't really say walking, it was more that she was floating towards me. I heard Oberon jump over the counter and land lightly right beside me. He grabbed my wrist and pulled it up behind my shoulder blades.

He spoke softly yet threateningly into my ear, his chin brushing the top of my shoulder. "You dare come into my tavern, try to charm me into giving you my hard-earned wares, and then you threaten me in front of my customers. I shouldn't let you leave this place alive." He took a moment and pulled my wrist farther up. I winced out in pain. "And you know what, I don't think I will."

When he said this, Peablossom reached behind her back and pulled out a long, thin dagger. She was still smiling, and now she began to giggle. If not for the large threatening dagger, the giggle would have been sweet, but it was absolutely terrifying with the knife. I tried pulling away from Oberon, but with my arm behind my back, any movement sent a flash of pain up my arm, into my shoulder.

There was nothing I could do, I couldn't get to my rapier, as I had left it with Andante, and my magic could do nothing against the fae. As a last resort, I drove my heel into the top of Oberon's foot, hoping he would loosen his grip for even a moment. Instead, he seemed unfazed by the hit as he pulled my arm even further up my spine. My fingers were now at the base of my neck.

All I could do was stand there as Peablossom came closer and closer to me.

Suddenly, Peablossom let out a gasp of pain and collapsed to the floor. Standing in her place was a tall, slender woman with long blonde hair that came to her waist. She was wearing silver armor, with a dark yellow cloak over her shoulders clasped over her chest with a palm-sized lily-shaped pin. Looking closer, I could see that the metal of her armor was stamped with a lily pattern.

"Clef, I see you've already gotten yourself into trouble."

"Hey Bon-Bon, how'd you find me?"

"Oh, I just followed the smell of trouble, and it led me to you." Fortunately for me, the shock of Bon-Bon's appearance froze Oberon in place. Unfortunately, I now saw Bonneville swinging a sword towards my head.

CHAPTER SIX

The Flower Shop

I barely had enough time to duck my head down before the blade went flying past. I tucked my chin into my chest and could feel the wind from the sword on my neck. Then I suddenly felt Oberon's grip release as he was hit in the jaw by the sword.

"You *killed* him!" I had known Bonneville for a long time, and typically she tried not to kill people as the first resort. When I saw she didn't react, I turned around expecting to see a dead body. I peered at Oberon's collapsed form on the ground, surprised to see that he was moaning quietly and holding his jaw.

"I didn't kill him. I used the side of the blade, the worst that could happen would be that he got a broken jaw. The other one will be fine as well. I used the hilt of the sword. She'll have a headache, but nothing else."

She put her sword back in its sheath and turned to walk out of the tavern.

Rolling my shoulder in its socket, I could feel the soreness start to leave. I hurried after Bon-Bon, jumping over Peablossom's collapsed form. I had to almost jog to catch up with Bonneville's quick pace. When we got out of the tavern, I was glad that Andante was still tied to the post. He was stamping his front hoof in the dirt and trying to pull away from the post he was bound to. I gave him another apple as I began to untie him. Halfway through undoing the knot, Bonneville came over to stop me.

"You can't just steal that horse, Clef. I mean, I would expect that from Kriv, but not from you." She started to pull me away from him.

"I'm not stealing him. He's mine! I bought him in Evenglade. His name is Andante." He shook his head up and down, helping me prove my point. I rubbed his mane and gave him some hay as I finished untying him.

Bon-Bon nodded her head and started walking beside me as we went down the path. We didn't know where we were supposed to meet up with the rest of the team, but I was sure we would find it soon enough.

"So, Bon-Bon, what have you been doing? I know it's only been about a month, but how have you been?"

"I've been doing well. I'm still working as a guard for that family back home. I just got a promotion, though. I get to help train the new guys and make sure they are up to par with what's expected. So how have you been? Are you still working at that tavern? What's it called… the Golden Unicorn, right?"

"It's the Brazen Unicorn, but yeah, I still work there. It's been going well, though I don't know how much longer I'll have a job there," I said solemnly.

"What do you mean, are you getting fired? What did you do, Clef?" Bonneville had always been the person on the team I was closest to. If Brand was the brother I never had, then Bonneville was the mother that I never had. I knew she cared about me more than just as a teammate, but rather as a friend. I felt the same way about her.

I told her what was happening. About Brand fearing the *Brazen Unicorn* would have to shut down, him telling me I might not have a job anymore.

She frowned a little and said, "Oh, Clef, I'm so sorry to hear that. If there's anything I can do to help, just tell me, and I'll try and do it."

We walked on in silence for a while, keeping an eye out for any sign or clue as to where the meeting would be. The Lily never told us where the rendezvous actually was, just the town it would be held in. They didn't want any chance of an interception of the message or the chance someone could stumble upon our meeting. While it was tiring having to deal with all of the secrecy, nothing would make me give up my job with the Lily.

We had been walking around town for a while, and I was beginning to fear we had somehow missed the meeting. I heard Bonneville stop walking, and when I looked back, she pointed at a sign. I looked up and read the sign—*Rose's Flower Shop*.

Bonneville and I glanced at each other and went over to the building. I tied Andante up outside, giving him another bundle of feed, and Bon-Bon and I walked in together.

Inside the room were multiple wooden carts. It looked more like they should have been outside, as if they were intended for a street market. Each cart was filled with flowers of every kind—irises, marigolds, daisies, peonies, snowdrops, and—in the corner—a small yellow vase with exactly five giant stargazer lilies. The flowers instantly caught Bonneville's gaze, and she jerked her head towards them to point them out for me.

Bonneville and I nodded our heads once at each other and split up so as to not look suspicious. As I strolled between the carts, I had to pretend to be interested in the wares. What I was really doing was seeing who else was in the shop.

I only saw four other people in the store. There was a mother with her young son walking around. The mother had to continually reprimand the son and grab his hand because he was trying to grab all of the flowers.

I was standing behind a cart of tulips when I saw the young boy crush a large marigold in his childish grip. His mother looked down at him, panicked. When she felt that no one was looking, she quickly threw the flower under one of the carts, kicking it farther under with her foot. She grabbed her son by the upper arm and pulled him away to another part of the store.

"Seems like a great role model," I said quietly as I passed Bonneville. She chuckled in response.

In the corner by the lilies was a man that seemed very frantic. He was bustling around the store, looking at flowers and then shaking his head, rushing to another bouquet. He eventually grabbed the vase of lilies and ran up to the counter where the fourth person was—an old lady. I'm assuming she was the Rose of *Rose's Flower Shop*.

The crazed man went up to the woman and said in one breath, "I need to buy these flowers. It's my wife's birthday, and I forgot. I need to buy these now." He reached into a pouch on his belt and pulled out a handful of gold, "How much for all of them?"

The woman looked him up and down and shook her head very slightly. "Well, I'm very sorry, sir, but these flowers are not for sale." She took the vase and placed it under her counter. When her hands came back up, she was holding a large bouquet of small white flowers. "However, I do suggest you take this bundle of snowdrops. Every woman *loves* a nice bouquet of snowdrops."

The man nodded his head and said, "Okay, whatever. How much for them?" Rose placed the flowers in a beautiful pink vase and pushed them into the man's hand while gesturing him out of the store, giving him the flowers and vase for free. The man thanked her profusely as he ran out of the store, off to remedy things with his wife... hopefully.

This odd exchange just confirmed my suspicions more that this was where we needed to be.

Rose then walked back to the small table, resetting the vase of lilies. She walked briskly and confidently for a woman of her age.

Bon-Bon and I had to wait until the mother dragged her son out of the store after he killed several more flowers. It was two peonies, a daisy, several more marigolds, and half a dozen tulips by my count.

Once they left, I made eye contact with Bonneville and tilted my head slightly towards the flowers, telling her to go first. Bon-Bon went over to the vase of flowers, grabbing a single lily out of it. She took it to the woman and placed it on the counter, saying nothing. The woman looked

Bonneville up and down. I saw her eyes lock onto the lily clasp on Bon-Bon's cloak. The old woman looked around the shop. I had been sure to have my back turned to them, pretending to look at a bundle of orchids. I could see the two women in the reflection on the window, though.

When Rose was sure I couldn't see them, she gestured for Bon-Bon to come behind the counter. She then led her to a back room. The woman came back to the counter a few seconds later alone and started rearranging a bouquet of yellow roses.

I waited a long count of ten and then went and grabbed a lily from the vase—leaving three. One would be for Kriv, another for Roscoe, and the final would be for Finnon. I walked confidently up to Rose.

"Hello, ma'am, I would like to purchase this *lily*," I put an emphasis on the word. She looked up at me, about to tell me they weren't for sale, but her eyes locked on my lily brooch.

She quickly gestured me back to the same room as Bonneville. She told me that as soon as everyone arrived, we would receive more information.

I thanked her and looked into the room. It was just a small one, practically a closet, only about ten feet by ten feet. The walls were covered in small glass containers, each with a bundle of fresh-cut flowers. The floral smell was nearly overwhelming.

In the center of the room, a round table had five wooden seats, each with a parchment bearing one of our names. In front of each placeholder there was a plate of food piled high.

Bonneville's had fresh vegetables with some sort of poultry and a glass filled with water. Two seats had meat and bread on a plate, with a large tankard of ale. I knew these would be for Roscoe and Finnon. I could barely look at Kriv's. He had merely a pile of raw meat, no plate. There were even a few white bones sticking out of it. I didn't make a habit of sharing meals with him, given his peculiar diet.

I was relieved to find mine had fresh bread that was still steaming, as if fresh from the oven, a stack of meat, and a pile of cooked vegetables. Though the best part of it was the golden goblet with mead inside it. When my stomach grumbled, I realized how hungry I was. I'd nearly forgotten that I hadn't gotten any food at *The Jolly Fairy*. The last time

I'd had food was early this morning, and it was past noon now.

Bonneville was already at her place eating her piece of bread. I went to my seat and was disheartened when I saw that it was next to Kriv's seat. I looked at his plate and had to fight for the food I'd eaten to stay down.

I grabbed his plate and name marker, gagging, and switched it with Finnon's. Bonneville laughed audibly when I did this and nearly choked on her food. I looked at her sheepishly and shrugged.

"I'd of done the same thing…" she said quietly. "I don't know how he eats like that."

I then sat down and started eating the meat from my plate. It was only a few minutes before a short man with frizzy copper hair and a bushy beard came strolling into the room. On his back was a large canvas pack nearly as large as he was.

"Hey, Roscoe. How are you doing?" Bonneville asked cheerily.

He took a moment to respond, and when I followed his gaze, I saw he was already looking at his food.

"Fine," he eventually answered as he sat down. Starting with a swig of his ale, he began to devour the food.

Roscoe was wearing a simple grey tunic with a yellow checkered kilt. Both of them seemed to be a very rough and coarse material. It kind of surprised me. Usually, the Lily sent the best quality of everything, but Roscoe's seemed to be very crudely made.

A few moments later, a man slightly shorter than Roscoe came into the room. He, too, had a head full of red hair, but his facial hair was kept to a short stubble. This was Finnon, Roscoe's half-brother.

He was dressed in the same fashion as Roscoe, yet he had a pale-yellow tunic and a gray kilt to match. They almost always wore the same style of clothes, making them seem more like twins than half-brothers.

Their food was gone in minutes while I was still slowly sipping my mead—which tasted fantastic—by the way.

I was pretty sure it was actually Brand's mead, though I don't know how that would be possible. I decided it was just another of the perks from the Lily.

They were always finding out information about us… like our favorite drink… or our hatred of peas—which I was glad were left out from my plate.

I asked Finnon about the clothes he had received, he and Roscoe traditionally wore armor, so I was confused by the simple clothes. In response, he took the knife from his setting and drove it into his left thigh. I flinched, but the blade of the knife snapped off and flew across the room.

Roscoe jumped in to explain, "It has micro-chainmail woven into it, so it'll stop nearly every blade. Plus, who doesn't want to wear a kilt… they're breezy."

Bonneville laughed and continued to eat.

The four of us participated in some idle chit-chat until suddenly Roscoe stopped mid-word.

Kriv had walked in. I was a little surprised—and grateful—because rather than his typical loincloth, he had on long, blousy gray pants. It seemed my complaints to the Lily had finally been answered.

Kriv said nothing and barely even looked at any of us before sitting down and eating his meal—if you could even call it that. I could hear bones crunching even across the table.

Bonneville made a disgusted face at me, and even Roscoe and Finnon seemed repulsed by his food. They both slid their chairs away from him, nearly rubbing elbows with Bonneville and me.

Kriv had crunched through several bones now, and I had pushed the rest of my food away. His eating habits had destroyed my appetite. I did, however, continue to sip my mead.

Rose came into the room once more. She had a very grandmotherly persona, yet also seemed very sprightly, like a woman half her age.

She walked to each of us and placed a scroll on the table beside our plates.

It appeared the same as the one I had received at the *Brazen Unicorn*.

A yellow ribbon was sealed around it by a white—lily embellished—seal.

Pushing our remaining food and drinks aside, my team looked at each other, nodded our heads once, and pulled the ribbon off our scrolls, letting them roll open in front of us.

I looked down and read what was on the paper.

> We have received word from the town of Brownstead, that every full moon, a swarm of goblins ransacks every home and shop. Last month the villagers tried to make a stand, but four men were killed, and nearly two dozen villagers were taken captive. The villagers no longer know what to do and are in desperate need of help. You must help them secure the village. Use any means you deem necessary to do so. Your contact is at the Erkling Inn. He will be expecting you.
>
> ⁓ The Lily

I was the first to finish the note, so I set it down, waiting for the rest as I began to think over the task ahead of us. We had dealt with goblins before. It seemed as though it would be a routine mission. I didn't know why the Lily felt the need to send us. We usually dealt with the bigger things, like dragons and manticores, not goblins. But I knew better than to doubt the Lily. There had to be a reason.

A bit later, they all finished, Roscoe being done much later than the rest. I looked at each person in the group and said very solemnly, "Well, I guess we better go teach some goblins a lesson."

Now I won't bore you with all the details of our trip to Brownstead. I rode on Andante for most of the trip, but we had to go slower than he would have liked to let Roscoe and Finnon keep up. They, however, were stubborn and refused to ride the horse. I let Bonneville ride Andante for a while as I stretched my legs. My horse seemed to take a liking to her. She did always have a way with animals.

I was surprised that we came across very few other travelers along the way.

At one point, when we were only a few hours from Brownstead, we came upon a family that seemed to be fleeing in panic. They were looking over their shoulders and clutching their small daughter's hand, who was dragging an old doll behind her. When I stopped them and asked where they were headed, they replied, "Anywhere but Brownstead," and proceeded to hurry on their way.

This gave me a familiar feeling. One of fear for what horror may lay ahead of us and one of excitement for a new adventure. To survive and feel alive. After that, it was only about a day and a half's journey to arrive at the town.

We broke through the forest late at night and found the inn quickly. The innkeeper had set aside a room for his "special" guests. I wouldn't typically want to share a room with all the others, but it was better than sleeping outside again. When we got up to the room, we, unfortunately, found that there was only one bed covered with tanned hides.

"I guess we better give the bed to Bon-Bon, given that she's the only woman." Typically, I would say lady, but I don't know if I would call Bon-Bon that… or if she would even allow it. All I got from her was a deep growl as she threw herself on the bed, falling asleep instantly. See what I mean? Not precisely lady-like.

Looking around for a place to sleep, I saw a padded chair over in one corner. I figured it was better than the floor, so I sat down in it and was glad it was somewhat comfortable.

I looked around and saw that Finnon and Roscoe had flopped down in the middle of the room, starting their symphony of snores, meaning it would be another night of difficult sleep.

Kriv, however, dropped his pack and walked right back out of the room, muttering under his breath, "Back later."

Kriv was never big on words, and I really didn't have the energy to think about whatever—most likely illegal—thing he would be doing. I just wanted to sleep, and somehow, I managed to, despite Roscoe and Finnon snoring like wild beasts.

CHAPTER SEVEN

The Lute

I *found myself back in my old mentor's chambers. This was where I had learned everything I knew about magic. Not just what it was, but how to use it. My mentor was the one that taught me that these talents should be used to help society, and that I shouldn't use these skills as a way to help myself.*

The place brought back the best memories of my life. I can still remember the smell of the cedarwood cupboards. I could still feel the aged parchment that had ancient songs and melodies written on them. I could hear the haunting harmonies that I had learned. I loved this place. It was the first place I ever thought of as a home.

It pained me to think of how many years it had been since I was there. I glanced around the room, remembering all the great memories I had from here—all of the accidental spells, the messed-up melodies, and the ruined sheet music. As time marches forward in life, it's nice to be able to look around and remember where we came from.

It wasn't until I looked over at the old workstation that I noticed someone else was in the room with me. Sitting in the chair was a man in his early forties. He had brown hair with auburn tones. His hair was ear-length, and he had a long, chest-length beard.

I slowly walked over to him, but I didn't know what I was going to do. How do you say anything to the person who raised you? When you repaid them by never coming to see them? I was about to put my hand on his shoulder when the door flew open behind me. I started gathering a spell until I noticed who came in—me.

Well, not exactly me, but my teenage self. His hair was much longer than mine. I had cut it shorter when I joined the

Lily. I found that having to brush hair out of my eyes wasn't practical in battle. The Clef standing before me was also a few inches shorter than I am now.

I was disheartened to see how weathered my face had become since then. While I don't look old, I definitely won't be mistaken for a teenager. I suppose it is the miles, rather than the years, that count… and I had traveled many miles— literally and figuratively—with the Lily.

That was when I realized this was all a memory. I wasn't actually back here. I was probably still asleep in the Erkling Inn, hearing Roscoe and Finnon's snores.

My past self spoke as if they couldn't see me, "Hey, Athelstan."

That name brought back another wave of memories. Athelstan Mylls. He had been like a father to me. In fact, he was the only father figure I ever knew. Being half-human and half-elf, I never really had a home to call my own. I left home early in my life, trying to live as a performer.

A few years later, Athelstan found me on the street and began mentoring me as a bard.

Young Clef continued, "What are you working on this morning? A new spell, a new song, come on, tell me what it is." I like to think I'm not as annoying now, but I'm sure any of my friends would deny that.

"No," Athelstan let out a deep chuckle that could warm any heart, "I'm working on something much more complex and important than that."

Athelstan's voice was enchanting. It was deep and rough. When he began to sing, it would make every head turn. It may sound cliché, but his voice was one of an angel. "This is something I have been working on for a while." He picked an item up off the table and handed it to my younger self.

I remember what it was, though how can I forget it. I still use it every day.

It was a masterfully created lute.

Athelstan spoke in his comforting voice, "It is yours now. I knew that you had the natural talent to be a true bard. This lute is made from the wood of a hundred-year-old birch, and the strings are interwoven with the hair of a unicorn. The strings will never snap or go out of tune, and the wood will never warp or break. Every bard needs an instrument that was made just for them. This will help you along your journey," he paused, as if debating continuing. In the end, he smiled and said, "And hopefully, we don't have any more mistakes like yesterday."

Both my past self and I looked down at the floor, hiding our faces. I don't know what event he was talking about. I had messed up a lot back then. Once I had been trying a levitation spell but instead turned my skin purple. It lasted for over a week.

Young Clef spoke, "I don't know what to say. Thank you doesn't feel like enough, Athelstan." This was the first real gift I had ever been given.

"Go ahead and try it. Just feel the power that is in it." I saw myself take a deep breath and begin to strum a simple melody on the lute. It wasn't a spell, just simply a song. But even the power from that was unexplainable. I remember that feeling as if it was yesterday.

There was a warmth that started in my fingers and continued all the way to my legs. My heart began to beat faster, and I felt goosebumps all up my arms. It was such a fantastic feeling that all I could focus on was myself and the lute. Nothing else mattered.

But now, seeing it from a new perspective, I could see the power that was in the room as well. Sheet music began to blow in a non-existent breeze. Even Athelstan's beard started whipping around his neck. That was when I noticed something I had definitely never seen before. Athelstan was smiling, and it wasn't just any smile. It was the smile of a delighted father.

I had always known that Athelstan respected me, and I had always loved him like a father, but I didn't know that he thought of me as anything other than a student. But now I see that he not only respected me, but he thought of me as a son. Just knowing that he respected—no—loved me made my heart beat with pride like it had when I played that lute. As I was coming to this revelation, Young Clef slowly finished the song, quickly stopping the last chord with a flat palm. Then, as the note cut out, everything fell back to where it was. By the time Young Clef opened his eyes and looked up, it was as if nothing had happened.

When Young Clef looked at his mentor, Athelstan said with what I now realized was pride, "Now you really know what it means to be a bard."

Then something very odd happened. The door to the room flew back open, and in charged Kriv. I definitely don't remember that...

CHAPTER EIGHT

The Barkeep

I awoke with a start as Kriv charged into the room. I don't know if he was returning from last night's excursion or if he had gone out again this morning. I didn't care, and if I was truly honest, I was too scared to ask. Plus, I doubted he would answer me… and anyways, it would likely be a lie if he did. Looking at the bed, I saw that Bon-Bon was already gone. Probably off on her traditional morning run. Finnon was still asleep on the floor, though I didn't see where Roscoe was.

As I scanned the small room, I heard a strange noise beside me. It sounded familiar—then I realized it was the strumming of my lute. I had never let another soul play my lute, so I wasn't prepared to hear it played by someone else.

I looked over and saw Roscoe holding my lute, messing with it. He had clearly never used an instrument before, as the meaty parts of his fingers were muting the strings unintentionally, leading to a hollow chord.

I quickly reached over and grabbed it from him. I'm generally not a possessive person, but with all the freshly dug-up memories, and given that it was Roscoe, I was horrified by seeing my lute in the hands of someone else.

Honestly, his hands always have dirt on them, I don't know how he does it, but his hands are *always* grimy. So I grabbed a rag from my bag and started polishing the dirt off my lute.

Looking down at it, I saw it still looked exactly as it had in my vision. There were no scratches on it, and the strings were still bright and strong, with a single metallic strand wrapping around each of them—the unicorn hair. Roscoe walked away from me, muttering something under his breath.

Kriv walked over to his pack and started unloading his pockets. I looked at him out of the corner of my eye, hoping he wouldn't see I was watching.

I saw him pull out several gold and silver coins, which is pretty typical of his excursions. But, strangely, I also saw him pull out a vial with what I think said "Griffin Grease." I shook my head in confusion and disgust.

I looked over to see that Roscoe had started his morning devotion praying to his goddess, Anar. His legs were folded under him, and he was running a strand of wooden beads through his fingers. His mouth was forming silent words.

Finnon groggily woke up, and when he saw that Roscoe was nearby, he scurried to the other side of the room. It seems that he and Roscoe were fighting again, though I don't know why. It's always something with them. One time they fought for three weeks because Roscoe accidentally took Finnon's sock. They are strangely weird about their socks, though all of them should be burned from the smell if you ask me.

By this time, Bon-Bon was back from her run, and her skin was glowing with sweat. I didn't know how, but she didn't even look tired. No matter what, she doesn't look tired.

If I went on a run like that, I—well—I wouldn't go on a run like that. I have always stayed healthy and have a fit body, but I was never a fan of running.

We all walked out of the inn and went to the local tavern to get some food. By the time we got there, I was officially irritable. When I'm hungry, really anything will annoy me. I mean, does anyone honestly need to breathe that loud.

We all ordered the same breakfast when we got to the tavern, and I quickly scarfed down the bread and salted meat. Having my hunger satiated, I found my mood to be significantly improved.

We decided to split up and get some information. I went over to the barkeep and started talking to him, asking what was happening. I tried to be sociable, seeming more like I was talking to a friend rather than prying for information.

The barkeep looked up at me with strained eyes and said very calmly and deliberately, "I don't want to talk about it, but I'm sure I'll remember in a moment."

He put his hand on the counter, rubbing his fingers together. It took me a second to realize he wanted money.

Seriously, some people, *I* am trying to help *him*, and *he* wants money. I could tell there was something wrong, and I didn't want to resort to magic, so I slipped a gold coin into his palm.

It took him a minute to start talking, but when he did, I realized that he was scared, "On every full moon, there is a horde of goblins that ransacks the town. They take everything they can grab—food, jewelry, money. Anything. We have a communal bunker where we keep our most valuable items stored away. Before each full moon, we send most of the women and children down there. We tried to fight back last month, but there were just too many of them. We had no chance. They broke through to the bunker. It seems they didn't care about valuables this time, but instead took villagers."

It looked like he was struggling to talk, but he continued, "Th-they took them, w-w-we don't know where they went, we just know they went o-out of t-t-town. M-my son was one of the o-ones they took. My W-Wren, my poor boy, they took him." Tears formed in the corners of his eyes. "We thought of sending p-people to try and get them, b-b-but everyone was too scared. I'm sorry, e-excuse me." He turned around to go into a room behind the bar, but before he left, his shoulders shook, and I could tell he was crying.

Now that he was gone, I saw a little box behind the counter with some money in it. Looking around to make sure no one saw me, I reached back and dropped several more coins into it. Then I went to see what the rest had found.

CHAPTER NINE

The Footprints

Finnon and Roscoe were sitting at a table still eating when I looked over. From the stack of plates on the table, it seems they had gone back for thirds, or even fourths. They obviously haven't done any real work. I walked over to them and saw them kicking each other under the table while shoving hunks of bread into their mouths. Pulling them apart, I drug them over to where Kriv was. They continued to bicker with each other the whole way. I was tempted to use a silencing charm on them but thought that might not be the best use of my time.

Kriv was going through his pack again, reorganizing it after gathering more illicit goods. This time he pulled out a ball filled with grey smoke, a small bag with pink dust, and a glass eye. That man, well, dragon, really is a mystery. I looked around the pub for Bonneville. Peering out one of the windows, I noticed that she was outside, so I drug Roscoe and Finnon out to her, hearing Kriv's heavy steps following.

Outside we found that Bon-Bon was crouched down, scratching a large dog behind the ears.

"Okay, guys, did any of you find any information? Because I talked to that barkeep and unfortunately didn't find out anything new. Though it's clear these villagers are terrified. With having all of their goods stolen each month, they've become accustomed to begging. Even though I was there to help, he still asked for gold."

I love all these guys—Kriv a little less so, if I'm honest—and we traditionally work well together. So I couldn't understand why they didn't do anything. Bon-Bon typically pulls *more* than her fair share, so it surprised me she didn't have any information.

"We really have to get going. We only have about a week 'til the next full moon so let's try and find out where the goblins went," I said, clearly frustrated at the lack of information.

Without looking up from the dog, Bon-Bon said, "They went to the south." I was glad to find that she had something to bring to the table. I should never have doubted her. Bonneville was remarkable with tracking. She seems to notice things no one else can.

"Uh, how did you find that out? Who did you talk to?" I asked.

"No one. I just followed the tracks and imprints they left behind. You can see the prints right here. They aren't shaped the same as a human's boot or even a bare foot. We are lucky that it rained the night the goblins came, and it hasn't rained since then. The prints have been mostly left intact," she pointed at the ground, and I saw prints that didn't look even vaguely human, "and here are deep grooves from where they drug those poor men and women out of town. You can tell that they go to the south. It's honestly quite simple if you just look." I wasn't surprised at all, Bon-Bon was as good with tracking and hunting as I am with music, and that's saying a lot.

"Alright, then, I guess we know where we are heading. Everyone, go grab what you need for the trip and let's go. We'll meet back up here in twenty minutes." We all split up to go about our business. I went back into the tavern and bought a few days' worth of bread and salted meat. The food Brand had given me was still good, but I wanted to be prepared. I also took Andante, who had been tied up at the *Erkling Inn*, to the local stable. I didn't know what we were getting ourselves into. It was one thing risking my life. It was another endangering the horse's well-being.

I paid the stable boy extra to take him out on a ride each day. I wanted Andante to be able to stay active while I was gone. He obviously had an excess of energy. I also told the boy that if I wasn't back within a fortnight, he should find Andante a new home. I had every hope though that I would be able to return and care for him myself.

After paying for that—and giving the barkeep a generous tip—I only had a couple of gold coins left. I had to hope the Lily paid us with gold this time and not gifts.

I headed back to the tavern to wait for the rest. Bon-Bon was already back and waiting outside for us. She was now holding a different dog than she was earlier. I really don't know how she does that. We waited a bit longer, and Roscoe and Finnon came to meet back up with us. They were fighting about something. I could faintly hear them saying, "I want to carry the mead" "No, I want to." "But you spilled it last time!"

Kriv still hadn't arrived after twenty minutes. All we could do was wait. After another ten minutes, our curiosity about what was keeping him was answered as Kriv finally showed up. He was bouncing up and down in his hand several gold coins. That guy really needs to get his priorities in check, we are about to go into battle, and he is worried about stealing money. I rolled my eyes. Luckily, I think only Bonneville saw it.

She smirked, knowing that Kriv annoyed me, and said, "Alright, let's head south."

CHAPTER TEN

The Sunken Fortress

As Bonneville had predicted, it was easy to follow the goblin prints out of town. There were still deep imprints in the now hard ground. When we got out of town, however, it was another matter altogether. Unfortunately, the main road was well-traveled and hard-packed, which hadn't allowed for prints to be made. We lost sight of the tracks the moment we left Brownstead.

Given that our destination was unknown and we didn't know what to look for, the party had to travel painfully slow.

We took turns, each taking a different position. First, one of us walked on the trail. Then one of us went about ten feet into the brush on each side, and then another person out another fifty feet or so on each side of that. We traveled like this for one whole day and didn't find anything.

Once the sun set, we knew we wouldn't find anything in the dark. So we made camp a few feet off the trail. We each took a turn being lookout, but I ended up staying awake all night. Part of it was from Roscoe and Finnon's snoring, and the other part was this odd feeling I had. I can't put my finger on what it is, but something felt different this time. It felt like this mission was going to be different than all the others. Not exactly worse or harder, but just different. I absentmindedly reached up and grabbed my necklace, running the long silver chain through my fingers.

Upon the sun rising, Kriv started waking everyone. Let me tell you. He was not gentle about it. He basically kicked us in the ribs grunting, "Up."

I'm sure he saw I was still awake, but he kicked me anyway.

I took the far-left position this time and started trudging through the brush. I saw nothing and was beginning to feel like we had been misguided. It surprised me, though, as Bonneville was usually so accurate in her tracking. I was about to call out and voice my opinion when I heard Bon-Bon shout.

"Hey guys, I think I've found something." She was on the main trail, so we ran over to her to see what it was. "Look here. There is this path flattened in the brush leading that way. It means something has gone this way a lot." She was crouched down, pointing out the flattened foliage.

"But couldn't that be deer? A game trail of some sort? It doesn't mean that it is the goblins." I wanted to believe Bon-Bon, but I was already concerned we were going in the wrong direction. I didn't want to continue on a wild goose chase.

"It could be…" she responded, "but I don't think so. Think back to the last several hundred yards. Have you seen any big animals? A bear or a stag—anything? Or even any evidence of their existence? Tree rubs, antlers… scat? I haven't. Something feels… I don't know… *wrong* about this place, as though even the animals are scared of it."

As I recalled our travels through the last day, I realized that she was right. I had not seen or heard anything, not so much as a bird chirping. There was absolutely no wildlife. "Alright, let's follow it then," I said.

We started heading down the thin trail, and not ten minutes later did we come to a strange site. Off in the distance, we saw several tall pillars. As we continued to follow it, the well-worn path led us straight to them.

What we found there was not what I was expecting. Rather than a building, we found a deep chasm in front of us. Looking down into it, I could see that there was an entire sunken fortress down there. It was in surprisingly good shape for having fallen into the ground.

There were parts of it that had split evenly. This led to stairs with no end and doors with no floor. Part of it was buried in dirt from apparent land- and mud-slides over the years. I kept looking around for a way down there but saw nothing. Kriv, however, was helpful. For once.

He grunted and beckoned us over. We walked to him, and he pointed down. About fifty feet down from where we were, there was a narrow ledge about as wide and long as I am tall. The five of us would barely be able to fit on it.

Looking back, I saw one of the prominent pillars about six feet away from the ledge, so I pulled the coil of rope out of my bag and started tying it around the column so that we could repel down the cliff. I started towards the ridge—ready to jump off—when I heard a screech from behind me. It was a sound I knew from previous encounters, and it sent a chill down my spine.

I looked back and saw that there were eight goblins charging towards us.

We all turned to face them, each of us pulling our weapon of choice in the process. I was confident we would dispatch this small horde of goblins quickly and get back to our discovery when, out of the corner of my eye, I saw something I could never have imagined.

Kriv was caught off guard. He turned too slowly and wasn't able to draw his sword before he was slammed into by the nearest goblin. He grabbed the creature that had dared touch him, but it was too late… the momentum of the goblin's tackle was already in motion. Kriv went over the edge, taking the goblin with him. Now Kriv can take a tackle and even a tumble like a champ, and I was sure he would survive the fall. But to the group's horror, the last thing we saw as Kriv disappeared over the edge was his head slam against a rock, instantly knocking him unconscious. Before

I could breathe, I heard the thud of his massive body hitting the ledge below.

Everyone froze. Even the goblins. They stared at the cliff with eyes wide in confusion. Perhaps that had been their leader, but we didn't care. Their hesitation was our fortune and their demise.

We would have to go after Kriv once we handled these goblins. There was no choice but to hope he was alive and that we would get to him before someone, or something, else did.

It was one of those moments that seemed to be in slow motion, taking forever to play out. Yet, it all had actually happened in about fifteen seconds.

Roscoe seemed to have read my mind as he charged forward, his battle-axe already in full swing while shouting, "We'll find Kriv after. NOW MOVE!"

Roscoe charged forward with his battle-axe swinging over his head. He quickly sliced two of the goblins in half and started going for more.

Finnon reached into a pouch on his belt and pulled out two small black stones. I saw him close his eyes for a second, and then I saw a red rune start to glow on each rock. His eyes then flew open, and he threw the stones. The two goblins that got hit were instantly incinerated in a burst of red flames, turning to dust.

That left three more goblins for Bon-Bon and me to take care of. I took care of one of them by pulling out my rapier and piercing it through the goblin's chest. While magic is my best weapon, that doesn't mean it's excellent in close quarters. If I had more time, then I could have gathered a spell to put them all to sleep or make them dance a satyr jig, but sometimes a sword is just best. Bon-Bon took care of the last two. She grabbed one by the shoulder and launched it over the cliff. The other one, she caught by the head and snapped its neck. She doesn't always need a weapon—her strength is enough.

We took a moment to look around, making sure there were no more goblins left hiding. Then we were able to worry about Kriv. We ran over to the ledge and looked down, expecting the worst, but we all breathed a sigh of relief when we saw him on the shelf below. When I called down to him, I didn't get a response, which made us all nervous. I quickly grabbed onto the rope and started repelling down. I got about ten feet down when I heard Finnon call down to me.

"Uh… Clef," he sounded more worried than he typically did, "you might want to hurry. That pillar is starting to break." Panicked, I started climbing down the rope quicker. I got another five feet, and then I heard a loud crash as I began to freefall the last thirty-five feet. Fortunately, Bon-Bon grabbed the rope at the last second, and I jerked to a stop about eight feet from the bottom of the cliff. I quickly slid down to the ledge and scrambled over to Kriv. He was indeed unconscious, and half of him was dangling precariously over the side of the shelf. At the bottom of the chasm, I could see two goblin forms—the one that had tackled Kriv, as well as the one Bonneville had thrown.

I quickly pulled Kriv entirely onto the shelf and looked for signs of life.

Aside from him kicking me or shoving past me in a tavern, I'd never actually touched his skin before. I was now desperately pressing my ear to his chest, trying to hear a heartbeat or feel him breathing through the incredibly thick scales that felt remarkably like stone. I was beginning to lose hope when I finally heard the faintest sound of a drum beat. At the same time, I felt his stony chest press against my cheek as he took a shallow breath.

I looked up at his draconic head and could see a bloody gash on his right temple from where he had hit his head while falling. I grabbed a cloth from my bag and pressed it against the wound, hoping to slow the bleeding. I could use my magic to heal minor injuries, but I knew that this was far beyond my capabilities. Some bards were good healers, but I was more of a fend-for-yourself-and-have-someone-else-clean-up-the-mess type of bard. But right now, I needed someone who was a talented healer.

I needed Roscoe.

"Hey guys," I called up to the group that was anxiously waiting for my report, "he's alive, but Roscoe needs to get down here. NOW!"

Another rope came over the ledge. I assumed this one came from Roscoe's pack. He somehow manages to fit everything one could possibly need in that pack of his. I hoped they had the sense to use a tree or a boulder or something other than another pillar seeing how that had turned out for my descent.

Slowly Roscoe, Bon-Bon, and Finnon climbed down the rope one by one. It took about ten minutes, but they all got down safely with no issues. Roscoe came first, and as soon as he had reached the ledge, he kneeled down and placed his hands on Kriv's chest. I kept the cloth to Kriv's head, and when I looked down, I saw that it was soaked through with dark red blood.

Roscoe began to mutter under his breath a prayer, asking for Anar, his goddess, to heal Kriv. As I watched Kriv, I could see a faint yellow glow around him. It slowly began to pulsate, growing brighter and brighter, beating faster and faster. I was pretty sure that it was following the beat of his heart. After a while, the glow turned solid and then went away altogether. Roscoe motioned me away, and when I removed the cloth from Kriv's head, I saw the wound was gone.

Kriv took a single, deep, shuttering breath and sat up abruptly. Bonneville and Finnon had made it to the ledge now, and we were cramped for space.

Kriv looked at each of us and said nothing. He did, however, look at Roscoe and give what seemed to be an appreciative nod. I handed the bloody cloth, which was beyond salvaging, to Finnon, who pulled a stone from his pouch and incinerated it. Then, I cleaned the dark liquid from my hands using some of the water in my flask.

After all the events from the day, it was getting to be dark again, and in the chasm, it was even more so. So I proposed that we take this as a chance to rest for the night.

While the ledge was small and sleeping would be cramped, we agreed it was doable and perhaps the best option to protect us from attack. We were well out of sight from the main path, and anyone attempting to reach us would be heard before they actually arrived on our ledge.

The ledge was cramped. My calf was being used as a pillow by Roscoe, who was snoring as usual. My head was closer than comfortable to Kriv, and my left leg was nearly falling off the cliff.

And there were other distractions that came with trying to sleep on a cliff. You know that feeling while you're drifting off to sleep like you're falling? Well, imagine that while on a cliff ledge, and you'll startle wide awake in fear, and at that point, it is extremely hard to doze off again. So, long story short, it wasn't restful. But that wasn't even the worst of it. The worst part was the rats, which I could hear scurrying around the lower ledges. I even felt one brush against my cheek at one point.

Rats are the one thing I can't deal with. I'm good with snakes, spiders, six-headed rabbits—yes, they are real—but a rat is too much for me. I don't know why I hate them so much. Probably because I had slept near them more than I would have liked after leaving home and sleeping in dirty street alleys.

Most people will say they are more scared of you than you are of them. However, they are dirty, grimy, and have long, sharp teeth. So, judge me all you want, but I am not getting bit by one of those.

I took the last shift of the night.

I waited until the sun came all the way up before I woke everyone. Everyone woke up a little groggy. We ate a bit of our rations as we planned our next course of action. Now that we were at the same level as the ruins, we could see that about five feet out from the ledge, at about the same height, was a flight of stairs heading down. We looked down at them and saw they led to a small door at the bottom. We decided to attempt to get to that door. It was the only quick way we saw into the fortress.

Kriv and I made the jump very easily. He was remarkably his old self when he woke up. You would never have guessed he had been nearly dead less than twelve hours ago. Roscoe and Finnon struggled a bit. Bonneville eventually had to throw them across the gap, and Kriv and I had to catch them.

She then joined us, basically stepping across the gap, making it look way too easy. We started heading down the stairs and found that we had to go very slowly. As we descended the precarious steps, which occasionally crumbled even under Roscoe and Finnon's weight, we were able to see just how big the fortress was. It stretched several miles in each direction. It would take us weeks to explore every nook, which was more time than we had.

We got to the bottom of the stairs and found just the one simple door. I looked around it but didn't see any traps or hear anything. I reached down and turned the knob. It was then that I noticed the string running along the edge of the floor. When I heard a faint click, I tried to jump back, but it was too late.

I landed on the ground in a pit, lying on my back. I looked around, wishing that I hadn't. All around me was my worst nightmare.

I was surrounded by half a dozen rats. Now these weren't normal rats. They were giant, at least a foot and a half long, not including their two-foot tail. I tried to gather a spell, but I just couldn't do it. I was too terrified even to think. All that came out was, "No, No, No… No…"

I heard the others run over to the edge. They saw what had happened. I heard one of them call out to me, but I didn't know who. Then, one of the rats started towards my leg. I tried telling my body to kick the rat in the face, as I knew there was no hope for a spell. But my leg ignored me, and instead, my body curled up into a ball. The last thing I remember was a shooting pain up my left leg as a rat latched onto it, and then—blackness. I told you, rats are nasty creatures with sharp teeth.

CHAPTER ELEVEN

The Faux Ears

I found myself standing in a very familiar field. There were large twisting oak trees all around me. There were raspberry and strawberry plants winding along the path I was on. Hanging down from the trees around me were ivy vines draping all the way down to the ground. It had been years since I'd been in this forest, but I couldn't forget it. In the distance, I could hear the faint sound of a river, one that I knew well. Those rivers and springs were the places I spent the hot summer days in. The trees were where I would hide *from my aunt. I could smell that there had been rain last night. This place brought back so many memories, and some of them were even good. I started walking around a bit, seeing all the great things from my past. The tree that I fell out of, the raspberry bush I had my first kiss next to. Even the rock that I tripped over when I was learning to walk.*

But then I remembered the bad memories. The fact that I had been pushed from that tree by an elf boy. That first kiss was because the girl had been dared to kiss the "freak." When I learned to walk, my parents had already been gone.

I didn't know what day this was, but I was sure it would bring back bitter memories.

I was either being relentlessly mocked or left alone back then. In the few moments when I wasn't ignored or alone, my aunt had endless lists of hard labor for me. Constantly reminding me it was the very least I could do as I was such a burden on her, and to punish me for being such an embarrassment to the family

There weren't many half-elves out there, at least not many that are publicly announced. Not only were the children emotionally tortured, but the parents were disgraced and shunned as well. Most of my kind's parents would hide their sons and daughters away, raising them in secret. My parents didn't do me this favor.

They decided everyone should know about it, that I wasn't a mistake—but a miracle. Then, a few months later, they disappeared. They were wrong that people would accept me, and when they realized this, they left in the middle of the night without telling anyone.

This left me to be raised by my elven aunt, Lyudmila, pronounced lude-me-luh. It means "graceful," which she believed was the essence of what an elf was.

Sadly, she did not live up to her name. She was a cruel-looking woman. All angles and bones. Her grey hair was streaked with black. She was 172 years old, still young for an elf, even if she didn't look it. With her always was a silver cane, which she was also willing to whack me with if she disapproved of my actions. Which was nearly all of them. She believed that her brother's mistake had ruined the family name, and she took that out on me.

She had tall, thin ears, which she was incredibly proud of. Many of the older elves believed that the height of your ears was a direct relation to your status in culture. Don't let her know I told you this, but once, I went into her room and witnessed her using a wooden device to stretch them out longer than they were. I ran back out before she saw me because I was sure this would result in a beating from the cane.

I kept walking, and then I heard laughter and talking near me. I followed the noise, then I realized what day it was. It was the Mid-Solstice Festival, the biggest celebration in elven culture. Elves from all around the region would gather for this one big celebration. It really didn't matter what type of elf you were. The archers, cobblers, magicians, toy-makers. Even the dark elves would gather together and forget all their differences—for this one day at least. Every elf was welcome. Well, almost everyone, pretty much everyone but half-elves like me.

We were never really respected as a real being, just considered to be some sort of mutt. All the jokes had us at the end of them, and we were horridly mocked. One of the jokes that hurt me deep down as a kid was, "What's the only thing worse than an unwashed ogre? A HALF-ELF!" Then all the other little elves would run away laughing at me, leaving me alone again.

My thoughts were cut short when I heard a whimpering sound to my left. I saw a large tree with a curtain of ivy covering the hollow at its base.

I remembered this specific celebration. I was about seven or eight years old at this point. My aunt had been particularly angry with me that day. She claimed that my ears weren't pointed enough and that I was embarrassing her. I had nearly mentioned the ear stretching I had witnessed but managed to bite my tongue, fearing more abuse. She claimed my ears were so short I should be treated as an ordinary servant, which was all I was in her eyes.

She had been yelling at me for hours this day, "You will never be anything!" She had a shrill voice that sounded more like a weasel than an elf. I pointed this out one day when I was around five. She made me scrub the dirt off the floor. It took me several hours to realize that we had a dirt floor in the house.

"I should have thrown you and your filthy blood out of this house long ago." That is what she called my human side—filthy. "Your father never should have fallen for that filthy human wench. He could have had a great life, but he had to fall in love with a human of all things." Her voice

then went so high that I couldn't even tell what she was saying, but I could tell that she was mad.

After her yelling at me like that, I had just run into the woods. As I ran, I could still hear her piercing voice. It seemed she hadn't even noticed I was gone.

I ran to a little nook in one of the trees that was the perfect size for me to hide in. With the wall of ivy, I was able to escape from my wretched life, even if only for a few moments.

I was now staring at this very same tree, hearing my younger self sob behind the curtain of ivy. As I watched, Young Clef hopped up and ran to find a young birch tree. I followed him and watched as he peeled the bark off of it and carefully carved it into two long triangle shapes with his knife. Young Clef then went to an oak tree and took some of its sap, plastering it onto the bark. He used it as an adhesive and attached it to the backs of his ears. Running over to a puddle, the small boy looked into it and was impressed with his craftsmanship. For the first time, I had felt like I was a full elf and belonged there.

Standing in the woods and remembering that moment made me tear up a little bit. Fine, if you must know, I was crying. *Those years with my aunt had been awful, and I wouldn't wish that kind of verbal abuse on anyone. I started to walk away, trying to escape the memories. I blinked the tears out of my eyes and looked around. I saw I was standing in a crowd of elves. None of them seemed to notice me—though that was probably for the better—as they would have mocked me once more.*

I heard a rustle in the bushes to the left of me. When I looked, I saw my eight-year-old self come sauntering into the festival with his prosthetic ears. I remember that moment. I was so proud of myself, and I felt like I could literally do anything. I felt like a genius, and I was finally happy.

Now seeing it as a bystander, I realize that nobody there was fooled. The faux ears weren't the same size, and they weren't laying exactly right on Young Clef's head.

All of the elves were stifling laughs and whispering under their breath to one another. They honestly were laughing at me more than they would have if I had just come in as my "filthy" half-elf self. But Young Clef was oblivious to this and thought that everyone had forgotten he was a half-elf and really believed that he was an actual elf.

I watched him practically skip over to the other young elf boys and girls. The shoddy masquerade didn't fool them, and they were whispering and laughing behind Young Clef's back. They went along with it for a while, though, just planning the most painful way to humiliate him.

We all played in the woods for most of the celebration— as if we were all elves. Honestly, even I had forgotten that I wasn't a full elf for a few moments.

One of the young elves then called out, "Hey, let's go over to the river," and now I could see that he had winked at some of his friends. Unfortunately, my younger self didn't seem to notice it.

The young elf boy who proposed a swim was one of those who had mocked me the most openly. I remembered one time that I wanted to play with the other elves, but when I had walked to the group, he turned and pushed me into the mud, yelling, "Get away from us, freak." The elf boys and girls then all ran away from me, making their awful half-elf jokes.

Though now that this boy seemed to be friendly, Young Clef trusted him blindly and followed the elves over to the river. What came next hurt terribly bad, even some dozen years later, that I almost couldn't look, but I forced myself to. I followed the kids over to the river. Sometimes, you just have to see how bad you had it so that you can know how good you have it now.

I watched as all of the kids ran over to the river and started jumping or diving into it. My past self was the last one to go in. Young Clef ran towards the lake and threw himself into the river, making a giant splash. All of the other elves had their heads out of the water, watching where Young Clef was going to pop up, already prepared to laugh. The boy broke through the surface with a massive grin on his face, proud of how big a splash he had made. I remembered very few times I had smiled back then, and even this time, it didn't last long.

The kids had already begun to laugh. The smile got washed off Young Clef's face as quickly as the fake ears had in his triumphant splash. The joy was instantly replaced with a look of pure confusion.

At the time, I hadn't known what they were laughing about. It wasn't until they had started to pull and tug on their pointed ears that the young boy realized what had happened. Young Clef reached up, felt his ears, and noticed that one of the faux ears was missing, and the other had shifted.

The water had dissolved the make-shift adhesive. One of the ears had rotated around and was hanging off the bottom of his lobe. Young Clef looked down, and he was now able to see the other one floating in the water in front of him.

If not for the fact that he was already soaked in water, you would have seen tears running down the child's face. I had been so sad. For once in my life, I felt like I had belonged, even if I was just fooling myself. But as soon as I surfaced from the water, I came to the rude awakening that I was wrong. I had felt like I would never belong anywhere and that I would be alone for the rest of my life.

I watched as my heart-broken and defeated young self slowly swam over to the shore, with the other kids still laughing and calling out "Freak!" and "Mistake!"

I followed my past self back to the secret nook in the tree and watched him curl up in a ball and begin to cry. The next time he came out of the hole, he would be a different person.

While lying there crying, he decided that he didn't need anyone else to be happy. He would need to make his own life, and if everyone decided he didn't fit in, then he didn't want to fit in. The next day the boy left the elven village and started forging his own path, but for now, he was curled up and crying by himself.

I wished that I could lean down and tell him that he would eventually have friends. Even if everything felt bad now, he would eventually have a family, even if he wasn't blood-related to them. There would be Athelstan, Bonneville, Finnon, Roscoe, and—yeah—even Kriv. There was Brand and Tillie. But most of all, I wished that I could tell him of Malia, that she would be there for him, for a while at least. Then I felt a tidal wave of water rush over my head.

CHAPTER TWELVE

The God of Death

Waking up, I found myself lying on a dirty floor in a dark room. I looked up to see that Kriv was standing over me with an empty flask in one hand. As I was looking at him, one last drop of water fell out and hit me right between the eyes. I sat up, spitting out a mouthful of water. I went to put my left leg under me, so I could stand up and hit him, but I fell back down.

Looking down, I saw that my right boot was off, and there were holes in the side of it. My bloody pant leg was rolled up above my knee, and my leg was wrapped in what had been a white bandage. I was sure it was one of the many that Roscoe always had in his pack. I should be clear that it *had* been white. It was now splattered with red stains and grime, presumably my own blood from the rat bite. When Roscoe saw me try to get up, he held me down, which was probably good. The bite was terribly deep. It felt at least an inch or two, and possibly that it was already becoming infected.

I ran my hands through my hair, trying to brush the water out, when Finnon leaned in, tilted his head, and said as an observation rather than a cruel joke, "I never realized how small your ears are, for an elf at least." Without thinking, I reached over and punched him right in the stomach. Hard. I heard all his breath leave him, and he gasped in a new one.

Under my breath I said, much more aggressively than I typically would, "Don't. Talk. About. My ears." He looked at me, shook his head, and walked away, probably to start studying one of his books.

I felt bad punching him, but I couldn't control myself between the pain from my leg and my freshly opened emotional wounds from my childhood memory. Looking down at my leg, I was confused for a moment. "Hey,

Roscoe." I saw him look up as if he was scared, like I was going to punch him as well. "Why did you just have to pray over Kriv, and he's all good, but I have to deal with this make-shift bandage?"

"I can only ask so much. It wasn't my power that healed Kriv. It was hers." He looked up at the sky, referencing Anar, "Apparently, she doesn't think a rat bite is worth her time." He then shrugged as if he didn't know what else to say.

"Yeah, I'd like to see her deal with this bite. That was in no way a normal rat." He smirked a bit and kept wrapping my leg. "You got any of your herbs or anything? I don't know if I will be able to walk for a few days with this. That bite was at least a few inches deep."

He nodded and replied, "I do have Stenogyne kanehoana. It's great for taking care of pain." He reached into his bag and pulled out a fuzzy green leaf, and handed it to me. I took it thankfully, and started chewing on it. It tasted very minty, which is a lot better than most of the things he uses. I will say one thing, Roscoe may be klutzy and loud, but he sure knows his plants. Within a minute, the shooting pain in my leg faded down to a dull throb. Roscoe helped me pull my pant leg down and put my boot back on my foot.

I slowly stood up but almost fell. About halfway up, my leg gave out from under me. Fortunately, Bonneville caught me and didn't let me hit the ground. I said thanks under my breath, and she let go of me. My leg still hurt terribly, but I could deal with it.

I finally got a chance to look around the room. It was an octagonal room about ten feet across. About halfway up on every other wall was a small window. Though now they were all filled in with dirt from when the fortress had sunken into the ground. There were a few rotten wood benches along the walls, upon which Finnon and Kriv were sitting. Littered on the ground were old bows and snapped arrows. Fortunately, everyone had cleared them away from the center of the room before laying me down. I was led to believe that it must have been an old archery tower. "Hey, where are we?"

Bon-Bon was the one to answer, "Well, we managed to pull you out of the trap before the rats did any more damage, and we wedged it closed so we could get past. Once we got through the door, we found a few goblins waiting for us, but they weren't that big of an issue. We then found this side room that came off of that main room. Oh, speaking of, sorry if you have a headache.”

Now that she mentioned it, I did have a slight headache, but the Stenogyne kanehoana was quickly taking care of it. “Uh, why is that your fault?” I asked.

She replied quietly and very quickly, “I may have used you as a human club.”

“YOU DID WHAT!”

Kriv now decided to pipe in saying with a faint smirk, “My suggestion.”

I glared at him again. That guy really knows how to get on my nerves. I was about to charge him, but Roscoe grabbed my elbow and simply stared at me. I got the message. That was not a fight that I wanted to start. It was not the time or the place, and I was not in the condition to win.

Roscoe felt my body loosen, and he let go of me. “That medicine should help for a while, but in case the pain flares back up, here’s a bit more.” He handed me a few more leaves which I tucked into one of the pockets of my pack. “You will have to let me clean that wound a few more times, or it could get infected, and that would take you out for at least a week, possibly longer."

I nodded and was about to tell the team to head out when I noticed something odd. There was no door in the room. I could see no way to get into or out of the room. There were just eight solid walls, a floor, and a peaked roof. "How do we get out of here?"

Finnon looked up from his book, saying, "That wall to your left is actually a door. Grab that brick that is sticking out and pull." I walked over to it and found the brick he was talking about. I held onto it like a door handle, and the secret passage swung open surprisingly easily and quietly. I looked around and stepped out into the larger room. It was another octagonal room that was completely empty. Well—empty except for the six unconscious goblins lying on the floor.

"How did you guys find this place?" I asked, turning to look back into the archery tower.

"Well, one of those goblins threw me against the wall, and it popped out of place." Roscoe seemed to be both proud and embarrassed at the same time. I blinked once slowly and tried to conceal my laughter. I then started walking forward. There was only one hallway off of the main room, so we assumed that had to be the way to go. We walked down the hall for what felt like forever, but it was actually only about fifteen minutes. At that point, my leg was starting to send a jolt of pain through my body with every step, so I chewed up another one of the leaves, and it started to feel better.

Bon-Bon jogged a few steps to catch up to me and said, "Are you alright? You were acting a little weird back there. Even though they can be painfully annoying, I have never seen you hit one of those guys." She paused, and when I didn't answer, she continued sounding very concerned, "Anyway, in all seriousness, are you alright?"

She had always been the motherly one on the team. When one of us seemed upset or in distress, she would always be the first to offer to help us, though with Kriv... she let him struggle for a bit.

I waited a moment and then said, "Yeah, I'm fine. I don't know what it is, but I've been thinking a lot about my past. Not everything has been bad, but all in all, I haven't had a life people would envy. It just... I... Well, it just puts me a little on guard," I looked down and said quietly, "If that makes any sense."

She laughed. It wasn't exactly a laugh of joy or one of mocking. It's kind of hard to describe, almost like she was trying to fill an awkward moment. "Yeah, I get what that feels like. I haven't had what you would call a shiny past either, but if you want to talk about it, I'm here to listen."

"Thanks, a lot of it is very painful, so I don't talk about it often, but I'll keep that in mind." We continued walking down the hallway. There were multiple times that we had to decide a path to take, and I boldly decided a direction each time, though I have no idea why I went each way. Still, I'm never telling them that.

The hallways had widened at this point, so we were all walking in one big cluster. We eventually got to one of the divisions in the path when we started to hear a commotion up ahead of us, but I couldn't tell from which direction. I feared choosing a course, knowing I may be wrong. Again, I didn't know for sure what was coming towards us, but I could only assume.

I grabbed my lute from my pack and hissed, "Goblins. Everyone, grab onto me." I then felt three hands grab onto me, two on the waist and one on the shoulder. Looking to my right, I saw Kriv just stare at me with his arms crossed. I did not have time for this. I kicked my good leg out, tripped him, and then planted my foot on his chest. I started to strum out a simple melody on the lute and sang under my breath.

Super nos ab illis,

nos hic facimus.

Nosque ab omnibus,

nolite ergo audire eos.

Instantly, I felt a chill pass over me, and I felt the others shiver. Looking down, I could see that the spell had worked. My hands and lute were slightly translucent, and gazing over my shoulder, I could see that the others were as well. Kriv was fighting me, but Bon-Bon stepped in and planted her foot on his stomach. Between the two of us, we were able to hold him down. I could hear the goblins getting closer.

Roscoe didn't seem to realize what was happening, and I could feel his grip lightening. I had to keep singing, or the spell would drop. Fortunately, Bon-Bon realized what was happening and whispered, "Stop, we all have to keep contact with him, or you won't be concealed with the spell. So, nobody move."

As she finished saying this, the goblins rounded the corner. There were at least forty of them, and mentally I breathed a sigh of relief. We wouldn't be able to take on that many normally, and with my hurt leg and the close quarters, it would have been a fight that wouldn't end well.

When the goblins got within a yard of us, I heard everyone take a deep breath and begin to breathe shallow, quiet breaths. The goblins then stepped right through Kriv's head, and he flinched, but I managed to keep contact with him. The crowd of goblins continued and walked straight through all of us.

Rather than the well-trained guards I had seen in the past at various castles, these goblins were sloppy. They carried their weapons poorly and couldn't keep a straight line. They would run into each other, and none of them were stepping at the same time. It gave me a small moment of relief, knowing how untrained the goblins were.

It took a few minutes for all of the goblins to pass. It wasn't until the goblins were well past us that everyone finally took a deep breath of air. I almost laughed. They obviously hadn't realized that—along with making us invisible and non-material—I also had hidden us from every other sense. Hence the goblins seeming to be entirely oblivious to us or that they didn't hear my singing. It wasn't until we couldn't hear the goblins anymore that I let the spell drop.

...nolite ergo audire eos.

I felt a warm breeze pass over me. Bon-Bon and I let Kriv stand back up. I had to take a moment to catch my breath. Not only is it hard to have to sing and play for so long, it's even harder to hold a charm for such extended periods of time. Spells like that drain you both physically and mentally. I wouldn't be able to do another spell that strong for at least an hour or two. It takes a while to regain all that energy.

Kriv got up and grunted at me angrily.

I replied, "Maybe next time, if you listen to me when I give a command, I won't have to pin you down to the ground." He, unsurprisingly, said nothing. We kept walking forward again, taking the path the goblins had just come down. We figured that they would be unlikely to retrace their steps.

Eventually, we came to the end of the hallway and found a simple wooden door. I made sure to check for a wire this time before I slowly opened it.

Inside was a very cluttered, messy room. There were several tables around it, with symbols cut into the walls. We looked around the room a bit, just seeing what there was. I saw Kriv pocket a few things. None of it seemed very religiously or culturally significant, so I didn't say anything. It still annoyed me, though.

In one corner of the room, we found a small altar with symbols and what seemed like religious drawings sketched and painted onto it.

I called Roscoe over to me to see if he could figure out which god or goddess it was worshipping. He looked at it for several minutes, running his fingers across the runes before he suddenly gasped, jumping back in fear.

"What does it mean, Roscoe?" I asked.

"Nothing good." He shook his head and said, "We need to be extremely careful around here, this is not a god we want to anger, and the same goes for his followers. This seems to be an altar to Mirgan, an ancient god of death. Specifically painful and horrific deaths. He savors any moment that someone suffers. There are only a few cultures that still worship him, but those who do are always violent and easy to become angered."

"Are goblins one of the ones that worship him?" Unfortunately, I didn't know much about the gods, so I had to turn to Roscoe anytime I had a question.

"No… goblins don't believe in any gods. They aren't evolved enough to have someone to worship. Of the ones that worship him, I don't think that any of them are around this area."

Suddenly we became aware of a whimpering behind us. We looked back and noticed that under one of the tables was a shaking creature covered by a blanket. It was crying and muttered only three things, "failed," "angered," and "Arkra."

I pulled out my rapier and slowly walked over to it. I poked it in the back, expecting to have a goblin greet me, but instead, I saw a long green tail pop out from under the blanket. The creature slowly rolled over, and the face of a giant green lizard greeted me. I jumped back, and the beast climbed out from under the table and stood up on its two back feet.

Its shoulders were still shaking while it was repeating the same three words.

The blanket fell off its shoulders, and I realized that it had the body of a human, just covered in green reptilian scales.

It looked similar to Kriv, but it was much more slender and weaker looking. While Kriv had draconic features, this thing was more like a lizard. Standing at its full height, it only came to about my chest.

He was now saying under his breath while looking at the ground, "Has failed my queen, deserves what comes."

Kriv pushed me aside and growled, saying a word that sounded like *uh-scab-o-late.*

"What was that?" Finnon asked Kriv.

At the same time, Roscoe whimpered, "Oh gods…"

"What's wrong, Rosc-," I trailed off. I knew what he was going to say from the look of fear on his face. I very rarely saw him look that scared, and it made my stomach drop, knowing that if he was frightened, we were in for a lot of trouble.

CHAPTER THIRTEEN

The Ascabolates

Roscoe said what I had been thinking, "The Ascabolates," which was what Kriv had called this lizard creature, "are one of the cultures that worship Mirgan. I thought they were all extinct. There has been no record of them for years. Our day just got a lot harder… and a lot more deadly." Roscoe sounded both fascinated with his discovery, yet also terrified for his life.

The creature now looked up, and when he saw Kriv, he jumped back and cried out, "No. Please, no hurt Zook. Zook mean no harm. He only try to do as queen say."

"Lesser kind, you are nothing," that was the longest sentence I had ever heard come from Kriv. The creature, Zook, I assume, seemed to be terrified of my dragon comrade. I wonder what that whole lesser kind thing means. I wasn't going to ask Kriv, though.

I quickly pushed Kriv away and said, "Hey, buddy, we don't want to hurt you," I spoke to Zook gently to calm his fears, "we're on a mission to discover why the goblins are attacking the local villages."

He jumped back again, looking terrified, and said, "No goblins, please no make Zook do that again. Zook already fail Arkra once, no do again."

So obviously, the Ascabolates were having an issue with the goblins as well.

"We won't make you see the goblins again. We want to get rid of them. We want the same thing that you do." He looked up at me, and I thought I saw a little bit of hope in his eyes. "Who is Arkra, though?"

"Arkra is queen. Zook must serve queen."

Bon-Bon stepped in at this point, "Could you take us to her, Zook?" She also spoke compassionately, much better than I was doing.

"Zook can't see queen, queen will be angry with Zook, he will be punished." His shoulders began to shake again as he choked on his sobs.

I looked at Bon-Bon and said under my breath, "You got this?" She nodded in reply, and I stepped back from her and Zook. It was tough to communicate with his broken speech. I heard her as she continued asking him more questions, trying to figure out what had happened, and figure out which way it was to the queen.

Even if they were a crazy, god-of-death worshipping race, they might be our best hope for taking care of the goblins—if we could come to some sort of agreement that didn't end in our violent and painful death.

I looked around the room a little bit more and saw that there were four other doors leading out of the area. I looked into the first one and found that it was a basic sleeping chamber. There wasn't much in there other than a few very well-used beds and a small chest. I opened the trunk, finding that it was just filled with loincloths. It looks like Kriv isn't the only one who favors this bold fashion choice.

The next room turned out to be an armory. I looked inside to see if there was anything that I could use. I found one well-crafted bow that was in pretty good condition, so I took that, along with a full quiver of arrows. I have always been pretty good with a bow. Maybe it was from my elven side, or I was just naturally talented with one. I had a feeling that we would need all the weapons we could get. Looking around a bit more, there wasn't much else that suited me.

Opening the third room, I found an even more elaborate altar inside. It was inscribed with more of the same carvings that Roscoe had identified on the other one. Though this altar was much more extensive, and the symbols seemed to have been filled with gold.

Littered around the altar were old bleached bones, that I hoped were not human—or elven, for that matter. There were a few small figurines on the altar and several that looked like ravens carved out of a very dark wood. Another was a humanoid figure with large raven wings sprouting out of its back. It appeared to be formed out of solid gold. It was a good thing Kriv wasn't in here, or he probably would have stolen it. When I pointed the golden figure out to Roscoe, he told me that it was a figure of the death god, Mirgan. There were a few other figures, but they were so worn down and aged that I couldn't tell what they were. To me, they were just formless shapes.

I left that room, about to open the final door, when Bon-Bon called over to me. I went to her and she said, "Hey, I finally got enough information out of him that I think I know what is happening. I don't know why the goblins are here or how, but I do know that they are attacking the Ascabolates the same way as the village. I don't know why they chose him, but apparently, Zook was sent to try and kill the goblin king and bring back his head. It seems that he failed and was ambushed here." That explains those goblins that came down the path towards us. They must have been coming back from beating him. "Because of that, the queen is going to punish him. He is scared to go see her, but he also knows that he has to accept the punishment."

Zook was back down on the ground shivering again, just talking about how he had failed and was going to be punished. He seemed to have a very broken form of speech.

"Did you find out where the queen is?" I questioned, "That might be our best bet for taking care of the goblins."

"No, he was scared that we were going to take him to the queen. He refused to say where she was," Bon-Bon replied in disappointment.

"Alright, then, I guess we better keep searching. We should probably take Zook with us, though. I wouldn't want to leave him here like this." Even though he was hard to speak to, and didn't seem like he would be much help, I didn't want to leave him to die. Either at the hands of more goblins or by the Ascabolate queen.

"The middle door there is an armory," I told the others, "If any of you want to stock up on supplies, I feel like we are going to need it." They went off to grab new weapons, all except Kriv, that is. He seemed to be disgusted at the thought of using an Ascabolate weapon.

From what I could determine, it seems that his draconic ancestors consider themselves to be superior to this smaller lizard race. The hatred had gone back centuries, and Kriv wasn't going to let it go.

Bon-Bon came back from the armory with a bow and quiver to match mine. Roscoe had grabbed a set of throwing knives, and Finnon grabbed one of the smaller spears.

"Alright. Let's go." I went over to the final door and pulled it open. Not paying attention, I didn't see the wire running up the frame—again.

This time, I jumped back in time. I would have been seriously hurt or even killed if I hadn't. Where I had been standing, a bucket of large rocks plummeted down and crashed on the ground, spilling pebbles as small as my fingernail to stones as large as my fist across the floor.

Unfortunately, that wasn't the only issue that we had. Charging out the door were six more of the Ascabolates. These ones were not nearly as dainty as Zook. They each held a spear in their hands and had a bow and quiver strapped to their back. I pulled out my lute and started singing again.

Stopio lle rydych chi,

Peidiwch â dod yn nes.

Nid ydym yn pwy ydych chi eisiau,

Ewch ffordd arall.

It was working, though I had to admit I wasn't surprised. This is one of the most powerful spells that I know. It is one that slows down the functioning of someone's mind. It doesn't leave any real damage to them, but it helps the rest of my team be able to prepare themselves for the battle, and allows me a few minutes to plan. It was working well, the Ascabolates' faces all went blank, and they stopped moving. They dropped their weapons to the ground. I continued singing.

Trowch yn ôl o gwmpas

Ewch gyfe-

"Owwwww!" I screamed. I suddenly had a shooting pain down my right arm. I looked down and saw an arrow sticking out of my shoulder. One of the lizards in the back hadn't been fully affected by my spell. He had shot an arrow at me. It hurt terribly, forcing me to drop my lute and pull my rapier out with my left arm. My right arm was useless now. I looked to my right and saw that Finnon had run forward with his newly acquired spear, ready to throw it. But I watched in horror as he slipped on the pile of rocks I had narrowly avoided being crushed by. One of the lizards threw himself on my friend and tied him up.

I saw Roscoe get overpowered before his throwing knife could even leave his hand. I'll never forget the desperation and the will to survive that was on his face as I saw him stuffed into a burlap sack, as if he was no more than a bushel of potatoes.

It was all happening at the same time, horrifyingly fast, and yet I felt I was watching it all in slow motion…

Three of the creatures had surrounded Kriv. I've never seen him defeated and beaten the way he was now. Kriv gave a valiant effort to win. I saw what looked like a nasty bite on one of the Ascabolate's arms that was pouring out blood… well, I assumed that thick yellow-colored ooze gushing out was their blood.

I raised my rapier with my good arm, ready to fight the lizard charging me, when I heard Bon-Bon call out from behind me. "Clef. We have to choose our battles. We need to live to fight another day."

I knew she was right. The two of us against this many lizards was a fight she and I could generally win. But with my useless arm, we likely wouldn't make it out of the battle. She walked forward to stand beside me, dropping her glaive, raising her hands to surrender. I lowered my rapier. Unfortunately, our idea of a peaceful surrender was the wrong choice.

I saw one of the soldiers raise one of the stones in one hand and bring it down over Bon-Bon's head. I attempted to call out, but it was too late. She collapsed on the ground.

Not even a second later, I felt something like a giant tail knock my legs out from under me. Then, everything went dark as I hit the floor.

CHAPTER FOURTEEN

The Necklace

*L*ooking around, I saw that I was in my old room. Not the one at the Brazen Unicorn. Or the one at my cruel aunt's house—not that I really had a room there—instead, I slept on the dirt floor in the pantry.

But this room was a different story. This was the one I had while I was training with Athelstan. While the room was small and cramped with nothing special about it, it was the first place I thought of at the mention of home.

I looked around the place and saw that everything was in disarray, which was typical of my room back then. There were rolls of parchment strewn about and old clothes on the ground. Every surface was covered in sheet music—the desk, the chair, the bed, and even the floor. Honestly, you could see more sheet music than you could of anything else. I had spent most of my time back then studying and trying to learn more songs and spells.

Honestly, seeing the room as such a mess brought more comfort than it would have if it was perfectly tidy. This was what it was like for me then. The best years of my life were spent in this messy, cluttered, simple room. Even now, I am not really known for my organizational skills. The only reason my room back at the tavern isn't more cluttered is that I have all the spells memorized and don't need so many parchments, though I do still have several tucked away as mementos.

The only item that was always carefully put away in its own special place was my prized lute. Though looking now at its shelf, I saw that the lute was missing.

After such a painful and chaotic day, I wished that I could go back to this moment and just stay there. I wanted to lay down in the bed and sleep for hours. I actually did end up going over to the bed and trying to move the sheet music, only to realize that my hand went right through the papers. That makes sense, though. I can't try to change a memory— just re-experience it. I decided to lay down anyway, documents and all. I couldn't actually feel the mattress, but I remembered what it was like.

The first night I slept there, I felt like I was lying on the most comfortable mattress ever, which it was. With one of Athelstan's unique charms, the bed would now magically mold itself to whoever slept in it, lending to a perfect night's sleep.

I lay there for a few minutes in the old bed, trying to remember what day this had been. I didn't have long to ponder as I was rudely interrupted by my past self barging into the room with the lute in his hand.

I wished I could have kept lying down, but I got up and stood in one of the corners, still trying to remember what day this was. He ran in, placing the lute Athelstan had made on the shelf.

Young Clef then started running around the room, tidying up. He was taking papers and shoving them into drawers.

Finally, he took the dirty clothes, pushed them under the bed, and then quickly pulled up the bed's blankets over the sheet music.

The only reason I had ever cleaned my room like that was when I knew she would be coming by. Even the thought of her name now made my heart beat faster. She was the one that was always there with me. She was the one that would laugh at my jokes even if they weren't funny. She was there to smile when I got a spell right, or to giggle when I messed one up. She was the one, the only one that mattered.

Young Clef had just finished shoving some more papers in a drawer when there was a faint knock on the door, "Hey, Clef. Are you all done hiding that mess in there, or should I make another lap around the hall?"

Her voice was the sweetest thing I had ever heard. There was not a drop of magic in her blood, but her voice was still the most enchanting thing that had ever touched my ears. My heart nearly beat out of my chest, and I had to remind myself she wasn't actually there with me. She hadn't been there in a while. But that didn't matter. I still felt like a teenager in love once again.

Lacking a response, she asked again, "Clef, can I come in?"

"Uhhh, yeah. Just… one… second." This whole time I had been using my hip to try and shove closed a drawer overly filled with old scrolls. I had then started spinning in circles, making sure the whole room was clean. The younger version of myself saw a pair of trousers on the chair's back. They were quickly scooped up and thrown in the wardrobe.

"And… uh… I don't know what mess you're talking about. My room was already clean." I know, for being one who uses words for magic, I wasn't a smooth talker, but that was because it was her. I was filled with joy even now just at the memory of her. Just remember what it was like being a teenager in love. Give me a little slack.

She gave a sweet little laugh and slowly opened the door. I would not have been surprised if an angelic chorus broke out when she walked in. She was beautiful. Not the type where men do a double-take, but the type where men will stop and stare slack-jawed at her, and she knew it. She was the most beautiful woman I had ever seen. Aphrodite herself was the only rival, and even then, the goddess of beauty had the disadvantage. While she was well aware of her effects on men, she didn't take advantage of it, and wasn't vain. Despite the fact she could have any suitor in the world, she chose me.

She stepped through the door, and my stomach was in my throat, both then and now. "Hey, Malia," my past self said.

This was Malia. Beautiful Malia Mylls. Malia, with the golden hair that seemed always to be shining. Malia, with the green eyes that the forests and meadows paled in comparison to. Malia, the one that would laugh, cry, and smile with me. Malia was the love of my life, and no one will ever compare to her.

"Hey, Clef. What was it that you wanted to show me?"

Young Clef had to remind himself to breathe before he could speak, "Oh, well, I learned this new spell today from your father, and I thought that you would want to see it."

With that, my past self grabbed a sad potted plant from the window that looked as though it hadn't been watered in weeks. It was brown and dead, barely more than a stick. He held it and placed it on a small table next to the bed. He then walked over and grabbed the lute from the shelf. While he was doing this, Malia sat down carefully on the edge of the bed. She could clearly tell there were rolls of parchment under the covers, but she didn't say anything. That was how she had always been, never rude or judgmental. The only way to describe her… was perfect.

My past self looked at Malia with a charming and charismatic grin. See. I wasn't totally awkward around the ladies. She smiled back, and her eyes sparkled. Then Clef looked down at the lute and began to play. It was a sweet song, slow and melodic. He played for a few seconds and then began to sing.

Fás plandaí fás,

cuid acu ar ais sa saol

Ná bí marbh níos mó,

bí glas arís.

The words were in a long-forgotten language. I didn't know what they actually meant—I just knew that there was power in them. Athelstan had told me they were from an old dwarven song that was meant to celebrate life and growth. As soon as I heard Young Clef sing this song, I knew what day this was, and I almost cried remembering it.

Caithfidh an saol,

arís eile fásann tú.

Glas a bheidh tú,

lig dom luí uirthi.

As the song continued, it became clearer that something was happening. As the music began to get louder, it sped up. The plant started to turn green again, growing taller and taller, reaching a height of about five inches. The song continued, and the plant eventually had a full blossoming daisy, but the spell wasn't done.

Teastaíonn uaim,

fás suas ard.

Cas go planda criostail,

bí i do bhláth anois.

The spell continued, but the flower wasn't growing anymore. It was instead beginning to sparkle and glow slightly. Malia leaned in closer to the flower in awe and wonder. She couldn't believe what was happening. It just didn't seem that something like that could be possible.

Lean ort ag fás,

glan ag fás anois.

Cas ar gem,

fás suas ard.

The last line of the song slowed down and became quiet and melodic once again. As the final note of the song died out, so did the ball of light that had been growing around the flower. The flower had undergone a complete transformation. Now, instead of a dead branch—as it had been— it was a clear crystal daisy that you could see all the way through. The flower itself was a perfect diamond, and the stem had become a flawless emerald. Upon tilting the flower in the light, you could faintly see images of Malia and me in it.

Watching this scene unravel again, I saw Young Clef pull the chair from the desk and sit down in it so he was facing her. Young Clef pulled the flower from the pot, put it in Malia's hand, and closed her fist around it. "This is so that you and I will always be connected. You will always have a part of me with you." She looked down at the flower, turning it to see the different images—the first time we met, our first kiss, the first time I said "I love you," and finally, the moment I was watching now. Then I watched as one single tear ran down her cheek. She brushed it away quickly, hoping I wouldn't see it, but both then and now, I had. At the time, I thought it was a tear of joy, but now I knew what it really meant.

She looked up at Young Clef, and kissed him on the forehead. She leaned back and said, "This means the world to me, Clef. I will never let this out of my sight." She placed the flower back in the dirt, and in the reflection, you could see the night we stayed out late to watch the stars.

Malia then reached up and took off a simple necklace she was wearing. It had a beautiful silver woven chain, and hanging from it was a single blue stone. Seeing it now, I reached up and felt the very same gem around my throat. "With this, I hope that you will never forget me. I want you to know that you will always be in my heart, and I hope that I will always be in yours." When she finished speaking, she leaned towards me and, with her gentle hands, clasped it around Young Clef's neck.

My past self looked down at the necklace for a moment. I hadn't ever been one to be big on jewelry, but the chain seemed to be perfectly in place. "I could never forget you, Malia. You mean the world to me. I would do anything for you."

She looked down, another tear fell off her perfect skin, and she said very quietly, "I know. That's why it hurts so much for me to tell you this." She paused for a moment. The following four words she would say were the most painful thing I ever had to take. More painful than my parents abandoning me, my aunt's abuse, or the constant mockery I had to endure. All of that was nothing compared to those four words.

"I have to go." Young Clef tried to speak, but Malia cut him off. "Please, don't talk. This is already painful enough. This has nothing to do with you, but I need to make my own life, go and live my own adventure. I can't do what you do. You know I can't use magic. I can't live my whole life in this small town. I have to go find my own way."

"Then marry me, and we can make a new life together. We'll leave and never look back," I begged.

She sounded sad when she responded, "Clef, don't do that to me. I would marry you in a heartbeat, but we're both too young. I can't ask you to do that. I can't let you do that. You have to stay here and finish your training. Father told me you are more talented than you could ever imagine."

"I don't care about what Athelstan says. I care about you. That's all I care about. I don't want us to be separated." I had been on the verge of tears. I was finally happy, but then

the love of my life had to be wrenched away from me. Even now, I had to reach up and brush a tear off my cheek.

"No," her tone had changed from sweet to reprimanding. "You will not throw away your training. You could be the best bard this world has ever seen, and I won't have it on my conscience that I prevented that. It was already hard enough to get father to let me leave. There is no way that he would let you leave as well. So you need to accept that I am leaving and you are staying here."

"But... Malia... I want to... go... with you." My past self choked on his words, trying to prevent the sobs from flying out.

"I don't want you to throw away your life for me. You have a future, and with your talent, you can do anything. Please, Clef, stop fighting with me. This is already hard enough. I wanted to say goodbye on a good note." She weakly smiled and leaned over, kissing Young Clef again— this time on the lips. It felt like the world had disappeared. The only thing that mattered was that Malia and I were together. I could still remember that kiss. It was like my lips were being burnt and frozen at the same time.

Sadly, the kiss seemed to end as soon as it began, and she stood up and walked to the door. Putting her hand on the knob, she turned it but didn't open it.

She said almost inaudibly, "I love you, Clef," This wasn't the first time we said it, but this was the most powerful. We weren't just teenagers saying we loved each other. She meant it this time.

"I love you too, Malia," Young Clef replied with as much conviction. I couldn't hold back the tears anymore. That was the last thing I ever said to her, and the last thing I would probably ever speak to her again. I had realized at that moment I had to stop fighting to keep her, but I had to be strong enough to let her go.

Malia said quietly, barely above a whisper, "Maybe if the fates allow it, I will see you again." We both knew how unlikely that was, but we didn't want to speak it aloud. She then left the room without saying anything else. It hurt to watch her walk out like that again. I knew it would do nothing, but I followed her out of the room, leaving my past self on the floor, clutching the necklace while crying.

Going out the door, I looked to my left and saw nothing, but I heard a noise to my right. Looking that way, I saw

Malia sitting on the floor, holding the diamond flower. She had her knees pulled up to her chest, and she was crying. Her head was tilted down to where her beautiful hair hid most of her face, but walking closer, I could see Malia was slightly turning the flower so that she could see more of our moments together. Looking at her face, I could tell that she was smiling. But it wasn't her usual smile—the one that lit up an entire room. This time it was a painful smile, one realizing all the great times we had together, and knowing that there wouldn't be anymore.

I walked over to her and sat down with her, watching as the flower showed new images, and I took a moment to remember all the great times we had together. Then, tears began to stream down my face once more, and it took all my energy just to prevent gasping sobs from erupting out of me.

Then, suddenly I found myself pitched sideways, and I hit my head on the floor.

CHAPTER FIFTEEN

The Prison

I regained consciousness, finding myself in an old rusty cell. I had hit my head on the ground when one of the soldiers had thrown me in. My shoulder was still throbbing from the arrow wound, but I did notice that it had been cleaned slightly. The arrow was gone, and there was a dirty bandage in its place. I was relieved to find I could move my arm again. Apparently, the lizards had some ounce of courtesy.

Immediately after noticing my arm had been tended to, another startling realization hit me. My shirt was gone, along with all my gear and lute. I had been left only my trousers and Malia's necklace, which I grabbed onto as if it were the only thing that could save me. With my other hand, I reached up and wiped the rivers of tears from my cheeks.

Looking down, I saw that the cages were filthy. There were a few inches of grime and sludge at my feet, which were sadly shoeless, so the filth seeped between my toes. I hoped that I wouldn't be here long enough to discover what the sludge was. I could only imagine.

I was relieved when I discovered I wasn't completely alone. While my team and I were all in the same room, we were each in our own cell, except for Finnon and Roscoe, who were forced to share one. I guess the Ascabolates assumed two small men made one whole. Zook, however, was not with us. I assumed he had been taken back to the queen to receive his punishment.

The cages we were in were much too small for us. I couldn't even stand all the way straight up in mine without hitting my head. Which was a good thing because the pain in my leg had come back, and I couldn't put any weight on it. I debated for a few moments and decided sitting in the grime was better than the pain in my leg. I sat down in the cleanest part of the cell I could find, but the ground still made an unpleasant squishing sound as I sat.

I looked at my comrades and saw that two of them didn't fit in their cells either. Kriv had to crouch down in his cell, and Bonneville's head just barely brushed the top of hers. Roscoe and Finnon, on the other hand, could have jumped up and down and still been fine. I guess sometimes it pays to be short. Who knew?

Along with all of our gear being taken, Bonneville's armor was also removed. She was now just wearing rough linen clothes.

Examining my cell, I found that the bars of the cage were about as thick as my wrist, with only a few inches between them. The bars were so rusted that I feared touching them. Sadly, despite the rustiness, they still seemed to be very sturdy.

One of the soldiers came over to my cage and unlocked it. This was the first of the soldiers I had seen wearing armor of any kind, and the other lizards seemed to respect him. I assumed he must have been the captain. I was disheartened when I recognized him as the one who had shot me. Coming into the cell, he turned and locked the door again.

He got uncomfortably close to me and ran one of his claws up my chest, leaving a razor fine slice on my flesh as he said, "Well, what have we got here?" When I looked down, I saw that he had Malia's necklace hanging on his claw.

"That is worth nothing to anyone but me." He ignored me, and I tried to pull away, but he held my right arm around the arrow wound.

"Let—it—go!" He ignored me again, and with a single flick of his wrist, he pulled it off my neck, snapping the chain in half. He laughed once and then walked out of the cage, locking it again.

He was about to leave the room when Bon-Bon threw herself against the side of her cage, creating a thunderous rattling sound. She practically growled, "That is not yours to take and is worth *nothing*. If you don't give that back, I swear to you, no cage is going to stop me from getting to you."

She then reached forward and started to pull the bars of the cage apart. The lizard was obviously scared enough because he threw the necklace back at me. I caught it before it fell into the grime.

The soldiers all left the room, obviously trying to get as far away from Bonneville as they could.

Once they were all gone, she called out to me, "I know a guy back home who can fix that for you, no problem. Just tell him you know me."

"Thanks… but why did you do that?" For all Bonneville knew, it was just a necklace. I had never told her the significance. I had never told *anyone* about the importance.

"I could see your face when he took it from you. It was like a part of you was being ripped away. Plus, I know you would have done the same for me."

"Thank you. This is one part of my past I don't want to forget." While we had been talking, I took the necklace and wrapped it around my wrist, tucking in the loose ends, making sure there was no way that it could fall off. Once I was sure it was safe, I leaned back in the cage, waiting to see what came next.

We were left in the cells for several hours. A guard would come to check and make sure the cages were still intact every few minutes—though they seemed to give a wider berth around Bonneville's.

Roscoe and Finnon didn't seem all that bothered by the grimy environment. Instead, they passed the time playing some sort of card game in their cage. I assume Roscoe had a deck stashed away in a pocket that the guards hadn't found. I don't really know how the game works, but there seemed to be a lot of punching in it. I think I even saw Roscoe bite Finnon at one point. Note to self, do not play card games with them.

Bon-Bon and Kriv just sat in their cages doing nothing.

I was sure Bonneville was trying to come up with a daring escape plan. I couldn't... no... wouldn't even begin to fathom what Kriv was thinking.

After a few hours of sitting in the cage, I realized this wasn't an issue at all. I was a bard, after all. All I needed were my words.

When the next guard came in, I started muttering under my breath again.

Stopio lle rydych chi,

Peidiwch â dod yn nes.

Nid ydym yn pwy ydych chi eisiau,

Ewch ffordd arall.

It was the same one I had used before. It was much harder to make it work now—without my lute—but I could still do it. The lizard had frozen about three feet from my cell. As I was singing, I started reaching out to try and grab the ring of keys off his belt. I was becoming light-headed and felt that I would faint. My fingers were a mere few inches from the keys when I collapsed. I was barely able to keep singing.

Bonneville picked up where I had ended and began reaching out for the keys.

I got about halfway through the next verse, and Bon-Bon was an inch away from the keys, when the same guard that had tried to take my necklace came in. He saw the soldier that had stopped in place and stormed over to my cage, I tried singing louder and pushing more will into my voice, but it seemed to do nothing to him.

He yelled at me, "Enough of that freak." Bonneville quickly pulled her arm back into her cell before the Ascabolate could stomp on her hand.

He didn't really seem to care about her, though. All of his attention was on me. The lizard pulled the cage door open, proceeding to drag me into the middle of the room, and he kicked me in the ribcage. I heard a crack and a sharp pain in my side. I cried out in pain, and in the middle of it, I felt a rag shoved into my mouth. It tasted like vinegar and grime. Another rag was tied around my mouth and cinched behind my head, ensuring that I couldn't spit the cloth out. I don't know when it happened, but there were now nearly a dozen lizards in the room.

They then pulled me back to the cell and shackled me to the back of my cage. I was on my knees, and my hands were behind my back—several inches higher than comfortable. I tried to fight, but with my hurt leg and shoulder and the freshly broken rib, there was nothing I could do to save myself—or the others.

The captain got down in my face while pressing the tip of his spear into the base of my throat and said very quietly, "You try anything like that again, and we won't be nearly as nice to you next time." He turned and walked out of my cage, slamming it on the way out. It hit so hard that a rain of dirt and rust showered down on me from the top bars.

He grabbed the Ascabolate that was closest to him and forced it in front of my cage, and said to him, "Stay here and guard him. There is to always be a guard at his door, and if

he tries something, feel free to deal with it as you see fit."
He looked right at me and grinned with squinted eyes.

As he was leaving the room, Bon-Bon threw herself at her cage again and growled at him. The captain quickly turned and hit her in the chest with the butt of his spear. He pushed her all the way back to where she was pinned against the wall, and his face was pressed between the bars. "Don't start that, or you'll wind up just like your friend did."

Bon-Bon reached up and pulled the spear out of his hand, snapping it in half. She threw each end at him, but he expertly sidestepped them.

"Bind her as well," he said, dismissing her with a wave of his hand. Then, without another word, he walked to the door of the room and left the others to deal with Bonneville.

Bon-Bon was also pulled out of her cage and was beaten relentlessly. They kicked her and stabbed at her with their spears. While I had quickly given up, she kept fighting. I saw several of the lizards get pulled down to the ground, and one was literally thrown all the way across the room.

Eventually, they subdued her and put her back in the cage. This time they shackled her as well. While I was cuffed kneeling, her wrists were cuffed to the top of her cell, so she had no way to rest her beaten body. She just had to stand. She, however, was not given the disgusting rag. I could not explain how envious I was of her at that moment. If I could open my mouth, I would have thrown up by now.

But then I saw how bad her beating really had been, and I only felt compassion for her. While I suffered a cracked rib, her abuse was much worse. She had a split lip, and a large bruise was already forming around her left eye. I could see that her clothes were now soaked in blood, and she was trying to keep her weight off her right leg. I would guess that she had several broken ribs as well.

One of the lizards said to my comrades, "If any of you want to be like them, just tell us now." He looked hopeful that one of them would react. Instead, Kriv sat in his cage, staring straight ahead with a look of defiance. I could just barely see Roscoe and Finnon huddled in the back of their cage, holding onto one another, shaking their heads vigorously. All of the lizards—except one at my cell door and one at Bonneville's—left us.

I looked to Bonneville again. I had never seen Bon-Bon look so bad. Once, I saw her battle with an ogre, and she came out of it with barely a scratch.

I rattled my chains, hoping to have Bonneville look at me. Sometimes we could develop a plan by merely looking at each other. She didn't move, but the lizard at my door slammed the butt of his spear into my chest.

"What are you trying to do?" he yelled at me. When I didn't respond and remained motionless, he turned away once more. I looked to Bonneville again, and she still hadn't moved.

Seeing her like this made me feel like this was the end.

I would never leave this cell…

I would never hold my lute…

Never sing another song…

I would never see anyone again…

Then it hit me… I would truly never see Malia again.

I was going to die in this dirty, rusty cell, handcuffed with my hands behind my back, with a vinegar-soaked rag in my mouth. My, how the mighty have fallen. Just when I believed that all hope was lost and that nothing was ever going to get better, the captain came back in.

"Take them. She is ready." He then turned on his heel and walked out of the room.

CHAPTER SIXTEEN

The Queen

The guards in the room started pulling us out of the cages. They sent several in each cell for Bon-Bon and me. The cuffs were kept on our arms, and the rag was left in my mouth. It was getting hard for me to breathe with the smell of it, and there were several times I had begun to gag on the taste of it.

The Ascabolates started marching us down a long, plain hallway. Bon-Bon was up front, and I was right behind her. I didn't know where the others were, but I could hear their steps behind us. I watched as Bon-Bon almost fell a few times, but the guards harshly pulled her back up by the shackles. They would then prod her forward, forcing her to go faster. Each time I heard her gasp out in pain. I had never heard her cry out in pain like that.

My leg gave out on me once, but I managed to avoid falling and therefore avoided being prodded along.

I wished that I could have helped Bon-Bon, but there was nothing I could do. Even if I had my whole pack and my lute, I couldn't think of any way to help her, given that I was still bound and gagged. Even if I managed to get away from the guards, I was still too weak to really do anything.

We were forced to walk about a mile in total, down several different hallways, taking many seemingly random turns. I assume that the guards were just trying to disorient us—and it worked.

The halls were just as dirty as the cells. The floor was covered in grime and filth. There were occasionally some lit sconces on the walls, but we had to walk in darkness for most of the time. Unfortunately, I could also hear rats running around our feet, though I couldn't see them in the dim light. At one point, a rat ran across my foot. I couldn't see it. I could only feel its claws and tail slide across my bare feet. When I tried to kick it, I accidentally hit the lizard to the right of me. He proceeded to punch me in the rib. I heard another snap and felt another rib crack.

I'm telling you—rats only lead to trouble.

We eventually got to some pitch-black and narrow halls. The only thing to guide us was the squeaking of the rats and the prodding of spears.

Walking for so long was the perfect amount of time to allow my leg to start having that shooting pain again. Man, I wished I had some of that minty goodness Roscoe had given me. But that was still in my pack, wherever that was.

Finally, our long journey ended. We came into a large expansive room that was ornately decorated. In the other rooms, I could have reached up and touched the ceiling if I hadn't been cuffed—of course. Here, I don't think I could throw a rock high enough even to come close to the ceiling. Given just the pure size of the room, I assumed it must have been the great hall of the fortress.

Unlike the rest of the building, the floor was immaculate. It appeared to be a white marble stone with gold streaks running through. The walls were also polished, and I could see that they were a light granite. The room was, surprisingly, extremely well-lit from silver sconces on the walls.

Interspaced between the sconces, the walls were adorned with large tapestries. None of them were the same color or pattern, but they somehow fit with the room. They seemed to be from every region, culture, and religion. I recognized a few of them as being from the east and a few more from the west. Some of them depicted animals, like one with a stag on it, while some had religious figures. I recognized one of the old elven gods on a purple tapestry. One that was very close to me was just solid black, but it seemed to shine and glimmer in the light. The only tapestries that seemed to ever repeat were four large black wall-hangings that had the same runes from the Mirgan altars embroidered on them.

The room was, all-in-all, beautiful, which felt wrong to say about anything related to these cruel lizards.

I don't know if it was just the vastness and extravagance of it, but something about the room made me catch my breath. Unfortunately, this led to me taking in a lungful of bitter vinegar, and I started gagging and choking on the taste.

Fortunately, one of the guards pulled the cloth out of my mouth, and I took a deep breath of fresh air.

I could still feel some vinegar and dirt in my mouth. I wanted to spit it out, but I feared the repercussions from the lizards.

I looked to my left, then right, and saw that we five Lily members had been lined up into a row, shoulder to shoulder, facing towards the majority of the room. Kriv and Bon-Bon were to my right, and Finnon and Roscoe were to my left.

We were forced to walk forward once again while staying in line. Finnon and Roscoe were practically having to run so they could keep pace with us. When we got to the middle of the room, the Ascabolates stopped us while saying nothing.

Right in front of us, in the middle of the wall, was a raised platform. Sitting atop it was a massive throne. It was carved out of pure white stone that had been intricately adorned in a mysterious pattern. Though when I looked closer, I realized it wasn't white stone. It was actually made out of bleached bones. I could see ribs making the back of it and some femurs and scapulas making the base. I felt dizzy when I saw humanoid skulls lining the top of it.

Two of the lizards near us marched to a door next to the throne. In their hands, they each had a stone club. They raised the clubs to their mouths, and I realized they were actually crudely carved horns. They blew into the instruments, and I cringed at the sound. Not only because I was a musician but also because I was a living being with ears. It sounded like an ogre dying, mixed with a cat yowling.

The lizards all stood abruptly at attention. They hardly seemed to be breathing. The door then flew open, and out of it came the soldiers' captain. He had now added to his armor a deep red cloak hanging over his shoulders.

He walked to the throne, stood to the left of it, and bellowed out to the crowd. "I now present to you, your queen, Arkra."

Out of the door came another Ascabolate, and I could tell that it was obviously a female. The other lizards were already very slender, but she was even smaller. While the other lizards were dark, like the color of an oak leaf, she was lighter, almost a white color. Around her shoulders was a red cloak, just like the captain's, and it ran all the way down past her feet. Beneath that, she wore a long white dress that stopped just above her ankle. On the top of her reptilian head sat a white crown, which also appeared to be made out of bone.

Following behind her were two other figures. The first one I recognized instantly. It was Zook. He was holding an oversized fan in one hand. He was still wearing just a loincloth, which allowed me to see the welts all across his back. I guess he was right about the fact he would be punished.

The second figure was wearing a large brown robe. The material looked to be very coarse and uncomfortable. It was tied around the figure's waist with a thick fraying rope. There was a large hood pulled up over the figure's head, and in their hands, they had a tray piled high with insects and bugs. Since they were wearing a complete set of clothes, I assumed them to be human or at least some civilized race.

The queen walked to the throne and stood in front of it, her back rigid and straight. She was glaring down at the five of us. Zook walked over and stood to her left, and the human knelt down in front of him, their head tilted down.

The captain called out and said, "Kneel before your queen." I felt the tip of a blade between my shoulders, so I knelt down, which is a tricky thing to do with your hands behind your back, but I managed to do it without falling and cracking my face open.

"I said—kneel—before—THE—QUEEN!"

I looked over to see that Kriv was still standing. He spit on the ground and said, "Not my queen."

"KNEEL BEFORE THE QUEEN!" the captain yelled this time, and several Ascabolates swarmed Kriv and forced him to his knees. Once he was kneeling, the queen finally sat, smoothing out her dress when she did. Sitting on the massive throne made her look even smaller, but she wasn't any less intimidating. Once she was seated, I tried to stand back up but was forced to stay down by the tip of a sword on my upper spine.

The queen then held out her hand, and the poor person kneeling down beside her reached onto the platter and picked up a giant beetle by one of its legs, and placed it in the queen's outstretched palm. I don't know if it was my imagination, or if what I saw actually happened, but I'm pretty sure I saw the beetle move. Arkra lifted her hand up to her lizard-like head and tossed the beetle into her open mouth. I kept myself from cringing, fearing what would happen if I did. Internally though, it felt as though my stomach was flipping in on itself.

Finally, the queen spoke and said, "I see you have already met my mate, Zedgrar. I do hope that he has made your stay… comfortable." She let out a chilling laugh and interlaced her fingers with the captain next to her.

So that means the lizard that abused us all was the king of these people. That made me worry about what the queen was capable of. "I know you have already met my… *spawn*," and she gestured at Zook. She said the word spawn with disdain, and I could tell that there was no love between the two. The cold relationship between them made the one between my aunt and me look better than it was.

"I do thank you for helping him," she continued. "I can't tell you how hard it is to find reliable servants. I only have this girl left, and even she fails me often." The queen crossed one leg over the other and went out of her way to knock the platter of bugs out of the servant's hands. The servant lunged and started piling the insects back up on the platter. As she reached for the bugs—several of which were scurrying away—the hood slipped from her head, and I could now see that it was, in fact, a woman. I felt horrid for her, I don't know how she came into servitude to these monsters, but it couldn't have been by free will. Who would choose a life like this?

"If he'd died," the queen said, gesturing at Zook, "I would have had to find a new errand boy, and that would have been horrible." She held out her hand again, and—still on the floor—the girl reached up, handing the queen a blue butterfly, which was eaten as quickly as the beetle.

"Your majesty," I spoke up. I didn't use any magic, but I tried to be as charming as I could. "My fellow companions and I beg for you—" I was quickly cut off when the queen pointed at me, and I gasped for breath when a spear was stabbed into each of my sides, right on the cracked ribs. They didn't press hard enough to break the skin, but with my broken bones, it still hurt terribly.

"I believe that my husband has warned you about these games, boy. We know all about what you can do, and we won't have any of that. If you care to speak again, we can get the gag out, and we can make it taste *much* worse." She put an emphasis on the second to last word, which was followed by a chilling cackle, "If I were you, I would let one of your companions speak for you." She held out her hand

and ate a massive worm from the girl. Then the queen reached over and smacked Zook, who started to fan her.

Bonneville spoke up to help me, "Your majesty, what Clef was trying to say is that we don't mean you or your people any harm. We simply came to your domain unknowingly to take care of the goblins. We didn't even know of you and your people living here." She spoke as if she knew exactly what to say to royalty.

"Yes, I genuinely don't care why you are here. All that matters is that you are here, and now you will do as I say. We, too, have been suffering from the goblins. So, you are going to take care of them for us. I don't care how you do it. I just expect to see that goblin king's head before me in two days.

"Why should we help you?" Finnon yelled aggressively while a guard held him back from charging the throne. He may be small, but he was feisty.

"Oh, only because it's in your best interest. My husband had a different idea of what to do with you," Zedgrar grinned devilishly beside her, "and if that's not enough inspiration, then your friend will stay with us... for a very long time."

She laughed, and multiple guards grabbed Kriv and forced him forward to the queen.

They forced him onto his stomach and bound his arms and legs. He tried to fight, but the king stepped down and pressed his spear into Kriv's back. I heard him cry out in pain, which I had never heard before. The king leaned down to Kriv and said so quietly that I could barely hear, "Oh, you and I are going to have some fun, aren't we," and he let out a blood-curdling laugh while the guards carried the bound dragon through the door. The king followed after them, probably deciding what horrid thing to do first.

The queen seemed indifferent to all of this and said, "I hope you do come back in time. I would love to see that false king dead, but torturing your friend will be quite fun too." She sounded as if she were debating which gown to wear—rather than the fate of two living creatures. "Though don't worry, we won't kill him—unless you fail, of course." Everything she said had very little emotion behind it, which was honestly more frightening than if she had been screaming like a raging lunatic.

I heard a scream from the back room and then silence.

The king came back out and said, "The hostage has been… subdued for the time being." Zedgrar seemed to be choosing his words carefully. He walked back over to the queen, grabbing a handful of bugs from the platter on the way. He put them all in his mouth at once and crunched down. I could hear the shells of the bugs cracking from where I was.

Bonneville said gently, "If you expect us to do any killing on your behalf, my companions and I will be needing our equipment back." Bon-Bon would be able to slaughter an entire army with just her hands, but without my lute and rapier, I wouldn't be helpful for more than simple charms.

"Yes, yes, we have all of your belongings set aside for you. My handmaid will show you the way." The woman kneeling beside the throne placed the tray of bugs at the queen's feet. She then walked over to us and headed back the way we had come. She had her head down, and kept her hands folded in front of her. She stopped at the opening of the hall and waited for us. The lizard guards unlocked the cuffs around Bon-Bon and me, though they both seemed reluctant.

Our team—minus Kriv—slowly stood up and walked to join the girl. I was surprised when I found that no guards had come with us. It was only us four members of the Lily and the girl.

CHAPTER SEVENTEEN

The Servant

She started walking down the hall, kindly walking slow enough for us to keep up. Bon-Bon and I were still in pain and limping. Roscoe and Finnon always had trouble keeping up with their short strides. We walked for a few minutes, and then I said, "So, uh, what brought you to this… well, place? This doesn't seem like a glamorous lifestyle."

She took a deep breath and said, "I made a poor choice when I was younger, and now I am paying for that." Her voice was dry and weak. She was obviously not treated well by her masters. I don't know why, but I felt a connection to her. Maybe it was her sickly features, or her dry voice, but I wanted to do anything to help her. However, I didn't want to pry anymore, so we walked in silence the rest of the way. We came to a room with a wooden door. Upon entering, we found ourselves in what seemed to be an armory, much larger than the one I had seen before our capture.

The handmaid said, "All of your items are over there," as she gestured to a table in the middle of the room. Everything was there. I hurried over and grabbed my lute from the pile. I started gathering all my other gear. Everything was there except the new bow and arrows I had grabbed. It seemed fair. I had stolen them from the lizards, after all. I was relieved to find my shirt, vest, boots, and cloak. I didn't want to go through this fight shirtless and barefoot.

I pulled my shirt over my head and then slipped on my vest. I was disappointed to find that they both were bloodied and torn. My cloak appeared to be intact, so that was a relief. As I was examining the tear in my shirt where the arrow had pierced my shoulder, the woman approached me and asked, "Is there anything else I can do for you or your party?"

" Well, I'd love clothes without holes in them, but I don't suppose there's a tailor here?"

She laughed. It was a bitter laugh, one that was a sign of years of suffering. "No, however, I believe we can find a solution." She looked up at me. She had eyes so sad, I couldn't tell what color they were, and around each one was a large dark bruise. Her cheeks were so sharp I feared they could cut someone. Stringy and oily hair framed her face. She had lips that were cracked and bleeding.

"If you are all ready, please follow me." We waited a moment for Bon-Bon to finish putting on her armor, and then we went out of the room. She guided us to the right, but kept checking every direction before taking a turn. It seemed that she was worried we would be caught.

The handmaid led us down a long hallway to another large wooden door. This one was adorned with a metal raven.

She looked in every direction and quickly unlocked the door, and pulled us in. She moved with remarkable speed—considering how sickly she looked—as she locked us into the room.

Looking around, I saw that it was obviously a sleeping chamber. From the elaborateness of it, I assumed it belonged to the king and queen. The handmaid gestured to one corner of the room at a wooden chest and said, "Take anything from in there. I'm sure something will fit you."

I quickly walked over and found that the chest was filled with clothing of all sizes. I had to dig past a beautiful silk dress, some very large black tunics, and a left shoe before I found anything that would fit. I pulled out a red shirt and a dark brown lace-up vest. "What are all these clothes? They don't exactly seem like something the king or queen would wear."

"They aren't," the girl replied, "whenever they take a new… servant, they strip all their clothes from them, leaving them with only these," she gestured down at her robe. "We are told that we will get them back when we have earned our freedom, but very few live to see that day."

She walked sadly over to the chest and withdrew from it a pale green tunic and sand-colored trousers. While she said this, I started pulling off my old clothes and pulling new ones on. "These were mine… before… before," she seemed at a loss for words, and I thought of anything to change the subject.

"You won't get in trouble for this, will you? I don't want to cause you any more pain." I wanted to help her. If not for Kriv being held hostage, I likely would have abandoned the whole mission just to save this woman from her cruel fate.

"I doubt they will even notice, though we should hurry," she said. She pulled herself away from her past life and hurried to the door, listening for footsteps.

I dressed quickly and noticed my necklace had come slightly undone from my arm. I started rewrapping it and asked Bonneville, "Are you sure that man you know can fix this? The chain is snapped through. I don't see how it could be repaired." I said it sadly. I couldn't imagine not having the necklace.

"Without a doubt." She replied confidently. "The family I work for *loves* jewelry, and I had to take much of theirs in for repairs. I've seen Frederick repair much worse than that."

"That's good," I still didn't see how it could be fixed, "I don't know what I would do without this."

The handmaid spoke up and said, "May I ask where you got such a lovely bracelet?"

I replied sadly, "Well, it was originally a necklace that I got a long time ago… from a girl I loved dearly, but Zedgrar broke it."

"That's nice," she replied, already listening at the door, and I saw that Bonneville stared at me with a look of confusion. She didn't know about Malia—she didn't even know that I had lost the love of my life.

I finished dressing, then went over to my pack. I made sure everything was there and put it on my back. "All right. Let's go."

The girl led us back the way we came.

My leg, ribs, and arm had begun to hurt even worse, and I saw that Bonneville was limping even more severely.

I suddenly remembered the leaves in my bag, so I pulled one out and started chewing it. I then handed one to Bon-Bon to eat. I felt the pain lessen in my body, and I saw the tension leave Bonneville's face. Sadly, the pain was so severe that even the herbs weren't able to help entirely.

The servant spoke again and said, "Oh, is that Stenogyne achenes?"

I had already forgotten the name of the plant—I only knew it helped. I was relieved when Roscoe answered, saying, "No, it's Stenogyne *kanehoana*. I always keep some with me. It's a great pain reliever."

"Oh, I have always been a fan of Salix bark for pain relief."

"I've always found that too hard to harvest, personally," Roscoe retorted.

They went on for several minutes, talking about their preferred herbs for different situations. Finally, we got to a metal door that had been barred closed.

"Everywhere past this point has been taken as goblin territory." She hoisted the large metal beam which had held the door closed. She was strong for being so frail and clearly malnourished. "But before you go—drink this," the girl handed Bon-Bon and me each a vial with murky green liquid in it. "It'll help with your injuries."

"How can we trust you, though?" I wanted to trust her, but she worked for the queen. This could have all been some elaborate plan that just ended with us all being dead before the day was over. For all I knew, Kriv had already been killed. It seemed just what Arkra would do, give us a glimmer of hope that only ended in our demise.

Still, I felt that the handmaid was sincere. She clearly hated the queen and wanted to help us in any way she could.

She looked up at me and said gently, "Because you can. I made this myself. The queen doesn't even know about it. I wasn't able to find the herbs I typically use, but this works just as well. I have to use it nearly every day. The queen and king are quick to anger, and they are more physical than verbal."

I looked at Bon-Bon, and with a slight tilt of our heads, we agreed the potion was safe.

Together we drank down the vials.

"I'm sorry about the bitterness," the handmaid said. "If I had any rebaudiana, I could help with that… but I couldn't find any."

She was right about the bitterness. The taste was awful, and it burned as I swallowed. I quickly felt a tingling in my shoulder, then my ribs, and finally my calf.

But I instantly felt the deep pain of my wounds disappear. I tried putting my weight on my leg, and rolled my shoulder in a circle. They both felt fine. I couldn't tell if they were entirely healed, but the wounds assuredly felt better.

I ran my hand down my side and didn't feel the pain of broken ribs. I looked down at my chest and was surprised to find that the cut from the king's claw was still there.

I looked up, and the girl could see the bewilderment on my face, "It won't do anything for minor cuts," she explained quickly, "I would have to constantly make tonics if I made one for every little scrape. But this one can do wonders for bones, muscles, and deep cuts… I can deal with bruises and scratches, but a broken leg hurts no matter what."

It was sad that she talked about these injuries as if they were something everyone deals with.

"Thank you so much for all of this… uh," I realized she had never introduced herself. "What was your name?"

"Oh, it's… Karina." It was as if she hadn't been asked for a name in years.

"Thank you, Karina," I finished. I then reached into my pack and pulled out a big piece of salted meat and a hunk of bread. I handed them to her along with my water skin. She took a large drink of water and handed it back. I looked at her once more, and then we headed through the door.

"Please be careful," I heard her call, and I looked back. She stepped back and waited. I could see she started to eat the bread and meat I had given her as if she hadn't had food in days, which wouldn't surprise me.

CHAPTER EIGHTEEN

The Goblins

I wished that I could just save her. Take her away from this awful place. But I had to remind myself that she couldn't be my main concern right now. The Ascabolates had Kriv, so we needed to find the goblins, kill their king, and save ourselves. I would just have to worry about Karina later, though, for some reason, I just couldn't shake the image of her face from my mind. I don't believe I had ever seen someone else so abused, and it made me furious.

We closed the metal door, and I heard the heavy beam fall back into place. There was no going back now. I looked around and saw the others do the same.

It was a dark and musty hallway that smelled worse than all the others. There were a few lit sconces, but most of them were broken off the wall and lying on the floor. We started heading down the hallway. The stench just kept getting worse and worse. It would have been a relief to have the vinegar rag right now.

We only had to walk about a hundred yards, which went much faster after the tonic Karina gave us, before we came to another metal door. I tried to open it, finding it was jammed closed. I tried to shove it open, but it got me nothing but a sore shoulder.

"Hey, Bon-Bon, can you take care of this, please?" I stepped aside with a humorous bow, gesturing for her to open the door. Anytime we needed some pure force, she was the answer. Don't get me wrong, I'm not weak by any means, but she far surpassed me in strength. Maybe all that working out does pay off.

She laughed while she walked over to the door. Squatting down slightly, she pushed her shoulder against the door.

Then in one sharp motion, she put all her weight on the door and pushed up. The door went flying off its hinges with a cloud of dust. From the open doorway, a colossal waft of that putrid smell came through.

As the dust settled, we looked through the door and were greeted by four pairs of angry goblins' eyes. I saw two more goblins behind them, but they had—fortunately for us and unfortunately for them—been crushed by the massive door. Scattered around the two dead goblins was a pile of broken furniture, which I assumed was the barricade that had held the door in place. I began to pull my blade out, but Roscoe and Finnon beat me to it. They rushed forward with their axes and charged the creatures.

I don't know if they were still in shock from the door flying at them or if it was because of the tiny men rushing at them, but they didn't stand a chance. The two small men ran at them and quickly sliced them in half before the goblins even got a chance to pull their weapons out.

Roscoe and Finnon barely even had a chance to celebrate before I called, "We need to go. That wasn't exactly quiet, and there will be more coming any minute. Come on."

We started to run down the hall but didn't get even ten feet before we started to hear goblins running towards us. I could tell that there were at least a dozen of them. I turned around to have the others grab me so I could use the same song I had earlier, but I couldn't see them anywhere. The footsteps kept getting louder and louder. Finally, I decided I had to just worry about myself, and I started playing the same tune as before.

Super nos ab illis,

nos hic facimus.

Nosque ab omnibus,

nolite ergo audire eos.

I felt the veil fall over me with a familiar chill. After a few more rounds of the melody, I realized it was a good thing I couldn't find the others because I didn't know how weak I really was. I was straining to be able to even hold the veil up around myself. I knew I couldn't do it around the whole group.

After a couple more rounds, I saw the goblins run past. There were at least twenty of them that charged past me, clearly oblivious to me standing there. Once they passed, I let the song's last note die out, and I felt the veil fall. From the strain of the charm, I felt woozy and nearly collapsed on the spot. It felt as if my brain were trying to fight its way out of my skull. I held a hand to my temple and closed my eyes. I just barely managed to keep my balance.

Unfortunately, at that moment, I heard another group coming from in front of me. Knowing it would fail, I tried to summon up the veil again, but—as I had assumed—I was too tired. I don't think I would have been able to hide even my scent at this point.

I felt the pain in my head return and had to shut my eyes, trying to hold down the contents of my stomach. I debated running down the hall but knew I wouldn't make it more than a few steps. My knees began to give out, and I nearly fell to the ground when I felt a hand grip the collar of my shirt.

I balled up my fists, ready to fight to the death, and felt myself get pulled backward. I turned around, already swinging, and found my fist hitting soft skin rather than the coarse flesh of a goblin.

"Stop fighting," a voice whispered, "I'm helping you." Then I realized that it was Bon-Bon that grabbed me.

I looked back at her and tried to act calm, saying, "Oh, uh, yeah, I knew that." My heart was still beating fast, and my head still throbbed with each word I said.

"That explains why the punch was so weak," she said with a grin.

She pulled me into a room off the hall, and I felt like an idiot for not seeing it earlier. She closed the door leaving a slight crack, and we watched as another fifty soldiers passed.

They fortunately didn't seem to notice that the door was cracked open. Unfortunately, that was the moment that Finnon and Roscoe decided to argue.

"Don't do that!" "What are you talking about?" "You bumped into me!" "No, I didn't. *You* bumped into *me!*"

The last goblin in the row stopped and looked at the door. He tilted his head to the side and then called to the soldiers ahead of him. They didn't respond, and the lone soldier took a few steps after the others. Very slowly, I closed the door, making sure not to make any noise. I turned the lock of the door and backed away.

I went over to Finnon and Roscoe, my face showing my justified anger. I hissed at them, "What were you guys thinking? You just alerted fifty goblins right where we are.

Do you want to fight that many? Well, do you?" They stared at me, saying nothing. They were obviously shocked by my anger. I usually tried to keep a cool head around the team, even though they aggravated me sometimes.

I heard the lock of the door rattling. I turned just in time to see the goblin barge into the room, luckily alone. He took one look at our group and ran back out, looking terrified. I could only assume he was planning on alerting the rest of the horde. I locked the door once again, knowing it would give us at least a few seconds of notice before the creatures came back.

"Come on. Now we have to find a place to hide. Hurry up." I looked around and didn't see much. Bonneville tipped over an old table, pulled it against a wall, and crouched behind it. I ran to one corner and used some discarded fabric and animal hides. Quickly I buried myself under them. It smelled awful, but it was the best I could do on short notice. I could see Finnon and Roscoe still standing in the middle of the room, looking for a place to go.

Behind them was an old wardrobe, which I tried pointing out to them, but they seemed not to notice. I sighed and ran over to them. Grabbing one under each arm, I forced them into the wardrobe. I was about to climb in after them when I heard a key turn in the door. I didn't have any time, so I slammed the doors closed and dove for the closest cover I could get, the now-opening door.

I got behind the door just as it opened. It flew back and hit me in the face. I felt my nose bend to the side, and then there was blood rushing down my face. I held back a cry of pain. Compared to the rest of today, this was nothing. I grabbed the door handle and pulled the door as tightly as I could against my body. Unless a goblin deliberately looked behind the door, I doubt they could find me.

The goblins came into the room and started looking around. Now that I could take a moment to breathe, I noticed that it was a sleeping chamber. I was able to peer through the crack in the door and the few inches of space on the other side. I still had a clear view of the wardrobe, but I couldn't see Bonneville's table. There were sleeping mats all over the floor and loincloths littered everywhere. I almost gagged when I realized that was what I buried myself under. What is it with these creatures and loincloths? I mean, come on, spring for a tunic and some trousers.

While I was contemplating the existence of loincloths, I watched as the goblins started looking for us. They weren't the brightest creatures. Their idea of searching for us was looking under the flat sleeping pads, or inside metal helmets. Maybe they thought we were mice or flies. Or perhaps they credited us as having more magic than we did.

One of them seemed to be a bit smarter than the others, and he went over to the wardrobe to check inside. I tried thinking of what I could do, but fortunately Bonneville thought faster than I had. I saw a flash of silver fly through the door, and I heard a clang of metal outside. She had grabbed a stray helmet and thrown it out the door.

The goblin at the wardrobe grunted a few sounds at the others, and half of them ran outside, though—to my disappointment—he stayed right where he was. He pulled open the cupboard and reached inside. I was about to charge him when he pulled out a few pieces of stray clothing. I tilted my head in confusion and watched as he stepped back and closed the door to the wardrobe, turning the other way. He grunted a few more sounds and then left the room with the rest of the goblins following. The last one closed the door on the way out.

My head was reeling. Why would the goblin just ignore the two of them? There's no way that he would just let them go. I walked forward, and while I thought, I reached up to feel my nose. It was broken, unfortunately, and bleeding—heavily.

Bon-Bon stood up from behind the table, and when she saw my bloodied face, she looked concerned. I waved her away, and when she looked for Roscoe and Finnon, I could see the same confusion on her face about where they were.

The first thing she did was walk over to the wardrobe and yank the doors open. "Hey Clef, you might want to see this." I walked over to where she was and found that the wardrobe was empty, save for a few pieces of clothing.

My head started to spin again. "How can they just be gone?" I knew that Finnon used magic, but he was never one that could do things like veils. He used fire and explosions. So we started looking around the room, trying to see if they had somehow slipped out while we weren't looking. But that also didn't seem likely. Neither of them were at all stealthy.

We looked for a while, and then we heard a voice behind us. "Hello! What's taking you two so long?" It was Finnon.

"Yeah, are they gone yet?" I looked around but couldn't see Roscoe anywhere, despite just hearing his voice. We kept looking and then saw both their heads pop out of the wardrobe, "Come on!" Roscoe called, and then their heads disappeared, and the cupboard closed once more.

Bon-Bon and I ran over to the wardrobe and pulled it open. They were once again gone. Then I realized what had happened.

Karina *had* poisoned us, Bon-Bon and I were dying, and we were now having hallucinations. I tried deciding when the symptoms had started. Were my headache and nausea really from over-exertion, or was it the first signs of poison?

I slumped down on the ground in defeat, thinking of all the things that I had survived, yet what took me out was a servant girl and a drink.

Then I saw Finnon's head pop out from the back of the wardrobe. A strange ambient purple light lighted it. He said, "Hurry up, guys!" Then he disappeared quicker than he had appeared.

I was going crazy. That poison must have been working fast. It had been only—what—thirty minutes, an hour at the most, and I was already delusional.

I put my hands to my face—waiting for the inevitable to happen—when I heard Bon-Bon say, "Hey Clef, you have *got* to see this." I looked up, and she was gone. I walked over to the wardrobe and looked around, but I couldn't find her.

"I have truly gone insane," and I realized I had said it aloud. I started looking around the room as the goblins had, under helmets, beneath the mats, though I still couldn't bring myself back to the discarded loincloths.

"No, you haven't. Get *in* here." It was Bonneville's voice, but I still couldn't find her. Her voice seemed to be coming from behind the wardrobe. Finally—deciding that my insanity was unavoidable—I climbed into the cupboard and pulled the doors shut.

I sat there cross-legged, wondering what would happen next, when I felt myself get pulled backward, tumbling head over heels and dropping down a few feet. I looked around and saw the room was lit purple, though I couldn't tell where from. I assumed that I had died and that this was the afterlife when Bon-Bon walked in front of me.

"Oh no! You died *too,* Bon-Bon," I cried out.

"No! We aren't dead. The boys found this little side room through the wardrobe. That's why we couldn't find them.

They were back here." She lifted a panel of the wall behind me up, and I could see into the closed wardrobe.

I then looked around and saw Roscoe and Finnon standing to the side of me. The thing I noticed immediately about the room, though, was the fact that there were no other doors or windows. There was absolutely no other way out of here. Also, the floors were clean, and the stench of the goblins was nowhere to be found. It actually smelled somewhat pleasant.

When I noticed there were no windows or doors, I had to wonder where the light came from. I finally saw that the ambient purple glow was coming from the sconces. Though instead of a flame on each sconce, there was a glowing purple fungus. Other than that, there was no source of light in the room.

While this description may surprise you, that wasn't even the most intriguing thing about the chamber. In the center of the room in front of me was a large fountain. There was a statue in the middle of it depicting an angel holding a large urn. I could tell that liquid used to flow out of the vase, but it had obviously been dry for a while. I walked over to it and looked at the couple inches of murky water.

The others came over, joined me, peering down into the fountain as well. Bonneville reached down and pulled back a skin that had formed over the top. The liquid beneath it was peculiar. Instead of more grimy water, there was a bright red liquid beneath. It was transparent, so we could see the bottom of the fountain, but it was also so reflective that we could see ourselves as if it were a mirror.

Finnon ran over to his pack and pulled out a book called *Exciting Elixirs, Peculiar Potions, and Baffling Brews.* "Hang on… I know I read about this somewhere… I just can't remember where…"

While he did that, I started talking to Roscoe. "So, how did you guys find this place?"

"Well, we were in the wardrobe, and then Finnon started pushing me, saying I was in his space."

"Which you were," Finnon called without looking up from his book.

"Keep reading," Roscoe barked to Finnon. Turning back to Bonneville and me, he continued. "Anyway, he pushed me, and when I hit him back, he fell back and disappeared. At first, I thought the gods had answered my prayers, but then he reached up and grabbed me."

"It's fortunate that you guys found that when you did," I told him. "A few seconds after the guards came in, they opened the wardrobe. I thought I was going crazy when I couldn't find you guys."

"We were worried about you as well," Roscoe said. "Once it got quiet, I was worried you guys were dead or something. Finnon thought you had abandoned us."

"No, you said that. Not me," Finnon pointed out, still not looking up.

Roscoe cleared his throat nervously. Bonneville and I looked at each other silently. Barely hiding our smirks, sometimes their bickering is annoying, but other times it's comical.

Roscoe continued, "It doesn't really matter who said that. Long story short… Finally, we peeked out, hoping you were still there and, well, you know the rest."

At this point, Finnon was done reading, and he jumped up, saying, "I knew I had heard of this. It's called *fuego brise*. It says here, 'Upon drinking this elixir, the user is granted the one-time ability to breathe a storm of fire.'" He pulled out a vial from his bag, filled it with the liquid, handed it to Bon-Bon, and said, "Drink up."

She looked around, stepped back, and said, "Why me? Why don't you drink it? Or Roscoe, he'll eat and drink *anything*."

"Some potions only work for different races," Finnon explained kindly. "And this one, unfortunately, only works for humans. So, you're the only one who can."

She looked hesitant and said slowly, "You're *sure* this is the potion you're talking about." She looked like she was disgusted at the thought of drinking that. She held it up to the light and looked at it. I could see some chunks floating in the bottom.

"Well, I'm pretty sure." Finnon looked in his book again and then said while reading, "Yeah, it says here that it would be fuego brise, or it's a potion that makes hair grow from your fingernails. Though I'm mostly sure it's the first one." He nodded his head, though I felt he wasn't all that confident from the grimace on his face.

"Well, I guess the only way we can know for sure is to drink it." She drank down the vial, and I gagged when I saw her have to chew part of it. We all stayed very quiet, watching her. I paid particular attention to her hands and fingernails. Then I saw her hit her chest and cough, and a small flame flew out of her mouth. "Ouch, that burns."

I laughed and said, "If you're the only one that can drink it, you better make good use out of it."

I was a little jealous of her new ability, but thinking back to the chunkiness of the drink, the feeling didn't last long. "We don't have much more time, so let's head out."

We headed over to the secret opening, and I went through first. I slowly opened the wardrobe, finding the room still empty. Thinking it was safe, I was about to call out for the others to climb through, but then the main door flew open. I saw a goblin head start to come through. I threw myself backwards and practically dove through the opening, making sure the false back of the wardrobe fell back into place. A few seconds later, I heard the wardrobe door creak open. A few soft thuds could be heard, and then the door creaked closed once more.

"Yeah, I think we are going to be stuck in here for a bit," I whispered to the others.

I peeked back through the opening. The wardrobe door wasn't entirely closed, and I could see over four dozen goblins in there through the crack. Most of them flopped down on the floor, falling asleep immediately. I watched as a few of them came over to the wardrobe, and I dropped back down.

Roscoe was starting to walk to the wardrobe, saying, "Whatever's out there doesn't scare me."

I grabbed him and had to hold him back, "There are no less than fifty goblins out there. Fortunately, they don't seem to know about this room. You already risked our lives once today, so like I said, we *will* be spending the night here."

It was effortless to intimidate most people with my build and height, especially when that person is barely at my waist. "With the fact there is a whole army of goblins right over there, we are going to take shifts as we sleep. Finnon takes the first shift, then you, Roscoe, followed by Bonneville, and I'll take the last one."

It seemed early to be sleeping, the goblins must run on a different sleeping pattern, but with all the abuse from the day, I savored the idea of sleep, no matter what time of day.

I went to one corner of the room and used my pack as a pillow lying down. While Karina's elixir had helped with the deep pain of my wounds, healing the broken bones and ripped tendons, it hadn't helped the topical soreness. My leg had started to hurt again, and my shoulder felt warm to the touch. On top of all that, now my nose was throbbing from the break. I chewed up another of the plant leaves Roscoe had given me.

Before I was allowed to sleep, Roscoe insisted on examining the rat bite and arrow wound. He said they both looked better than they should—thanks to Karina's potion. The arrow wound looked like it would become infected if not properly cared for.

Roscoe cleaned the wounds with a liquid I could only explain as smelling medicinal. I was disheartened when I discovered it stung painfully. After *thoroughly* cleaning the injuries, he wrapped both once more with clean bandages. He gave me a clean cloth and some water to let me clean the blood from my face, and—fortunately—it was no longer bleeding.

I realized I had used the last of the herbs. When I asked for more, Roscoe said, "Sorry, that's all of the Stenogyne kanehoana," which I had already forgotten the name of again, "I had brought with me. I haven't had a chance to harvest any for a while. Sorry, I have a few other mild pain killers, but they won't do anything for this."

He looked sorry that that was all he could say, but that didn't prevent him from lying down and starting his snoring. Luckily Finnon was keeping watch, so I only had one set of snores to listen to.

While my leg, shoulder—and now nose—were throbbing with pain, I would have to deal with that tomorrow. But I could just lie down and rest my eyes for now. Within seconds of closing my eyes, I was asleep.

CHAPTER NINETEEN

The Street Performer

I found myself on the corner of a rundown street. Around me was a large crowd of people, all looking at the same place. I could hear humming from the middle of the group. I walked over, about to ask people to move aside, but I found I could walk right through them. I got through a few rows of people when I finally found what they were staring at—me.

Standing next to the tavern door was a much younger version of me, probably around the age of eleven or twelve.

He looked tired, and worn down. His eyes were drooping, and his cheekbones were very pronounced. His clothes were tattered with stains and tears in them. In his hands was an old and mostly broken lute. The edges of it were chipped, and the strings were on the verge of breaking. His fingers were harshly calloused and sore, but he kept playing— knowing he had to.

I remembered this time in my life. It was before Athelstan had taken me in as his apprentice. I had to hope that I would earn enough tips each day so that I could afford food and a room that night. Sadly, there were still many nights that I had to sleep on the street from the lack of money.

The only companions I had were the stray cats and dogs that lived on the streets, which I had come to call home.

I had to live a life of constant travel. I could never really stay in one place for much longer than a week. People will only donate money to a musician so many times. Once they have heard all your songs, they become tired of you, and you become merely a nuisance.

This night, however, I could see quite a pile of money in front of Young Clef. The song that he was playing was slow and sad, yet it held the crowd's attention. It seemed like they couldn't look away from the small troubadour in front of them. He continued to play his song, and I watched as a few people dropped copper coins at his feet. Young Clef's eyelids were drooping, nearly closing at some points, but he kept playing.

He played on for about ten more minutes. I looked around the crowd watching their faces. They seemed fixated on him, and they hardly ever even blinked.

The music went on for a while, and several of the tavern patrons came out to the street and started watching. At this point, the door to the tavern was completely blocked off. People were flocking from businesses and homes to watch this young and—dare I say—extremely talented musician.

Even I was entranced by Young Clef's voice and songs.

In the middle of a lively jig—which caused several men in the crowd to stamp their feet and even one of the women to lead a man forward, dancing with him—an angry man pushed his way out of the bar holding a wicker broom in his hand.

He looked over at Young Clef and started screaming at him. "YOU BETTER GET AWAY FROM MY TAVERN, BOY! YOU'RE TAKING AWAY ALL MY CUSTOMERS, AND IF I LOSE ANY MORE

MONEY, I'M GONNA' HOLD YOU ACCOUNTABLE!" He was shaking with anger and waving the broom threateningly.

"And all of you," he said to the crowd, "if you aren't gonna' buy something, then go!" The group quickly dispersed, leaving only a few who kept a far distance from the barkeep.

As he was throwing this tantrum, several of his guests walked out of the bar and, looking at him concerned, dropped a few coins at Young Clef's feet, giving the boy a sympathetic grin.

This obviously threw the man over the edge, and he started beating my younger self with the broom. Young Clef fell to the ground, and the lute fell out of his hands. The man continued to beat the boy, who was curling himself up into a ball. I had been crying out in pain, but none of the people around did anything.

I remembered that feeling. Each time the barkeep had hit me, the wicks of the broom scratched against my skin, cutting my face, arms, and exposed feet. Watching it now, I wanted to beat the man senseless—make him feel the pain he had inflicted on me. I raised one fist and cracked it down over his skull—only to find my hand pass right through him. I could do nothing but watch my past self be abused.

The beating went on long enough for Young Clef's face and arms to become covered in thin scratches, and large red welts could be seen forming all over his flesh.

The man obviously decided he had administered enough of a beating, and so he finally stopped. He reached down and grabbed the money on the ground, throwing only a few bronze pieces to Young Clef. He then picked up the lute with a vicious grin on his face.

Young Clef reached out for it timidly, thinking the man would hand it to him, but what the man actually did was smash it against the wall of the building, completely destroying it. Young Clef had to cover his face to prevent shrapnel from cutting him, but he received several more cuts on his arms.

Young Clef lay on the ground crying. He reached out and gathered the broken remains of the lute into his arms— which was only held together by the strings at this point— pulling them into him as if his hope could heal it. But it couldn't.

He was crying deep, gasping sobs. It had been hard for me to breathe while crying like that.

I stood there, watching my younger self sob for a while, knowing I could do nothing to comfort him. Then a man came by and helped Young Clef up, wiping some dirt from his clothes.

Now I could see that my eyes had been bright red, and my cheeks were covered in fresh tears. The man who had helped him was about to say something when Young Clef grabbed the few pieces of money, along with the broken lute, and ran down the street, still crying. I started to follow him when suddenly I had the desire to look back at the man. He watched as Young Clef ran off, and I realized who it was.

Standing in front of me was Athelstan, the night he saved me from my life on the street. I watched as he followed after my past self, being careful not to be seen by the boy. I followed closely after him until we all arrived at the local inn. Athelstan walked inside, and I could see my past self standing at the counter, on his tiptoes to see over it. He placed the bronze coins on the counter, but they were pushed back, and the innkeeper shook his head. The boy gathered his money back up and headed to a door to the left with a sad look on his face.

I remembered that conversation. I had wanted to get a room and some food. When I realized that I didn't have nearly enough money, I lowered my expectations to just a hunk of bread. I passed the money to the man who told me he couldn't help me. He needed twice that amount. He had said I could sleep in the stables, though he couldn't do anything about the food.

Once Young Clef was far enough away from the counter, I saw something new to me. Athelstan quickly walked up to the man and said a few words, and the man nodded his head. My soon-to-be mentor then reached into his pocket, pulled out a handful of coins and threw them on the counter, and hurried out of the building

"Hey, boy!" The man at the inn called to Young Clef, who stopped in the doorway and hurried back to the counter. The innkeeper told Young Clef he had an extra room he couldn't rent out because of mildew and that the boy could stay there. Clef started running up the stairs, ecstatic at the prospect of a bed, no matter how moldy it was. I followed Clef, and as I

stepped on the first stair, I saw that Athelstan was now back in the room and was holding a tray piled high with food.

I followed Young Clef to the room, and when he opened the door, we stared into a rundown room with a mostly broken bed. The walls were covered in mildew and grime, and the floors were water-logged and moldy.

Young Clef scurried in and sat down on the floor at the foot of the bed. He held the broken lute in his hands, staring down at it.

That was the first thing that had been mine. I worked at a stable, cleaning up after the horses, for nearly a year to be able to afford it. Even though it had already been used and was worn down, it had been the one thing that I always had with me then.

There was then a knock on the door, and it slowly creaked open. Young Clef started pushing himself backward away from the door, still sitting. He was mentally telling himself what an idiot he was for not locking the door. Up against the back wall, he was ready to scream, but then he relaxed. The face that greeted him through the door was that of Athelstan.

"Hello, boy, would you mind if I came in?" He said it so nicely and sincerely that it was hard not to trust him.

"Y-y-yes, sir." Clef slowly stood up.

Athelstan laughed and said cheerily, "Oh, calling me sir is not necessary. My name is Athelstan Mylls. Please call me Athelstan. What may I call you?"

"C-clef Cantatio sir... I mean, Athelstan."

"A fitting name for someone with your talent." I hadn't known what he was talking about, but Athelstan didn't give the boy long to think about it. "Would you like some food, Clef?" It was then that Young Clef had noticed the tray of food Athelstan was holding. Young Clef nearly grabbed at it, but refrained himself.

"Don't worry, it's all for you," and Athelstan handed the tray to the boy. There was meat and bread, along with vegetables and fruit, both fresh and dried. I couldn't remember ever eating a meal that filling back then.

Young Clef was halfway through devouring a piece of meat when Athelstan looked at him and said, "Can I talk to you about something, Clef?" The boy nodded with a mouth full of food. "Do you know what you were doing back there?"

Young Clef looked at him confused and, with food still in his mouth, said, "Singing?"

He laughed again, not mocking, just amused, and said, "I mean besides that." Young Clef shook his head back and forth. "I assumed as much. How do I say this?" He said it more to himself than he did to my past self. He then pursed his lips and squinted his eyes. He was quiet for a second and then said, "Have you ever heard of a bard, Clef?"

Young Clef swallowed a large bite of food and then said, "Isn't that just a performer, you know, like in a tavern or something?" He then took another bite of bread, savoring the fact he didn't have to avoid mold.

Back then, I hadn't known how much more it meant to be a bard rather than a typical performer. But once I did, it would change my life.

"That's a common mistake. Your words have power, more so than other people's. If I may ask... Have you ever found that you could easily get something you want, or—like tonight—people seemed mesmerized by your singing?" Young Clef remembered the crowd of people and nodded his head quickly, now eating some of the fruit.

"That isn't just because of your voice, though it is beautiful. It's because of the magic *in your voice. Very few people are gifted with this talent, and even fewer realize the*

gift they have. The people who have this gift are referred to as bards. They are able to use their words to perform spells and incantations. Unlike other magic users, your power comes from the heart, from your very soul. Those people around you gathered because you told them to, even if you didn't know you were."

I had been staring at him, with my jaw hanging open, an apple being held just below my mouth.

"I want to train you. I want to make you into a bard."

Young Clef looked excited and was about to say something, but then he paused, looking sad. "I don't have any money. I wouldn't be able to pay you anything." The boy gestured at his broken lute and said, "I don't even have a proper instrument. I don't see why you would want to waste your time with a freak like me."

"You aren't a freak. You are one of the most talented musicians I have ever seen. You haven't even come of age yet, and you charmed a whole town without even knowing it. That's why I want to train you, so that someday I can say that I trained Clef Cantatio, the most powerful bard ever known. Now what do you say, would you like to come home with me? You will have your own room and all the finest *clothes, and I will train you every day. I even have a daughter, Malia, who would love to meet you." Athelstan then added as an afterthought, "Of course, we'll have to check with your parents first."*

"I don't have parents," Young Clef replied as if it wasn't as sad as it was.

"I see... so would you like to come live with me, Clef?"

The boy on the bed started crying and nodding his head quickly. He couldn't say anything. Athelstan stretched his arms out, and Young Clef dropped everything, ran over to the older man, and hugged him. It was the first time anyone had ever hugged me that I could remember. All I had ever gotten was beatings and slaps on the wrist.

"Now grab your stuff, and let's go."

The young boy looked around the room, grabbed the lute, despite it being broken and said, "This is all I have."

"Well, we are going to have to fix that aren't we," I now realized that he was talking about both the broken lute and my broken heart. Athelstan reached down, grabbed Young Clef's hand, and led him out the door. They walked out, and while I couldn't see it, I knew that the small boy was grinning wider than he ever had.

I, however, was left in the moldy room alone. I remembered what had happened next. Athelstan took me around the town, buying me anything that I could ever want. He bought me several sets of nice clothes. I got several rolls of parchment. My soon-to-be mentor had even taken me by a little shop that just sold sweets. He let me pick out anything I wanted, and when I came back with just a tiny plain pastry, he told the clerk that we would take one of everything. I remember the stomach ache that came from eating all that food.

The final stop we made was at the local luthier, who took one look at my lute and said it was unfixable. Athelstan pulled him aside, just out of earshot, and spoke to the man privately. The luthier looked over at me once, nodded his head, and walked back over to me. He took the lute from my hands, saying that it could be ready the following day. I was thrilled to hear that.

Athelstan then got us a proper room at a fancy inn. It was the most comfortable bed I had ever slept on at that point.

Now, standing in the moldy room by myself, I was confused when I heard a woman start calling out to me,

"Clef. Clef! Wake up, Clef!" The voice sounded oddly familiar, though I couldn't place who it was.

225

"Clef. Clef! Wake up, Clef!" The voice sounded oddly familiar, though I couldn't place who it was.

225

CHAPTER TWENTY

The Transformation

Bon-Bon's face was hovering over mine when I woke up. "Hey, Clef, you might want to come to see this." She led me over to the panel in the wall and slowly pulled it open. "Be quiet. Every single one of them is awake."

We climbed into the wardrobe, and Bonneville held her finger to her lips, obviously telling me, again, to be quiet. She slowly cracked open the wardrobe, and I could see a horde of goblins gathered at the opposite wall. They were shouting and yelling at each other.

Most of the goblins were wearing simply loincloths, however, against the wall facing us was one wearing a full suit of armor. Both the goblin and the armor looked like they had seen many battles. He clearly seemed to be the leader. I saw that under one arm, he was holding rolls of parchment.

The goblin quickly unrolled the papers and—from his belt—drew several nails. He turned his back on us and drove the nail through the parchment, attaching it to the wall. He repeated this three more times, two of the papers being attached lower on the wall, and then turned back to the crowd. I was worried that he would see the narrow crack in the wardrobe, but he was too fixated on the group in front of him. I tried seeing what was on the parchments, but I quickly became distracted when the goblin started screaming at the soldiers in front of him.

When he began to speak, I realized that the goblin sounded different from the others. While all the others had a raspy and deep voice, this one was smoother and higher. It was then that I realized the captain was a woman, not a man.

I couldn't tell what she was saying, but suddenly my stomach turned, and I had a feeling she was talking about my group. I tried straining to see what the posters had on them, when I almost fell out of the wardrobe. If not for Bon-Bon catching me by the back of my shirt, I would have fallen out into the horde. I gave up hope of seeing what was on the posters and began trying to figure out what the goblin was saying. While I couldn't understand the words she was speaking, I started to understand the purpose of it. She was trying to rally the troops. I've heard Bon-Bon speak in a very similar way before we would go into battle.

Suddenly the goblin captain drew out a dagger from her belt and drove it into the middle of the far-right parchment. I still couldn't tell what was on it, but I started having a feeling I knew what—or should I say who—it was.

The goblin woman started walking around the room, punching the goblins or pushing them down to the ground. Suddenly—when she pushed one of the creatures down to the floor—I saw what was tacked to the wall, and I was horrified to find that my hunch had been correct. On the wall staring back at me was a crudely drawn image of myself with a dagger through my nose. Next to it was a drawing of Bonneville, and on the two lower posters were portraits of Roscoe and Finnon.

The goblin woman was starting to come closer to the wardrobe, so Bon-Bon and I decided to climb back into the hidden room.

"I cannot believe this," I said.

"I know," Bonneville replied, "I had been cleaning my sword when I heard a commotion out there. I looked through the opening and saw that goblin woman come in. She started to kick the goblins awake. That's when I decided to come and get you."

"Not only that, but did you see those drawings of us?"

"What?" She sounded shocked.

"Yeah, those parchments each had a drawing of us on them. I don't know if I'm more impressed that goblins can do art like that or insulted about how they messed up my forehead. It's not nearly that big. I mean, it's not like I have a forgettable face. The least they could do is have a well-drawn picture before driving a dagger through it." Bonneville looked at me with a mixture of disgust and disappointment. "Fine, I guess that's not the biggest of our concerns. But how did they know what we looked like?"

"It must have been that scout that came in while Finnon and Roscoe were bickering. He must have assisted in describing us."

"Now, every goblin is going to be on the lookout for us. I could prepare costumes and makeup if I had more time, but I don't think that would work. You and I are much taller than the goblins, and no amount of makeup will change that. And Roscoe and Finnon are too short" I started talking to myself as much as I was to Bonneville, "And on top of that, we only have one more night to find the king, or else Kriv will… well, I don't think they plan on just killing him. I can't even imagine the things they'll do to him."

Bon-Bon interrupted, "We'll find a way, but with all those goblins out there, how are we going to get out of this room, let alone find their leader? I mean, we could just kill them all, but I feel that would just call along more goblins. We could try tying them up, but that…"

"But even if we get out of this room," I then interrupted, "we are going to stick out like a troll in a unicorn field."

She laughed, and I gave a half-hearted chuckle with her, "Hey, why don't we use that song again? You could just veil us. They'll never even see us. We could walk anywhere without leaving any trail." She seemed excited about her idea, and I felt bad letting her down.

"It doesn't work like that. Playing the lute is one thing, but forcing that power—that magic—into it is hard. Simple magic, like charming someone, is easy, yet even that would be pushing it right now. Fine magic, like a veil, is even harder to do. It uses a lot of energy. There is no way I could cover myself, let alone all of us. With my injuries, I won't be able to do anything like that for a while." She seemed disappointed, "But don't worry, we'll figure something out. Now get some rest. I'll keep an eye on the goblins."

"All right, but I don't know how much it will help," she replied sadly.

Bon-Bon went to one side of the room and fell asleep. I climbed back through the trapdoor to watch the action, careful not to let the wardrobe door open too much.

The room was different now, though. Rather than an unorganized group of goblins, I spied into a room of four perfectly formed lines. Each one was facing a different poster. Every goblin now had some sort of weapon as well. They were mismatched, and I could tell they were retrieved from their victims. I saw a few elven bows, some dwarven axes, and even a fey blow-dart. The female captain was standing to the side of my poster, and that was when I noticed that beneath each head was a roughly drawn outline of a body. Suddenly the captain grunted a short syllable, which made the lead of each line let their weapons fly.

I watched as an arrow pierced my heart, an axe sliced Bonneville's head down the middle, a javelin sunk into Roscoe's stomach, and a dagger flew next to Finnon. When the captain saw the dagger miss Finnon, she pulled a whip from her belt and cracked it at the goblin's back. I saw a thin run of crimson begin to drip from an already forming welt.

The goblins went to retrieve their weapons and went to the end of the line. The next goblins had much better aim, and each outline had new weapons lodged in them. They went through a few more rotations with several more goblins. Nearly a dozen goblins' backs were now adorned with dripping welts.

Finally, I watched as a goblin threw what looked like an axe made of rock at my outline. It hit the poster right between my drawing's legs. I flinched instinctively. The goblins cheered, and I cringed thinking about that aim. I did *not* want to meet that goblin on the battlefield.

I watched as several more rounds of goblins took aim. Several lodged weapons in Bonneville's torso and a few in my head. The soldiers seemed to struggle when aiming at Finnon and Roscoe though. I assumed they weren't used to such short targets.

Another goblin took aim with a dagger. As I wondered where he was aiming, the dagger flew backward towards the wardrobe and lodged itself in the door. In the process, it pushed the door closed, pinching my fingers. I bit my lip to keep from yelping.

I could see the tip of the blade sticking out this side just a few inches from my head. The captain called something out, and the goblin trotted over to the door. I debated heading back to the fountain room, but realized I didn't have time. I was worried that I would reveal the secret room to the goblins.

I heard the goblin come over and grab the blade, pulling it out, but unfortunately, it slightly pulled the door open. Knowing I was too weak to conceal myself, I prepared a small charm I had learned. As the door swung open slightly, I made eye contact with the goblin and watched as his eyes widened. Just before he let out a cry of alarm, I muttered under my breath, "*Difracta.*" It was a simple distraction spell taught to me by Athelstan that even a beginner could use, yet even that simple amount of magic made me feel like I would faint.

Fortunately, the spell was just enough. The goblin blinked twice, closed the door, and walked away.

I could now watch the room through the new dagger hole, allowing me to keep the doors shut, making me feel slightly safer. A few more goblins took aim at the outlines. Their accuracy continually improved, though that may have been from their apparent fear of the whip. Eventually, the captain spoke up, gesturing for the goblins to leave the room.

I realized this was our only chance to get out of here, so I hurried back into the room to wake everybody up. "Get up. Come on, guys. No, Roscoe, you cannot have five more minutes. They left the room. This is our chance."

They finally got up, though not without complaint. Finnon recovered quickly and ran for the door after grabbing his pack. Bonneville caught him and said, "What about when we get out into the hallway? We still haven't figured out what to do then."

I realized I hadn't thought that far ahead, but I didn't want to admit I didn't have a plan.

"I think I have a solution to that." Roscoe said this while he was still sitting up, yawning loudly. We looked at him expectantly, "We become goblins."

Our looks of hope quickly turned to stares of disappointment and confusion. "We're looking for a real solution. Do you want us to swap bodies with a goblin? How are we going to do that?" Finnon sounded annoyed. He could very easily be exasperated by his half-brother. Though even I admit, it wasn't the best of Roscoe's ideas.

"No, that's dumb, Finnon. We aren't going to switch bodies. We are going to *change* our bodies." He stared at us. When he had an idea, he liked rubbing it in that he solved the problem. "While I was up last night, I did a little bit of research. I knew I had seen this fungus before." He gestured to the glowing fungus on the walls. "It's called *shaep morphite.*"

He pulled out a book from inside his pack, and I could see the title *Fungi and Herbs of the Underground.* "See. Read this entry here." He handed the book over to me, and I read over it while he was explaining how it worked. "This is a rare fungus that—when ingested—will allow you to take the form of any creature you want… Well, I shouldn't say any. You can't become a horse or a giant. There has to be *some* semblance to your regular form."

"Roscoe, that's amazing!" I was genuinely impressed. Roscoe's ideas typically gave us a jumping-off point of what we should *not* be doing. "How long will it last though? I can't be a performer looking like a goblin… the women will run screaming."

"I can't give a definite answer. If I had the time to analyze the nutrients and humidity of the room, I could give a more accurate time. Though the longest it could last is forty-eight hours, and the shortest would be around an hour."

"Well, if nobody else has any solutions, I'm going to say this is our best chance." When no one else spoke up, I gestured at Roscoe to gather the fungus. He nodded once swiftly, pulled out a knife, and went to collect the growth. He reached up to grab the shaep morphite but found he was about two feet below the lowest growth, even when jumping.

He said, "Uh, can I get some help, please?"

Bon-Bon chuckled and walked over to lift him up the wall. He gathered a handful of the shaep morphite, then patted Bonneville's shoulder to let him down.

Now the idea of eating fungus was in no way appealing, but it was clearly our best bet, so I decided to go along with it. He handed us each a piece of the growth, and we all looked at each other. "All right, well, here goes nothing."

I placed the piece of shaep morphite on my tongue and nearly threw it back up. It tasted worse than Roscoe's feet smelled, and that is saying a lot. I ran over to my bag and grabbed Brand's mead, taking a large swig to wash away the awful taste. I passed it around to the rest of the group, and they were all very grateful.

It took a few seconds for the effect to start, but let me tell you, having your fundamental anatomy change hurts— badly. The feeling started in my feet. I could feel my arches flattening and my toes growing longer and thicker. I quickly reached down and pulled off my boots. While I was doing this, I could see my fingers becoming slimmer and shorter. My nails became rough like a porous stone, growing to points. Next, I felt my lower jaw start to push forward, and my lower canines grew longer, nearly cutting into my upper lip. I could feel my skull changing shape. My eyes were growing farther apart, and my forehead became longer.

I felt a strange sensation on my head. I reached up and felt my hair pulling back into my scalp. I looked down and saw that my skin was slowly becoming dark green and thicker. Finally, as if someone flipped a switch, my vision turned entirely brown and gray.

Looking over to the rest of the group, I saw that their changes were just about to complete as well. The only way that I could tell them apart was through their clothes. Roscoe and Finnon's clothes were much too small on them, and Bon-Bon's armor had nearly fallen off her. Looking down, I saw that my typically slim-fitting tunic was now uncomfortably tight around my waist, and the sleeves hung several inches past my stony nails. My trousers were much too long now, and my belt was cutting into my rough flesh.

"Well, I fink it worked," I found it hard to speak with my underbite and long teeth.

"Yeah, but we need to figure somefing out about fis," Bonneville gestured down at her armor.

"Well here, take fis," I handed my cloak over to her—I figured my dark grey cloak would be more discreet than her yellow one. "Try to cover yourself as much as you can." The rest of us turned around and let her take off her armor and wrap the cloak around herself, covering her whole body. "It seems that the men wear only loinclofs or nofing. My vote personally is for loinclofs. So, I guess we're stuck wif fose. Wait here."

I climbed through the trapdoor again, feeling clumsy in my new goblin body. I regretfully walked to the pile of loincloths, suppressing my gag reflex as I dug through the discarded clothes. I tried to find the least stained ones I could but eventually gave up, refusing to touch another one of the repulsive garments. I managed to find three that were not quite as disgusting as the others. I went back through into the fountain room and handed the loincloths to Finnon and Roscoe.

Bonneville kindly returned the favor by turning around while the three of us undressed. After taking off my tunic, I discovered that there was a rounded green belly rather than my usually fit body. Every inch of my body was covered in coarse green flesh, with the palms of my hand and soles of my feet being a bit paler and *slightly* softer. I undressed all the way and quickly tied the loincloth around my waist.

I shoved my other clothes into my pack, along with Bon-Bon's armor. It seemed the Lily's strange magic was showing once more. Somehow Bonneville's heavy armor managed to fold down to the size of a large dinner plate and fit into my bag quite easily. I put the pack over my shoulders and would never believe there was a complete set of armor in there.

I fastened my lute to the side of Bonneville's pack—under the cloak—so that I could access it quickly and so that it would be hidden from immediate sight. Finnon and Roscoe had just finished dressing and shoving their clothes in their packs as well. Now that they were only wearing loincloths, I couldn't tell them apart. However, I believe that Roscoe was the more muscular of the two.

I had to hope that none of the real goblins would be suspicious of Roscoe, Finnon, and I wearing packs, which I hadn't seen any of the other goblins with, and I hoped none of them would think anything about the bulky cloaked goblin.

"Well, let's make the most of our time. Let's get going." I lead the way out into the main room, grateful to find it still empty. I called for the others, and they climbed through to join me.

Bonneville and I weren't used to being so short, and Roscoe and Finnon didn't seem to like being so tall. They each hit their heads on the trapdoor on the way out.

We made our way out to the hallway and once again had a stroke of luck. There were no goblins in sight.

The moment of truth came as we turned a corner. Five goblins were coming straight towards us. However, our assumptions of the goblin's intelligence levels stood to be correct as they didn't even glance at the packs or at Bon-Bon's cloak.

We picked up our pace with a new confidence that our disguises were, in fact, working. Unfortunately, looking like a goblin did not include speaking like a goblin or interpreting their language.

We had discovered the goblins seemed to greet each other with a word sounding like "Krubitz." We managed along fine.

For the most part.

CHAPTER TWENTY-ONE

The Princess

We had been going down the halls for about twenty minutes when two goblins came towards us. I was about to greet them by saying, "Krubitz," however, Roscoe interrupted me and butchered the word. Instead, he said "Kravinz" as they passed us. Apparently, rather than a greeting, this is some sort of threat or challenge.

Both goblins instantly stopped mid-step and turned to look at the four of us. They squinted their eyes and said something that I couldn't understand. When we didn't respond, they grabbed their weapons—a spear and a crossbow. They began to walk towards us menacingly. It reminded me of a wild animal stalking its prey, moving slowly, only taking a step every few seconds.

"Roscoe! What did I tell you about speaking?" He began to answer, not realizing it was a rhetorical question. I cut him off and shouted, "I said not to do it… like, *ever*. You aren't supposed to talk. *I* am."

This whole time the goblins were getting closer and closer to us. Fortunately, they seemed to be focusing on Roscoe and didn't see Bonneville slip behind them. They got to be about four feet from us when Bon-Bon stood between them, a few steps back. She reached out with her goblin arms and cracked the two soldiers' heads together. I heard a crunch, and they collapsed to the ground.

"Fanks, Bonneville. But what are we going to do about feir bodies?" She gave no response, simply shrugging her shoulders. I looked around and saw a door a few feet away.

I slowly opened it and found it nearly identical to the sleeping chambers we had come from. However, instead of a wardrobe in this room, there was a large wicker basket.

I assumed it to be for dirtied clothes. I grabbed one of the goblins by the arm, and Bon-Bon grabbed the other by the leg.

We pulled the goblins into the room. I lifted the lid of the basket. The stench was awful. It smelled like something had died, been born again, and then was killed. It nearly forced me to throw up what little food I'd eaten. We quickly lifted the goblins into the large basket and put the lid back on. We had to push it down to make it look natural, but we managed to make it work.

I was sure someone would find the bodies eventually, but hopefully I would be back home by then. We went back to the hallway and kept walking in the same direction. Roscoe started to speak, but I just walked past him and his words never even formed.

Bon-Bon and I were walking several feet ahead of the others. I spoke quietly so that they couldn't hear. "Hey, Bonneville, if your offer still stands, I'm ready to talk." I was surprised at the words I was saying.

She looked over at me, equally surprised, and said just as quietly, "I'm always here for you."

I nodded my head slowly, gathering myself to speak. I told her everything. I talked about my childhood, my aunt, living on the street, Athelstan, and most of all, I told her about Malia. I was surprised at the words I was speaking. I guess this adventure had been so different. I somehow just felt I needed someone to know who I was—or at least how I had become the man they would fight beside and for.

The only other people I had told even some of my story to were Brand and Tillie, and they didn't know nearly as much as I had just told Bonneville.

As I was talking, I realized I was used to speaking with the underbite now, and words came more easily. I was even able to pronounce words better, almost normally. Bonneville seemed to improve as well. It's incredible how quickly the body can adapt.

"So, this… Malia, she's the one who gave that necklace to you." I nodded again and didn't say anything. If goblins had tears, there would have been one running down my cheek. "I understand what it's like to not fit in, Clef. As a child, my mother always wanted me to be proper and lady-like." I almost laughed at the thought of her being proper. "I just wanted to be able to play in the dirt and go on hunts with the men. She never understood me. She would always say, *'A lady is always proper. Getting dirty is beneath people like us.'"* Bon-Bon said this in a high mocking voice, like a woman pretending to be more important than she was. It made us both laugh, a sad laugh, like someone remembering better times.

"I finally had enough of it," she continued. "I left home before I was even an adult. I spent several years just… *living*, and then eventually, I found the Lily. It was the perfect opportunity. Not only was I allowed to fight like a man, but it was encouraged of me. I jumped at the opportunity, and… well, you know the rest." She had joined the Lily around the same time I had. We had always been on the same team and had been promoted together. "I still write to them every few months. You know, they may not respect me, but they are still my parents."

"I understand. Even though my parents abandoned me, I would still love to meet them. You know, prove that they shouldn't have left me. Prove that they should be proud of me… should… love me." I choked out the last few words.

Bonneville looked at me with as much seriousness as she could with a goblin's face and said, "Clef, if you remember even one thing from this journey, I pray that it's this… you don't need to prove yourself to them or anyone. I think it's natural to feel that way, but you have proven to *yourself* that you are a survivor. And while they were able to walk away, you never turn your back on your friends. You stay, and you fight the good fight. Blood doesn't make you family. Loyalty does. Your broken past is the perfectly paved path to this very moment."

Bonneville's words sounded like music to me. I felt a glow within me that was stronger than any spell I'd ever experienced. I looked her in the eyes, and all I could say was, "Thank you." I could tell how deeply she meant every word of what she said.

We gave each other a nod of respect, and she continued on. "The worst part of writing them though is when they write back—and that is very seldom—they don't sign it 'Mother and Father.' No, it's always signed, 'Fondly, Richard and Rowena.'"

I choked and stared at her, "Your parents are Richard and Rowena," she squirmed a little and nodded, "as in *King* Richard and *Queen* Rowena." She nodded again, looking embarrassed. "As in the people who rule this whole kingdom. But… I never heard of a Princess Bonneville."

She responded slowly, "Yeah, well, I don't prefer to talk about it often. I changed my name when I left the palace, wishing to leave all that behind."

Everyone had heard about the long-lost princess, but I never knew that Bonneville was the one they spoke of. We had always been led to believe the princess had died or some terrible tragedy had befallen her—it seemed that the stories were wrong.

"Bon-Bon… you're a princess. Sorry, I should say, *Lady* Bonneville… you're a princess," I said this with a mocking tone, and I dipped one knee and bowed my goblin head to her.

She pulled me up by the ear and said, "I may be born to royalty, but I sure don't act like a princess. And I swear to you right here, if you tell another living soul—that will be the last thing you ever say." She said it with a smile, but I could tell she was serious.

"Alright, alright, let go," I said as I pulled away from her, "I won't tell anyone," then I said under a cough with a smirk, "Your majesty." She glared at me. I smiled at her and laughed. She joined in. This time it wasn't a sad laugh—it was a real laugh of enjoyment. Despite being in a goblin's body, her contagious laughter rang through, and it even made Roscoe and Finnon laugh as they caught up to us.

"What are we laughing about?" One of them asked this. I think it was Finnon.

"Oh, we were, uh, just talking about our pasts," I replied through the laughter. Bonneville and I looked at each other and smiled. I cut off the moment by saying, "Okay, we only have until tonight to get the crown, or we aren't going to see Kriv again."

"Well, typically, the guards will check in with the King every few hours."

"How do you know that, Bonneville?" I think this was Roscoe.

"Oh, because I wa—" She realized she almost let her royal past slip and changed to say, "Just some reading. Anyway, I would suggest that we find a group of guards, and we try to blend in."

"Well, it's better than any other plan we have. So, let's go," I said.

We kept walking, keeping an eye out for any groups of goblins that appeared to be heading to the king. We walked for a while when we suddenly heard a commotion ahead of us. Out of instinct, I ran towards it, and I heard the others following behind me.

I came to a split in the hall and followed the sound to the left. After several more yards, I came to a dead-end, and in front of me I saw a large wooden door. The metal frame of it was embellished with gemstones of different sizes, I couldn't tell what color they were with the goblin eyes, but it was magnificent.

The others caught up to me, and Finnon stated the obvious, saying, "Well, this looks like an important room to me."

Real observant there—a blind centaur could have figured that one out. But, given my previous hostility, I decided to be kind instead and replied, "Seems like it. Now everyone, let me do the talking," I looked mainly at Roscoe and Finnon, "and we'll go in. *Try* to look like you belong."

I walked up to the door and slowly pushed it open. I expected to find a room in complete chaos. What I found instead shocked me.

CHAPTER TWENTY-TWO

The Cathedral

My expectations were to find a room that smelled like death, draped in sorrow, with piles of rubble and old loincloths everywhere. In the back of the room, there would be a monstrous throne made of bone and old hides with a fat goblin war chief perched on it, likely gnawing on a large piece of charred meat.

I could not have been more wrong.

Instead, I found an elegant and neatly organized cathedral. It was a remarkably welcome contrast to the vile, filth, and despair we had been experiencing in this horrible place. Lining the room were wooden pews. Each one was covered in shimmering silk cushions without a single tear or stain. The wall directly across from me was composed of a large stained-glass window.

It was remarkable that the glass had survived the drop when this palace had sunk into the earth, and equally impressive how it was now clearly holding up the avalanche of dirt that pressed against it. It was almost as if it was enchanted to withstand the pressure and still sparkle with no light shining through it.

The marble floors were spotless. And below the window was a large marble altar with metallic embellishments on the sides.

I hardly had time to admire the beauty around us before I was rudely brought back to reality by the familiar, yet always upsetting, sound of snoring. I turned to hush Roscoe and waken him, ready to scold him and remind him this was no time for a nap.

However, upon turning around, I saw Roscoe, very awake, still in goblin form, standing by the door. He waved and pointed. Looking in the direction of his gesture, I was horrified to discover that there were goblins sleeping on the floor between each pew. There had to be at least a hundred of them in here. However, instead of loincloths like all the others, these ones were wearing silk dresses of different colors, though I couldn't tell what hues they were. I quietly walked towards the altar and saw that these pews had goblins in shining armor sleeping on them. Beside each of the armored goblins was a large sword. I looked down at my measly loincloth and felt wildly underdressed.

It seemed that the commotion we had heard was the goblins settling down to sleep. I thought it was odd that these goblins were sleeping now, as the other soldiers had just awoken. They must all sleep in a sort of rotation.

I stopped walking and went back to the group and quietly told them what I saw.

"They must be the royal attendants and guards," Bonneville said, "That means we are close to the king's quarters." Roscoe and Finnon looked at her, confused. "I… uh… read it in a book about royal daily life," not wanting to explain how she was so knowledgeable about royal schedules and palace layouts from growing up in a castle with first-hand knowledge of the changing of guards.

Suddenly, Finnon's eyes went wide, and his gaze went past me. At the same time, I heard something behind me. I slowly looked back and saw one of the armored guards stand up and tilt his head at us. It alerted the goblins around it as well, and they started heading towards the door.

"Divgrits," the one closest to me said.

"Uh… Krubitz," I replied quickly. I hoped to sound confident, but instead I sounded confused.

It quickly picked up on my hesitation and said more aggressively, "Bindgiz firdzen drig?" I couldn't be sure, but it sounded like a question. I assumed he was saying something along the lines of "Why are lowly soldiers like you in here?"

"Krubitz," I tried again, hopefully. He pulled his sword out and began to advance towards me until he was only about ten feet away. I could see the handle was encrusted in red gems. Then I realized what I was seeing.

Colors.

I shouldn't be able to see like that as a goblin.

"Clef…" I heard Bonneville say slowly, "We have a problem." I looked down and saw my skin turning tan again, and my fingers were lengthening. The fungus was wearing off.

The guard's eyes went wide, he cried out, and the goblins in dresses stood up and looked at him. Then they noticed my part-elf, part-human, part-goblin self and looked terrified.

Suddenly it looked like a wave of colors rushing away from me through a door off of the cathedral. Purple, green, blue, yellow, and pink all flowed away from me as the goblins fled in terror. Fighting through the tidal wave were heavily armored soldiers, each brandishing a large, lethal-looking sword.

I was surprised I was even aware of my surroundings, though. I have to say body transformation is painful every time it happens. However, I did manage to fight through it and choke out, "Lute," to Bonneville.

Bon-Bon understood and reached under her cloak and threw my lute to me with her lengthening arm. I could see the agony on her face.

I caught it one-handed and, with my still goblin fingernails, strummed out a chord pushing the remaining energy I had left into the word, "*AIRESE!*"

Through my darkening vision, I saw the goblins fly through the air past—what I could now see as red—pews into the multi-colored stain glass window.

The pain of the transformation ended. I looked down and saw my fully half-elf body. Unfortunately, my vision started to swirl and darken, and I watched as my lute fell down to the ground. My grip had given out.

My vision went entirely black, and I realized I had pushed myself farther than I should of. That burst of wind put me past my limit, and now I was paying the consequences. I collapsed to the ground and passed out.

CHAPTER TWENTY-THREE

The Invitation

I was back in the Brazen Unicorn. I could vaguely hear music in the background and the chattering of patrons. I heard Brand calling out to Tillie to refill a man's tankard. I felt like I was underwater, my motions were slowed, and my vision was blurred. I wondered for a moment if I had died. I never imagined that the Brazen Unicorn would be heaven. However, my vision continued to clear, and I realized I was very much alive.

Up on the small stage where I usually perform was a slightly younger version of myself. I was having another one of my flashbacks, though I couldn't be sure what day this was. It looked like any other time I had performed at the tavern.

Walking forward, I stood in a corner to the right of my younger self. I was looking at a very familiar picture.

Young Clef was sitting on a stool playing the lute, singing an old song.

I must say, I do sing well—incredibly humble, remember?

The song Young Clef was singing was one I knew well. I played it nearly every day, after all. It was a lively and bouncing song that was easy to follow along with, no matter how drunk the men at the tables were.

So, come boys, and drink a tankard

Hear the music from the lute

Now, lads and lasses, hear the bard

Raise your glass and cheer 'Salut!'

Every person in the tavern called out this last word, and each of them emptied their mug. Young Clef went through several more verses of the song as I watched the crowd. I saw in the first few chairs young women staring intensely at

Young Clef. They were each trying to steal his attention from the others and ignoring the men they were with. Fortunately, the men were all too drunk to realize, or I'm sure I would have been punched by many jealous men. I recognized several of the women as being regular patrons, one of whom was the woman that had followed me to my room and barged in, demanding my affection.

Raise your glass and cheer 'Salut!'

Tillie had gotten very quick at refilling the men's tankards, so when Clef called that final word with the men, they each were able to empty their mugs once more. Brand always appreciated when I played this song as the men would empty two or three tankards of mead in a matter of minutes. None of them wanted to admit that they couldn't keep up with the man next to them.

I had never been much of a drinker, so I couldn't quite understand that mindset. There had been one night that Finnon and Roscoe challenged the group to a drinking contest. It was then that I discovered—despite their small size—those tiny men could put away some alcohol, and after one or two mugs of ale, I had to quit. I believe Finnon won after drinking twelve rounds of ale, living up to his family name of Aleslosh. I can't recall the exact numbers, though, as I spent the rest of the evening sick in a flower pot.

Young Clef changed songs now to a slower one, and I knew that meant it was coming to the end of his performance. This was always my closing song. It had no words, but it was beautiful and melodic. Suddenly I heard Tillie make a slight gasping sound to my left. I looked over and was horrified to realize I knew exactly what day this was. Tillie was refilling a drunk man's mug when he suddenly put his hand on her waist.

Tillie was used to the men being very forward like this— especially when they were as drunk as this man. But this man was more aggressive. When she flinched back and tried to pull away, gently moving his hand, the man grabbed her small wrist and said in a slurred voice, "Hey, pretty lady, what's your name?" He stood up, looming over her, leaning down to try and kiss her. She pulled back, turning her head, but even through his drunken state, his grip was firm.

Even though I was watching from a dream, I wanted to run to Tillie. Fortunately, I heard an out-of-key note strum through the air and saw my younger self doing just that.

"HEY!" He shouted it with so much authority that even I was startled.

At the same time, Brand dropped a tray of food he was holding and yelled at the man as well. The man ignored both of them, leaned down, and kissed the side of Tillie's neck. Despite her fighting, she couldn't get away. She even hit him in the ribs with her pitcher—spilling mead all over the floor—but he was undeterred.

The people at the tables surrounding the scene quickly backed away as Clef and Brand ran over to him.

Brand got their first. He punched the man in the jaw. The drunk man's grip loosened around Tillie's wrist, and she stumbled back. Brand grabbed her before she fell and pulled her back to the bar.

She was extremely distraught and quickly wrapped her arms around Brand, burying her face in his chest. She looked like a small child afraid of a storm in his large arms. I could see that she was crying. He wrapped his arms around her and rubbed her back.

Now that she was out of the way, Young Clef could take care of the man. He was still holding his lute in hand, so he pulled it around his shoulder and swung it like a bat, hitting the drunken man in the face. The man was still tottering from Brand's hit, and after the lute hit him, he went down to the ground. If it weren't for the lute being unbreakable, it would have shattered on his skull.

Surprisingly the man recovered quickly and started to pull himself up by a table. His weight overturned it, and the food and drinks came sliding off it over his head. He still tried to stand, but halfway up, my past self kicked him in the side, and he fell back down. The man had tried to grab Young Clef around the ankle, but because he was drunk and I was agile, I had easily avoided it, stepping down on his hand. Young Clef reached down and grabbed the man by the front of the shirt, pulling him partially up while leaning down to him.

My younger self was a mere inch from the man's face when he said, "If I ever see your face even near this tavern, you will regret the day you decided to drag your sorry drunken behind in here. Now get—out."

I had said the last word with such force that the man quickly stumbled his way out of the bar. He looked back once, but when Young Clef stepped towards him, he promptly ran out the door, falling on his way out.

THE INVITATION

Now that the man was taken care of, Young Clef went over to check on Tillie. Without saying anything, Brand passed her over to him. She wrapped her arms around him, putting her face in his arm nook. He could still feel her crying and could start to feel the dampness of her tears through his shirt. Young Clef slowly led her up the stairs to her room. They went slow, taking the stairs especially carefully. I watched as my past self and Tillie turned the corner at the top of the stairs.

I remembered what had happened next. I led her into her room and laid her down on the bed. She wouldn't let go of my arm, so I laid down in the bed next to her. I imagined this was how a father would comfort a small child—not that I ever had an example of that. The bed was so small that I was almost rolling off the edge of it, but I didn't want to leave her.

I had never seen her so upset. She was still crying, and I let her—gently brushing her hair with my hand. I was trying to help her calm down. Slowly I felt her stop crying, and her breathing slowed, then finally, she fell asleep. I rolled out of her grip and covered her up with a blanket.

I wasn't actually watching any of this, though, as I was still currently down in the tavern. As soon as Tillie and I had left the room, Brand called for everyone to leave the pub. Men protested, but Brand was intimidating enough for them to sober up and quickly go on their way. Nearly everyone left except for an older woman in the back of the pub. Brand didn't seem to notice her.

Brand was cleaning up the tavern from the debacle, and when he turned, I saw the surprise on his face, "Lady, I said we're closed. Get out." He wasn't mean or aggressive about it, but it was still forceful.

"I will," she said gently, "but I need to take care of something first."

I recognized her, but I couldn't place where from.

She reached into a bag she had with her, and Brand flinched back, likely fearing it was a knife. Instead, she pulled out a parchment envelope with a yellow string around it. Brand's tension faded away, and he walked over to her. I followed him.

Brand sat down in a chair across from the old woman, and she slid the letter to him. He started to untie the string, but she stopped him, saying, "That isn't for you."

Brand looked confused and said, "Then why are you giving it to me, lady?"

I was still trying to figure out who she was when she replied, "I need you to give it to Clef as soon as he finishes helping Tillie."

"How do you know their names?"

"I know a lot more than you'd expect, Brand."

He looked shocked hearing his name.

"I can't tell you much, but I will tell you this. I work for an organization of sorts. We search out the most talented men and women from the region to recruit for tasks no one else could handle. While we don't pay extravagantly, I believe Clef would find he will be happy with the rewards." She could see that Brand's shoulders dropped in disappointment. He would never say it, but he didn't want me to leave the Brazen Unicorn. She quickly added, "He could stay here and work for you. We would only hire him out as needed." Brand looked relieved.

She continued, "We have had men watching him for quite some time, and after that... ahem... display tonight, we are sure he is right for this group. I am sure we also have a space for you if you wish to join as well."

Brand laughed, "I haven't been a fighter for a long time, but that sounds perfect for Clef. I'll let him know."

"Please don't mention this meeting to him. The organization thrives on secrecy. Please just give him the letter. It will explain everything." She quickly gathered her belongings, and as she walked out the door, I realized who she was.

At the same time I realized this, Brand called out, "What's your name?"

She paused for a moment and said quietly, confirming my suspicion, "Rose." This was the woman from the flower shop—though several years younger. She then quickly went through the door, leaving Brand alone.

After seeing this, I had a hunch that she was more important to the Lily than she had initially let on.

Brand looked at the letter and then called out, "Hey Clef, can you come down here, please?"

I watched as Young Clef ran down the stairs and came over to Brand. "Brand, I am so sorry. I didn't mean to take it that far, but I know that Tillie isn't able to fight for herself, and I was jus—"

"Clef, I threw the first punch. You did the right thing. I'm proud of you." I remember how much that meant to me. Very few people had ever said those words. "This is addressed to you." He handed the letter to me, and I saw written on the envelope four words.

For Master
Clef Cantatio

"Where did you find this?" Young Clef asked him.

"Oh, it was just… um," I could now see that he was debating telling the truth. "I just found it on this table and saw your name." At the time, I didn't know he was lying, but now I was surprised. This was the only time I was actively aware of him lying to me. "Huh, weird." Young Clef opened the letter slowly and found a folded piece of white parchment with a Lily drawn delicately on the front. He sat down, unfolded the paper, and read the words scrolled on the parchment.

These words are meant for Clef Cantatio, only. We have been watching you for quite some time now, and are very impressed with your skills... both with charms, as well as with blades. More information may be provided to you at a later time. For now, we will share this...

We are an organization known as The Lily. The Lily contracts out men and women that are willing, and able, to maintain safety and freedom in the kingdom. We only employ the best of the best, and you have proved yourself worthy. You will be compensated for skills, not always with gold, but we assure you will not be disappointed.

You will be able to continue your employment as a performer at the Brazen Unicorn. Your skills will be called upon as needed, should you choose to join our elite group. Upon acceptance, more information will be provided to you. And only you. This letter, and all future communication with The Lily, must be kept a secret.

If you will be joining us, we will need your response tonight. Simply sign your name on this parchment, and place this letter on the window sill outside the door of the Brazen Unicorn.

We wait with great anticipation of your response.
～ The Lily

I read over the letter a few more times and looked up at Brand, saying, "So you say that this was just left on the table?"

"Uh, yeah." He said it quickly, like the faster he said it, the less of a lie it was.

"They want to hire me out to an organization called the Lily. They somehow know about my... talents." He was one of the few people who knew that my songs were more than just words. "They said I can stay here except for when they need me." I paused, "What do you think I should do?"

He waited a moment to respond as if thinking, "I think you should do it, Clef. You're meant for more than just performing here. You need adventure. You need a... purpose."

"Then I need a quill." He handed me one, and I signed the bottom of the paper.

We wait with great anticipation of your response.
～ The Lily

CLEF CANTATIO

I watched as my past self walked out the tavern door, and I watched through the window as he put the letter in the window sill. As Young Clef came through the door, everything began to shake. I didn't know what was happening, but I was worried the building would collapse. Then I realized my past self and Brand were unaffected. I noticed it was me shaking, and I woke up.

CHAPTER TWENTY-FOUR

The King

Waking up, I could see and feel Bonneville shaking me. However, she wasn't quite looking at me. I saw that she was fully human again and was once more wearing her armor. I looked around for Finnon and Roscoe, noticing they also had their clothes on. All of their goblin disguises were gone. Finnon and Roscoe also seemed to be keeping their eyesight off of me.

"Alright, I'm up, I'm up. Stop shaking me." I sat up and found that I was sitting on one of the pews in the chapel. I looked around and saw that nearly two dozen goblin guards were crumpled at the base of the stained-glass window. When they had hit it, it shattered, so there was colored glass surrounding them, and packed dirt spilled into the room.

Then in the aisle, there were half a dozen more goblins collapsed on the ground. I looked at Bonneville and tried to stand up. I fell back down to the seat. That last spell had taken a lot more energy than I had expected. I had pushed myself more than I should have the previous two days.

Bon-Bon was still looking past me, over my right shoulder, when she said, "I'm glad to see you're up. We were all worried about you."

"I'm fine," I put my hand out, and she helped me stand up. "That spell drained me. I'm not going to be able to do *anything* for a while." She was looking directly away from me now, and I finally said, exasperated, "Why won't any of you look at me?"

"Ah…" she coughed and laughed a little, "You're still just wearing a loincloth."

I suddenly became very self-conscious and grabbed at the skimpy cloth, trying to cover as much of myself as possible. In the process—because of letting go of Bon-Bon—I fell back down on the seat. Still holding the cloth in place, I said, "Oh, I see. Then can one of you grab my pack?" Finnon ran over and threw it to me, though he still wouldn't look in my direction. "Thanks."

They all turned around, and I quickly put my tunic and trousers back on. I grabbed out my boots and the new vest I had taken from the lizard king. Bonneville reached her hand back to pass my cloak to me, and I put it around my shoulders.

"All right," I said, and they all turned back. "So, what have I missed?"

Bonneville answered my question, "Well, after that windblast, you collapsed to the ground. You took out most of them, but a few got back up and charged us. Each of us took out several goblins. Only a few got away. Those—what I'm assuming are handmaid goblins—still haven't come out of that room. Surprisingly none of the other goblins have come in here. I used several of the pews to barricade the door in case any others were coming, but none have so far.

"After we were sure everything was taken care of, we came to check on you. We were scared, Clef," I saw a tear form in the corner of her eye. "You weren't breathing, and you didn't have a pulse. Roscoe tried to heal you, but for some odd reason, he couldn't. He kept trying and trying, but nothing happened."

She paused and pulled in a shuttering breath. "I thought we'd lost you, but a few moments ago, we heard you take a gasp of air in. That's when I started shaking you awake."

I was sad to see her so emotional. I hated that I made her so worried, but I didn't know what to say. We looked at each other, and thankfully our eyes said it all. We nodded and got back to work. "Alright. So, Bon-Bon, if you think those goblins were handmaids, they would probably be heading to the king, right?"

"That would be my guess," she said.

"Well, then, let's head that way." I stood up to walk towards the door but stumbled. Bonneville put her hand out to help, but I gestured it away. "I'm fine, but thanks."

We moved towards the door the goblins in dresses had fled through. Upon reaching the door, we discovered that the goblins had the same idea as Bon-Bon. When she tried to open the door, we found there was a barricade preventing us. Once again, Bonneville put her shoulder against it, and in one motion, the door swung open on its rusty hinges. There was the sound of furniture falling away, and I heard creatures screeching.

The room inside was, once again, not what I had expected. I was anticipating some sort of demented bedroom, but what I found instead was a nursery.

I was confused. In the middle of the room was what looked like a stone crib with hides within it. Scattered around the ground were items that resembled children's toys.

I could see a rattle that seemed to be made of bones and a pacifier made out of rock. There was an old, dark wooden desk to one side of the room that looked like it hadn't been touched in years. I looked to the back of the room and saw the goblins there, huddled as a group. In the middle of them was a goblin handmaid holding a small bundle of furs and cloth. I looked closer at the bundle and noticed that there was a golden shape perched on the pile.

Bonneville made the connection before me and said quietly, "It's a child…"

Once she said it, I finally connected the pieces. The goblin king we had been searching for was this tiny little thing, not even old enough to stand for himself. She asked, "Do you think Arkra knew?"

"I wouldn't put it past her," I replied. "But Bon-Bon, we can't kill a child."

"But what about Kriv?" Finnon asked.

"I don't know, but we'll figure it out," I said annoyed, not at him, but at myself. I put my hands on my head. I couldn't even *think* of a solution.

We stood there for a moment and considered our options. The handmaids were cowering away from us. They were not being aggressive, clearly just trying to keep themselves between their infant king and us. These goblins clearly weren't fighters. I knew we couldn't kill them, but I didn't know what else we could do. "Bonneville, any ideas?"

She paused, then slowly said, "I'll take care of it. Everyone, go back into the cathedral."

"Bon-Bon, no, you can't kill him," I said in disbelief.

"Clef." She said it sternly. "Let me take care of this." She looked directly into my eyes like she was trying to tell me something, but I couldn't figure it out this time. I returned her gaze, confused, but I trusted Bon-Bon with my life. I had to trust her now. I made my way back to the cathedral with the others. Bonneville slowly closed the door, looking deliberately at me with serious eyes.

Once in the cathedral, we waited. For a long while, it was silent. It felt like the calm before the storm. Finally, a wild scream from Bon-Bon broke the silence. Then we heard a sound that was painfully similar to a baby's wail, which then suddenly stopped. It was silent once again. We had just enough time to wonder how long we should wait before going back in for Bon-Bon when she emerged. In one hand was a golden crown. In the other was a round object wrapped in cloth.

I looked at her wide-eyed, shocked. I was about to ask her how she could do that when a boy popped out the door behind her. I jumped back, surprised. He couldn't have been older than sixteen. He appeared to be sickly and thin. His ear-length black hair was in knots and greasy, and his brown eyes filled with despair.

"Bon-Bon, who's this?" Roscoe asked, always ready for a fight.

The boy answered for himself with a parched voice. "My name is Wren. These goblins have been keeping me prisoner. I've been a sort of jester for the…" he shuttered and looked at the bundle in Bonneville's hand, "…king."

"When I… took care of the king," she seemed to be careful with her words looking right at me again. I still couldn't figure out what she was saying. "I found him in the huddle of goblins."

Wren. I had heard that name before. It took me a moment to place it. Then I remembered the conversation I had with the barkeep in Brownstead. I asked Wren, "Your dad runs the tavern. Doesn't he?"

His eyes lit up at the mention of his father. "Yes, he does. Have you seen him? Is he alright? What did the goblins do to him?" He was babbling, so I couldn't get a word in.

"Wren, Wren," I said, cutting him off. "He's fine. He's still back in town. The only thing wrong with him is he is worried about you." He nearly started crying while smiling at the same time. "Wren, we know you've been under horrible stress and abuse, but we need to know… do you know what has happened to the others? The other people that were taken from the village?"

Holding back tears, he said, "They're in that room over there." He nodded to another door to the right, "We were all made into servants for them. I had it easy compared to them, physically, at least. This is the worst I got." He held up his hand, and I could see small teeth marks on the tips of his fingers.

It seemed he was often a human pacifier for the late king.

He continued, "The others were made servants for the guards. They had to prepare the food, clean the weapons…" he gagged, "wash their feet, anything that the goblins didn't want to do for themselves. Then if the goblins weren't happy with them, they would be…" he shuttered again, "punished. And we're all starving."

As he spoke, I walked over to the door he had gestured to. I was surprised to find it unlocked. When the door swung open on its rusty hinges, I was disgusted with what I saw.

CHAPTER TWENTY-FIVE

The Villagers

Placed sporadically throughout the room were metal bars that ran all the way from the floor to the ceiling. Chained to these poles were men and women of all ages. I could see the youngest was a girl around the age of eight, while the eldest was a woman who was clearly well into her eighties. In total, there were about a dozen and a half prisoners. They all looked malnourished and in even worse shape than Wren. I saw whip marks on several of them, and when I saw that the little girl had bloody knuckles, clearly from being hit with something, I became furious.

Bonneville looked through the door a few seconds after me, and—from the sound she made—I could tell she was even more enraged than I was. She dropped the crown and the bundle to the ground, which caused a thud. She reached over and pulled an axe from Finnon's pack. Swinging it furiously, she began to hack the chain links apart. It was fortunate for her that the goblins didn't seem to care for their property, unlike the Ascabolate's sturdy cells. While the chains were thick iron, they were in such disrepair that they were rusty and no match for Bon-Bon's rage.

In a few strikes, she had broken every chain. We found ourselves in the middle of a new, unspoken plan. These people had to be saved. Everything started happening quickly.

My team and I began handing out the last of our rations, but there wasn't nearly enough.

The young girl we had saved suddenly started crying. Bonneville scooped her up, allowing the girl to bury her tear-covered face in her shoulder. Bonneville gently nodded towards the crown and bundle on the ground, telling me to grab it. Goblin children must be stocky because I was surprised at how difficult it was to lift the package. I looked at her, confused, and she shook her head gently. I still felt like she was trying to tell me something, but I couldn't figure it out.

"So, uh, does anyone know the way back to the lizards?" It wasn't until that moment I had even considered that we could get lost in here. I had been solely focused on finding the king, and now that we had, I wished we hadn't. I looked around at my team, hoping that one of them had an idea, but everyone had confused looks on their faces.

Well, almost everyone.

I couldn't find Roscoe in the crowd of people, which is typical given his diminutive stature, but I was still surprised not to see him—or at least hear him. Suddenly behind me I heard his yelp. I looked back and saw him staring at the marble altar.

"My gods!" he cried, "I can't believe I didn't figure this out sooner." He hit his forehead as if he felt like an idiot. Running to his pack, he pulled out another book. On the cover, I saw the words *Folklore, Fables, and Other Myths.*

He flipped through the book, and finally found the page he was looking for. He handed the book to Finnon.

Finnon read over the page and said hesitantly, "Are you sure, Roscoe? If this is what I think it is, you are onto something big."

"I'm *sure*." I rarely heard Roscoe sound so confident. He looked at the rest of us and said, "We are standing in the Fortress of Elpis." When everyone looked at him confused, he continued, "Really, you haven't heard that story? My mother used to use this as a bedtime story all the time."

"Oh wait… I think I know that one," Wren's voice didn't sound nearly as raspy now that he had some water. We looked at him expectantly, and Roscoe nodded for him to continue.

Wren spoke up hesitantly, "Well, there is this story about a fortress that was invaded by some evil race of creatures. Some say it was trolls. Others say it was a dark race of elves," he looked at me apologetically. Elves all knew about our darker kin, yet we didn't speak of them often other than the Mid-Solstice Festival. "But the one thing that everyone did agree on is that they worshipped death itself." I thought back to the Ascabolates and their altars to the goddess of death, Mirgan. "The original inhabitants of the fortress were too weak to fight."

Roscoe interrupted to clarify, "They were followers of the goddess Elpis, the goddess of hope, hence the name of the fortress. They lived for joy and peace. They knew nothing about fighting." He then nodded for Wren to continue.

"Yeah, thanks," Wren said sheepishly. "But the moment that the last man was killed, Elpis heard in the heavens a cry of distress and sorrow. When she heard this, she looked down and saw her followers' bodies lying there dead. The usually peaceful goddess was filled with fury and—with the little bit of anger she had—sent a terrible quake through the fortress, sinking it into the ground, never to be seen again." He paused and then looked at Roscoe with his head tilted slightly to the side. "But isn't that just some old tale? It isn't true, is it?"

"I didn't think so at first, but all the signs added up. I was a fool to miss them from the start. It wasn't until I saw this that it all made sense." He pointed to the altar. I stood next to him, looking at a symbol etched into the stone. It was a cornucopia, with a bundle of flowers growing out the end.

He then showed me a mark in his book, and it matched perfectly.

"But how does this help us, Roscoe?" This was great and all finding this lost city, but that wouldn't help us get back to the queen. At this point, he was just wasting our precious time.

"Because, if this really is the Fortress of Elpis, which I guarantee it is, the priest's chamber will have a map in it." I looked at him, confused. "Every head priest of the monastery has a map of the temple."

"But how can we know that it's accurate?" Bonneville asked.

"They always have to be spot-on, to the inch. They have to know the exact locations of different rooms to conduct their ceremonies. If they were even a few feet off, it could anger the gods."

"So then, where would the priest's chamber be?" Bonneville said.

"Well, it would have to be near the cathedral, directly off of it, I would guess, so I would say right there." He pointed slowly to the nursery. I shuttered, imagining the massacre in there.

"Well, let's go check it out." I didn't want to go back in there, but if there was a hope for a map, it was worth it.

Bonneville spoke up suddenly, "No, just me. I'll go take care of it. Where do you think it would be, Roscoe?" Why was she so adamant about being the only one to go in there? Then it clicked, I think I understood what she had done in there, but I didn't quite know *how* she had done it. I smirked at the thought.

"It would probably be in a desk. He would want to keep it safe," Roscoe explained.

I remembered the dusty desk and told her, "I saw one in there, Bonneville. It was to the right." She thanked me and set the crying girl down. One of the female prisoners came over and started comforting the girl in Bonneville's place. Bon-Bon headed into the room while we waited. A few moments later, she came back out holding a large roll of parchment. She unrolled it on the altar, and we were pleasantly surprised to see a very accurate drawing of a castle. In the top right-hand corner, the same cornucopia symbol was drawn. Bonneville also threw down on the table an old leather-bound journal, which was stamped with the cornucopia.

"I thought you might like this, Roscoe. It seems to be the priest's notebook." His eyes lit up, and he grabbed it, putting it in his bag, clearly restraining himself from reading through it immediately.

We started to examine the map as Roscoe quickly pointed out key features—the cathedral, the priest's quarters, and the door Karina had led us through. "Clef, you aren't going to believe this," he said. "You would say that the lizard queen was in the great hall, right?"

I thought back to the room and remembered I had thought the same thing. "Yeah, I would think so. Why?"

He started laughing and said, "We are a lot closer to the queen than you think. Temples used to have secret passages in them. Many still do," he explained. "Clearly, this one is no different." He pointed out the chapel on the map and then the great hall, which was only two rooms to our north, though there was a maze of hallways leading back to it. "Look here," He pointed to a thin column that was drawn on the map in dashed lines. The path went from the altar to directly by the entrance to the great hall.

"The high priest wouldn't have time to go all the way from here to the great hall for every meal, so they put this passage in here. This made it easier for him to travel so that he could spend more time in prayer each day." Now that he pointed it out, I noticed several other passages on the map like this. When it came to religious facts and knowledge, I always trusted Roscoe.

"Roscoe. You are amazing." We rolled the map back up and started examining the altar, it took us a moment to figure out where the passage was, but finally Bonneville found it.

"Look at this," she was pointing to the ground beside the altar. Brushing away some of the dirt and broken glass on the ground, we could see that there were scratch marks on the otherwise flawless floor. "Clearly, something has rubbed against this part of the ground a lot, so I would guess…" she paused and walked to the other side of the altar and pushed on it as hard as she could. The large piece of marble began to slide away slowly. Underneath, there was a staircase leading back under the chapel.

The villagers looked shocked and peered down into the opening, appearing frightened. "Okay. Roscoe, Finnon, you take the lead. Bonneville and I will follow behind."

Just as I finished saying this, I heard a crash near the chapel door. I looked over and saw some of Bonneville's barricade fall away.

The goblins were trying to get in. Clearly, the news about the invaders had left the cathedral. The soldiers were coming to protect their king. "Go, hurry. Hurry!" Bonneville and I started rushing everyone into the tunnel. We had to hope that the goblins hadn't discovered this path, or we were doomed.

It took a long time to get the villagers through, given how weak and tired they were—but we managed. Two men were helping the elderly lady, and several of the women were carrying the small children. As the last of them went through, Bonneville and I jumped in behind them. We found a small handle on the underside of the altar and began to pull it back in place.

When there was only about an inch left, I heard two sounds. The first was the crashing of the chapel door with dozens of pounding footsteps.

The other confirmed my suspicion of what Bonneville had done. It was the cry of an infant.

CHAPTER TWENTY-SIX

The King's Head

I looked at Bonneville as we pulled the altar the last inch, and it silently slid into place. She smiled at me timidly. She had obviously heard the baby's cry as well and knew I had figured out the plan. Fortunately—when we looked at the others—it appeared that no one else seemed to have heard it. The rest of the group was huddled together, staring at us, waiting to see what we would say.

"Everyone, we need to get to the other end of this passage as quickly as possible. When we get there, all of you will stay in here, and we will go to the queen. Everyone needs to stay as silent as they can. The Ascabolates are vicious and would love to have another servant." I thought back to that poor girl Karina. "Once we give the queen the…" I looked at Bonneville with a smirk only she could notice, "package, we will come back to get the rest of you." I didn't know how we were going to sneak this horde of people out of the temple, but I was sure we would find a way.

"But what if they find us before you come back?" Wren sounded terrified.

I looked at the group and asked, "Who here is any good with a weapon?" A few of the men raised their hands, and so did the elderly woman.

I looked at her surprised, and she replied, "Give me a crossbow, and I can hit a pixie from a mile away."

I smirked—impressed with her confidence—and we distributed weapons. Bonneville held onto her glaive, and I kept my rapier. Roscoe and Finnon each kept their hammers and an axe. The rest of the weapons were entrusted to the few that could use them. Finally, I handed the dagger I kept tucked in my boot to Wren.

He took it with his nibbled-on fingers and looked at me nervously. I spoke to him quietly, "Now I need you to keep the rest of them safe, buddy. No matter what happens, never give up." He puffed up his chest and looked proud of himself. Despite his young age, I felt that he could defend himself. He was also in much better physical shape than the rest. It seemed the goblins were not as severe with their punishments against the boy.

Now that everyone was well-armed, we started heading down the passage. We went as quickly as possible, but it still took us a few minutes to get to the other end. While we walked, however, Bonneville and I spoke about her plan. Since we were bringing up the rear, no one could hear us.

"So, when were you planning on telling me that this *isn't* the king's head," I asked while bouncing the bundle in my hand. Bonneville was the only person on the team I would allow to make a plan without telling me, but I still liked to know what would happen.

"I don't know what you're implying," she replied indignantly with a smirk on her face.

I unwrapped the bundle and found a large stone rather than a decapitated goblin head. I looked at her with an eyebrow raised.

"I couldn't kill him," she said. "He may have been a goblin, but he was still just a child. When the three of you left, I dropped my weapons and slowly walked over to the handmaids. They were more afraid of me than I was of them. I stepped on that bone rattle. That's why I screamed," I could now see that she was limping a little, "It frightened them and several screeched, so I slowly reached out and took the crown from the king. He started to cry, but the one holding him covered his mouth. Then I grabbed a stone from the ground, wrapping it in some of the extra hides. I couldn't tell at first what they were doing, but then they pushed Wren towards me. Although I couldn't really understand what they were saying, and they couldn't understand me, they seemed grateful."

I laughed and said, "I knew you were trying to tell me something, but for the life of me, I couldn't figure it out. I'm glad you did it, but I hope it's enough to fool the queen."

"I was thinking about that, and I had an idea." She looked at me but didn't continue.

"Well, are you going to tell me, or will I have to guess this one as well?"

She smiled and simply said, "I'm sure you'll get it."

I was about to say more as I heard Finnon call out quietly that we had reached the end of the tunnel. I reminded the villagers to stay here, and then Bonneville interrupted. "Wren, I need you to come with us." His eyes went wide with fear. "I promise you'll be okay, but I need you to trust me." She gestured him over, and he came to stand beside her. She whispered in his ear for a moment. He looked at her, thinking, then slowly nodded in agreement with a slight grin on his face. He then came and stood beside me.

I didn't bother to ask Bonneville what was happening. I knew she had a plan that would work, I just couldn't see how Wren was involved in it.

I pushed on the wall we had come to. It turned out to be a false panel.

It noiselessly swung out into the hallway directly behind two lizard guards. The team rushed out and pushed the panel closed before the lizards could see the passage and the prisoners—who were now concealed within.

I cleared my throat, and the guards spun around, frightened, with spears raised.

"Not very observant, are you?" I bounced the rock-head in my hand, which was rewrapped in the hides, and held the crown in my other hand, saying, "The queen won't be happy if you kill her servants, will she?"

Their spears lowered. When we asked them to lead us to the great hall, they seemed disappointed to miss out on a kill.

As we entered the room, we found it very similar to when we left it. Arkra was sitting on her throne with Zedgrar standing beside her. Karina was kneeling near her with an almost empty tray of insects, while Zook was fanning the queen again.

"Ah, I see my champions have returned with… Well… Who is this?" She was looking right at Wren. I began to worry about what the plan was—and what would happen to him if it didn't work out. Wren ducked and hid behind me.

"The goblins had taken him," Bonneville answered in a matter-of-fact way. "He's my son."

I fought very hard to conceal the confusion on my face, managing to just barely raise my eyebrows in shock. I was relieved that the queen was still staring at Wren intently and missed it.

"I was just so relieved to find him still alive. I feared they had… killed him." Bon-Bon worked up a sob that was so real, even I was convinced. When she said this, she knelt down, looking at Wren, who ran over to her, wrapping his arms around his "mother's" torso. Clearly, this was part of the plan, but I couldn't figure out why it was necessary. Why did we even need Wren in here?

"Fine, whatever," Arkra replied, "Have you brought the king's head?" She asked this with a venomous hiss in her voice.

"Yes. Clef has it," Bonneville replied while convincingly finishing her fake tears. Bonneville continued, "We brought you both the false king's head *and* his crown. We thought it would please you."

The queen's eyes lit up with what I assumed was joy, and she gestured me forward.

I walked towards her, and I could hear two guards following behind me. A guard grabbed my shoulders a few feet from her throne and forced me onto my knees, which was more manageable now that I was unshackled.

I grunted, and the guard took the crown and "head" from me.

Arkra gazed at me and said, "You would make quite a fine entertainer for me, bard. How would you like to stay with me?" I was not too fond of the way that she spoke but stayed silent, fearing another vinegar rag.

The guard handed Arkra the bundle. Finnon spoke up before she could unwrap the cloths, "What about our friend?"

"Oh, you people do ruin all my fun," Arkra replied with a pout. "Zedgrar, if you would please get the prisoner?" He left and went through the door I had seen them use earlier. While Zedgrar was doing this, Arkra ate the last bug from Karina's plate, which seemed to be a millipede. As the servant ran off to fill it, I could have sworn I saw her wink at me

We stood in the throne room in a frightening silence, with Arkra looming over us from her carcass throne. She said nothing, but her eyes told a story, and it was not one I wanted to read.

After several long moments, Zedgrar came back with Kriv behind him. I had never seen my comrade look so terrible. He had large red gashes across his whole body. Whether from a whip or blade, I couldn't tell. His torso was covered in purple and green bruises where it looked like stones had been thrown at him. I couldn't imagine what else they had done to him. His long trousers were now torn, and I could see that they were stained with blood and grime.

The king drug the dragon behind him. Kriv was barely even moving his beaten body.

Zedgrar got within a few feet of me and pushed Kriv over. I caught him before he hit the ground and led him back to the group. Arkra was about to unwrap the bundle when Bonneville called out.

"Your majesty, my son here already had to witness the death of the king. Please don't make him view… *that*… again." She wrapped her arms around Wren once more, burying his head in her shoulder.

So that was her plan, hoping the queen wouldn't unwrap the rock before we left. I just didn't see why she claimed he was her son. I hoped whatever they planned worked. Karina came back in again and winked at me once more, but it seemed only I noticed.

"You *dare* tell the queen what to do," Zedgrar bellowed this as he came towards Bon-Bon, raising his deadly spear. Bonneville continued her motherly guise and pulled Wren behind her.

"Zedgrar, that is quite enough." The queen said as she took a bug from the freshly refilled plate. She turned to my party, "I am feeling generous today. You may leave with your lives. You have completed my task, now begone before I change my mind."

We turned to leave, internally rejoicing our victory, when suddenly a group of lizard guards burst through the door we had come through only moments before. I jumped back in fear but then saw something that made my stomach drop.

Being led by the Ascabolates was the group of villagers we saved. I was surprised, however, to see that the lizards had left them their weapons.

I didn't know if this discovery was part of Bonneville's plan, but from the look of shock on her face, I doubted it was.

"Your majesty, we found these *humans*," the guard spat the word out like it disgusted him.

Arkra was furious now and turned her rage upon Bonneville, "What was your intention of hiding them from me?" She reached down and grabbed a handful of bugs from Karina, crunching them with her sharp teeth.

Bonneville thought quickly on her feet and stuttered, "Y-y-your majesty, we merely wished not to frighten you with such a large group. These were prisoners of the goblins that we rescued." This plan was falling apart quicker than I could have ever imagined, but then I saw something that filled me with hope. A flash of light came from where Karina was kneeling. Her hand was holding something. I looked closer and couldn't quite tell what it was. Was that a flower? I couldn't be sure.

Arkra yelled at Bonneville, "...and don't you think I would have liked some new servants. These ones are getting worn out." She gestured to Karina and Zook. The girl quickly shoved the shimmering item back into her pocket before the queen could see it. The queen continued, "I think I'll just take a few of them as consolation for your insolence." She gestured for the guards to bring a few of the prisoners forward, and I was horrified to watch as one drug Wren away from Bonneville's embrace.

Bonneville cried out and lunged for him but missed and fell. A guard planted his foot on her spine and held her to the ground.

"Now, what else were you lying about," she said wickedly as she unwrapped the stone. When she found a rock in her lap rather than the head she was expecting, I saw a level of rage I had never seen in a creature before, not even my aunt. "WHAT IS THIS!" She bellowed, "KILL THEM. KILL THEM ALL!"

Everything began moving in slow motion. First, I saw Wren spin around, pulling out the dagger I had given him. He plunged it into the chest of the lizard holding him, who instantly fell to the ground dead. Another lizard dove for him, attempting to bludgeon him with a club, but Wren rolled out of the way and stabbed at that lizard as well.

Two guards charged my group, but I suddenly saw a blaze of bright red fire erupt from Bonneville's mouth. I had nearly forgotten about the fuego brise elixir she had drunk. When the flames subsided, all that was left were two piles of black ash.

Unexpectedly—through her yelling—the queen grabbed her neck and began gasping for air. Zedgrar ran to help the queen, but a crossbow bolt hit him right in the heart, and he collapsed to the ground. I looked back and saw the elderly woman holding the crossbow Finnon had given her. She loaded another bolt, and a guard beside her fell to the ground.

I looked back at Arkra and saw her still holding her throat. She fell back to her throne and began to writhe in obvious pain, which finally ended as she lay motionless, halfway off her throne, one hand still clasping her throat.

I looked around. To my left, Finnon pulled out several small stones. Glowing blue runes lit up on them. He threw them at a charging group of lizards, and the Ascabolates instantly froze, shattering into millions of ice shards.

The lizard guards holding the prisoners were now taken out by the men we had given swords to. I was about to run to help when my attention was drawn back to Karina. I saw another flash of light. She had pulled the item back out, and I could now tell what it was.

It was a crystal flower. Malia's crystal flower. Her eyes locked onto mine, and they sparkled like the eyes I knew from so long ago. I saw a faint smile appear on her face and could tell that one had appeared on mine as well. I couldn't believe what I was seeing, but I never wanted it to go away.

I was looking at Malia's beautiful eyes right now. I was staring at the love of my life. Drawing my rapier, I began to run towards her. Nothing else mattered now. I could vaguely hear Kriv fighting to my right. I thought I heard Finnon cry out in pain behind me, but I didn't care. I had found Malia.

CHAPTER TWENTY-SEVEN

The Reunion

A few lizards charged at me, but I quickly dispatched them with my blade. I was a few paces from Malia when Zook stepped out in front of me, holding his dead father's spear. I had to skid to a stop, and as I did, I watched as an Ascabolate grabbed Malia by the wrist and held a wicked-looking knife to her throat.

"Zook, don't make me do this." I didn't care what I had to do. I was going to save Malia.

"Down," was the only response I received. He repeated it, pointing down.

I looked down and felt the spear graze the back of my neck. Then I heard a cry of pain from behind me. I looked back quickly and saw that Zook had impaled a lizard that was attempting to sneak up behind me. Zook pulled the spear free from the lizard's throat.

"Zook want free, Zook come with." He then ran off and began to fight several other Ascabolates at the same time. He now seemed quite capable of defending himself. When the other lizards had seen his traitorous act, several lizards ran towards him, ready to avenge their fallen comrade. He used the spear both as a weapon and as a way to block the other lizards' attacks.

I continued my path to Malia and cried out her name. With a flick of my wrist, the lizard holding her found a river of yellowish-brown blood dripping into his eyes, blinding him. He released the love of my life and began to stumble away. He only made it a handful of steps before he stumbled. When he looked down, he saw an axe lodged in his chest. I didn't care, though. Malia stumbled towards me, and I grabbed her before she fell.

She wrapped her arms around me, saying, "Clef. I thought I'd never see you again." We held the embrace as she kissed the side of my face, but suddenly she winced and grabbed her rib, "Ow!"

I was about to let go, but when she felt my embrace loosen, she said, "It's worth it. Don't you dare let go." She cried out in pain again, and I pulled away but still held onto her arms.

"What happened to you?" I asked.

"The king discovered I had given away his clothes. He was furious," she winced, still holding her rib.

"No, I mean, how did you get here?"

"I'll tell you later, but for now, we need to get out of here." She grabbed my arm and pulled me towards the main door. "Come on, Clef! We need to go. More guards will be here any moment."

She was pulling me through the chaos while I called, "Everyone! Let's go." The rest of the group heard me and followed behind. The old woman took out two more lizards as one of the men helped her walk. Wren slashed at another lizard—barely missing a fatal blow. Finally, my group, the villagers, and Malia were running down the hallway. However, we heard lizards close behind us.

Quickly we turned a corner, and Malia pulled a vial from her smock and smashed it on the ground. The corridor soon filled with smoke, and I couldn't see anything. I felt someone push me to the side and briefly saw Malia's face through the smoke. I was shocked.

What had happened? Was she under some sort of curse? Was she mad at me for not finding her sooner? But how was I to know she was in trouble?

Then I tumbled through a wall of cloth and found that I was in a passage very similar to the hidden one we had used earlier. I was staring at the back of a tapestry when the rest of the group fell into the passage as well. Malia came through a second later and told everyone to be quiet. We saw the shadows of lizards run past, and as they did, the little girl that Bon-Bon was holding started to cry. The lizards stopped and came back to the tapestry, Bonneville put her hand over the girl's mouth, but it was too late. The lizards knew we were here. A lizard's claw began to pull back the wall hanging.

Suddenly, another shadow joined the picture. The sounds of weapons hitting weapons and screams of agony rang out. Then it was quiet, and only one shadow remained. I could tell the figure looked left and right before popping its head behind the tapestry.

"Zook, come on. Hurry up," Malia called.

"Zook, coming."

"You can drop the act now, Zook. These are the good people."

"Oh, yeah, I'm sorry about that. I guess I was so used to the façade," Zook said perfectly clearly. Then, he looked at me and said, "That was a crazy fight back there, wasn't it? Sorry I couldn't explain more."

"Oh, uh, yeah, I guess it all worked out fine…" I didn't know what else to say. Had I just heard that right, did Zook make a complete sentence? What was going on?

"What is *he* doing here?" asked Finnon and Roscoe at the same time. Kriv grunted in anger.

"He's fine. He's with us," Malia answered.

"And who are you?" asked Roscoe angrily, turning his annoyance on her, "a spy for the queen, just leading us to our death." He stepped menacingly towards her, reaching back for his axe.

"She's good, Roscoe," I said defensively, pushing him backward, "if she tells you to do something, you do it, or you and I will have an issue. That goes for all of you, you hear me?" Everyone nodded their head timidly. I didn't realize how angry I sounded, but I felt I needed to do everything to protect Malia now.

Malia took the lead before I could ask any questions, "This tunnel leads back to the entrance of the fortress. From there, you'll see some rickety stone stairs. Follow them up to a rope. Those of you who are able, please help the elderly and children up the rope. No one is getting left behind."

My message had clearly gotten across about trusting Malia, and the group started hurrying down the passage without question.

The sharp-shooting old lady began to fall behind, but Zook ran forward, picked her up, and charged ahead. Malia and I had the back of the line so we could talk while we ran.

"What is going on here?" I cried with a mixture of confusion and annoyance.

"Zook and I have been planning an escape for a while, and when I saw you, I knew that this was the time to do it," she panted back.

"What was with Zook speaking like, you know, a normal person?" I questioned.

"Well, when I first showed up here, he could barely form a sentence, so I started to teach him. After a while, he was able to speak coherently. However, we needed to keep the act of his ignorance up so that the queen and king wouldn't suspect anything. He hated them. They never treated him like a son. They treated him worse than me…" she paused and held her rib for a moment as we ran, "sometimes. We managed to find this passageway a few months ago. We snuck out so that I could gather herbs outside. We began to prepare for today."

"But how did you get here?" I panted.

"After leaving home, I began studying plants and alchemy. There were some very rare herbs in this area I wanted to examine, and while I was examining one, I felt a bag put over my head, and then I went unconscious. Next thing I knew, I was here, wearing this…" she gestured down to the sack she was wearing.

It was all starting to make sense, but I was still confused about a few things. "What happened to the queen?"

"That's an easy one. It's a mixture of several different plants. Cowbane, strychnine fruit, hemlock, and oleander flower. It makes a very potent and effective poison. When I went to get another tray of…" she paused over the word, "food, I drizzled some over them. They usually make Zook test the insects, but through all the chaos, they didn't think twice about it."

I nodded along. I now wish I had joined Bonneville on her daily runs because I was out of breath. However, I managed to gasp out, "Why didn't you tell me who you were the first time? We could have saved you then!"

She looked sad at the question, "I had never expected to see you again. I lost all hope. I was so heartbroken I just stopped really seeing faces. It was all just shapes. So, to be honest, I didn't realize who you were at first. But when I saw your necklace, it was like waking up from a nightmare. I realized what a fool I had been not to see who you were. That was why I gave you those elixirs. I wanted to provide you with the best chance you had of surviving.

"You don't know how much I wanted to run away with you, Clef, but the poison wasn't ready. I was worried if I told you the plan, it would distract you from what you had to do. And the queen still had your dragon friend, and if you had failed, she would have done worse than kill him.

"Zook and I still had to plan a few more things, so we decided to wait until you came back. We weren't expecting you to try and trick the queen with a rock, though. That made the plan more challenging. I'm glad you noticed the flower. After Zook and I became close, he stole it back from those monsters. When the queen asked where it was, he told her he had broken it. The king beat him worse than you could imagine possible. I never let it out of my sight since then."

I felt terrible for not recognizing who she was. With her knotted hair and sunken eyes, she didn't look like the Malia I had known and loved. And while I didn't love her only for her looks, even her aura of joy was gone.

I had never expected to find her. I had lost all hope that I would see her again. Despite the million apologies and sweet things I wanted to say, I gasped out, "How... much longer... is this... tunnel?"

"It should be just around this corner." Sure enough, we were met with sunlight in just a few moments. With our talking, the rest of the group had gotten quite a bit ahead of us, and I could see that they were already climbing the rope. I saw several men helping the women and children climb up. I was impressed when I saw Wren helping out as well.

Malia and I had just hit the stairs when I heard a lizard behind us shout, "There they are, they're the ones who killed the que—"

A bolt from a crossbow in his throat cut his words off. I looked back at the rope and saw that the old lady was already at the top of the cliff. She went to load another bolt, but her frail hands dropped the crossbow over the ledge, and it clattered at the bottom of the rope. I heard her mutter a word I was surprised to hear from such an old woman, but she couldn't do anything now.

Malia reached into another pocket and pulled out a bottle with a blue liquid in it that looked like it was boiling. She handed it to me and said, "Drink."

"What is it?" I asked, already uncorking it. I drank it, and I could feel a warmth grow through me.

"Mainly the plant aspidistra, but there are a few other things as well."

"What does it do?" I asked as the guards got closer. I threw the bottle to my side, and Malia backed away from me and ran for the rope.

"You'll see," she called over her shoulder with a wink. I rolled my eyes and prepared for the fight. There were five soldiers against me, not odds I liked, but I've had worse. I knew I was still too exhausted for any spells, so I had to rely on my swordsmanship.

One of the guards charged me, and I raised my rapier. I pointed it straight at the Ascabolate as he charged me. He ran right into the blade, and with a flick of my wrist, I pushed him to the side into another lizard. The two of them went plummeting off the side of the stairs, and—a few seconds later—I heard a thud.

Two of the other guards charged me, but I didn't have time to react. One of them swung their sword to the left, the other to the right. Then they went to swing the blades together, with my body in between. There was nothing I could do but hope for a miracle—and one came.

When the swords hit my clothes, they ripped through, but when the swords hit my flesh, nothing happened. The blades stopped as if hitting stone.

"Figure it out yet?" I heard Malia call jokingly. I stepped backward and felt the blades run across my skin, ripping my shirt more, but that was it. There was no pain, just a slight tickle. "Makes your skin impenetrable by blade. The effect only lasts a few minutes, so you might want to hurry."

Taking her advice, I kicked at the lizard on the right while he was still staring at his blade, trying to figure out what had happened. I caught him off balance, and he went plummeting off the cliff after his two comrades. The other guard, unfortunately, recovered faster than his friend and reached out, grabbing my leg. He tried to set me off balance, but I was able to recover quickly and slashed at his wrist with my blade, forcing him to let go. He backed away quickly.

There was only that lizard and one other, and they both looked hesitant.

One of them fought his fear and started coming closer to me. When he was a few steps away, a dagger became lodged in his chest. I quickly looked over my shoulder and saw

Wren looking very proud of himself. I was getting more and more impressed with that kid every moment.

The lizard dropped. I charged forward, leaning down to pull out the blade from his chest. I jumped over him to take care of the last one, when I stumbled. That dagger hadn't killed the lizard as I had believed. He had reached out and grabbed my heel. My rapier dropped to the ground, with the dagger landing beside it. I saw the world spin out above me, and the next thing I knew, I was falling. I tried to grab the ledge, but it didn't help. I slipped. I knew the ground was coming soon.

I was trying to prepare myself, knowing it was impossible.

Suddenly, I saw a blue streak above me, and then something grabbed my leg and jerked me upwards. It was Kriv—and he was flying. "KRIV! YOU CAN FLY?" I yelled to him.

I don't know how I had never noticed his wings before. I now realized that what I had thought were large scales on his back were—in all actuality—wings tucked together.

"Superior race," was all he replied as if that was an answer. He lifted me back up to the bridge and dropped me down on it. Not gently, I might add. He tucked his wings in, and once more, I could barely see them.

He reached down and handed me my rapier and dagger.

We turned to face the remaining guards. Putting aside all differences, we stood there as comrades, each willing to sacrifice ourselves to save the other if it came to that.

As we prepared ourselves for battle, half a dozen more lizards appeared from various doorways.

I was preparing to tell Kriv to run when I heard a bellow in his throat, and then a line of blue fire shot out of his mouth. It lasted only a few seconds, but when the smoke cleared, all that was left were large piles of ashes, which began to blow away in the slight breeze.

"You can breathe fire too?" I feel like these are things that could have helped out a *lot* in the past. He went to open his mouth, but I cut him off, saying, "I know, superior race." I shook my head and looked out for any more guards. I couldn't see or hear anyone, so I hurried over to the rope with Kriv close behind.

CHAPTER TWENTY-EIGHT

The Plan

We started climbing the rope quickly. Everyone else was already at the top of the precipice. I pulled myself over the face of the cliff and saw the rest of the party ahead of us. There were only a few wounded, but none of them seemed to be fatal, which was a huge relief. I saw a few of the men had wounds from spear points, but they were healed quickly with a prayer from Roscoe's divine intervention and a few of Malia's tonics.

Bonneville was distracting some of the smaller children with some help from Wren. I walked over to her and asked the question I had been wondering the whole time, "So what was that about Wren being your son?"

"Well, I had hoped to have a child in there so that we could avoid her opening the *head*," she said the last word sarcastically. "I decided to say he was my son because I figured she would be less likely to take a child from his mother than a stranger, though clearly that didn't work. But I guess that everything worked out. Wren, can you take over for a second?" She pulled me aside from the group and said quietly, "So, is that girl her? Is that Malia?" She sounded like she was filled with disbelief and excitement at the same time.

I swallowed and smiled, "Yeah, it is. I don't know what will happen now, but all that matters is we can be together. Come on. I want you to meet her."

We walked over to Malia, who was currently speaking with Zook. "Malia!" I called out. She looked over, "I want you to meet someone."

She looked at Bon-Bon and frowned a little, and I could see she looked disappointed. I was confused at first and then realized she was jealous of Bonneville. I laughed and said,

"No, it's not like that. Bonneville and I work together. She's like a mother to me." When she heard that, I could tell that she was relieved. I quickly told her about the Lily and why we had even been sent out here.

"So, what do we do now?" Malia asked.

I paused for a moment, thinking. Eventually I said, "Well, I would say we need to get these people back to town, then we need to check in with the Lily." I suddenly looked at Bonneville, filled with fear, "I just realized this is the first time we've failed a mission. Brownstead was having a problem with the goblins, not the Ascabolates."

"What do you mean?" Zook asked. It was still odd hearing him speak coherently.

I briefly told him about the Lily and then said, "Every full moon, the goblins ransack Brownstead, and recently they started taking prisoners." I gestured to the men and women we had saved.

"Well, we have explored the perimeter of this pretty extensively, and there are only a few ways to get out of it. We could just take out the few ropes, ladders, and such that are left, and they would be trapped in there, right?" Zook suggested.

"Couldn't the goblins just build a ladder or something?" I asked, fearing what would happen if we had failed the Lily. That had never happened before.

"Clef, they can't even tell their left from right. I know for a fact they couldn't build a ladder," Malia said with a grin.

"Then that sounds like our best bet," Bonneville said, and I had to agree with her. Hopefully, the Ascabolates and goblins would kill each other out, I had to hope they wouldn't form an alliance, but I doubted the cruel lizards would work with such a primitive creature.

I called Roscoe, Finnon, and Kriv over to us. "Roscoe, Finnon, stay here and protect the rest. We are going to go and take care of something. If anything happens, send a firebolt into the air, Finnon." They nodded, and Roscoe went back to bandaging a man's leg.

Wren ran over to me and asked, "Do you need any help from me, Clef?" He looked excited to fight.

I bent down to look him straight in the eye, "I need you here, okay." I handed him back the dagger Kriv had retrieved, "That was a great shot you took. I probably, no, I *definitely* would have missed that. If there's any danger here,

I want you to be the one to protect the others." He smiled and tucked the knife into his belt.

"Alright, I understand." He then headed back to entertain the kids.

CHAPTER TWENTY-NINE

The Old Lady

We started our trek around the fortress. It was several miles around, so it took us a while. We came to multiple locations that Zook and Malia pointed out as being paths out. There were half a dozen ropes like the one we had used to climb out, but Bonneville took care of them with a quick swing of a blade.

We even came to the location where my team had entered the chasm, and I had to admit that seeing where we started, I realized I would never have imagined how complex this mission would have been. We expected a simple goblin issue. Instead, we found a cruel death-worshipping race, possibly discovered a long-lost society, let the goblins live, and I found the love of my life.

At one point, there was a large stone staircase that led directly to the ledge. But Kriv flew down, ramming his body into it. It shattered into thousands of pieces, and I had to shield my eyes from the debris. We were nearly back to the camp when I saw a purple ball of fire shoot into the air. Bon-Bon took a quick swing of her blade and cut through the final rope, and we ran back to the group.

Upon arriving at our makeshift camp, it appeared everything was peaceful. Then we saw it. On the far edge of the cliff, two of the men were fighting with the older woman. It looked as if they were driving her off the cliff.

Finnon was running towards us, but we were already heading towards the fight, so he changed course to run with us. We were all shocked as we heard one of the men shouting and pleading, "Ada! Stop! We won't let you go back there!"

She fought back and called for them to let go. It seemed that they weren't trying to push her off, but instead, they were trying to prevent her from going back down.

We got there just a moment before she pushed them off of her to start climbing back down the rock face, given we had already destroyed the rope. "Ma'am," Malia said gently, "Why are you trying to go back down there? We just saved you from them?"

The woman, Ada, I assume, stopped fighting and—through tears—said, "They hurt my baby," she gestured over to the young girl, who was currently climbing a tree with help from Wren. It seemed the girl was Ada's granddaughter. "She didn't do anything and they forced her to clean their feet. She was forced to endure that wretched task for weeks, and there was nothing I could do. They hurt my Bella. They are going to pay. I'm going to kill them all. I won't stop until every single one of them has paid."

"Ada…" I said gently, "Look at her. She's okay. We are going to take you all back to town. Everything is going to be fine."

She was still fighting the sobs, "But they hurt her. I had to watch her cry as they beat her."

"But she's okay, Ada. *You're* okay," Malia added. "What you did back there with the crossbow was amazing. I've *never* seen anyone shoot like that. You're a real sharpshooter." This led to a small laugh from Ada, and Malia wiped away some of the woman's tears.

While they were talking, I called over to the girl, "Hey, Bella," she looked over at me from a low branch she had climbed to. "Can you come over here?" She looked disappointed to have to climb down from the tree, but Wren helped her to slide down the trunk, and the girl came running over to me.

"Hi!" She called out. It is amazing how resilient children are. She had just barely gotten out of this prisoner encampment, and then almost died at the hands of vicious Ascabolates. But now, she was acting as though everything was fine. Children will never cease to amaze me.

I knelt down to her and said, "Your grandmother is a little upset, and I thought you might comfort her."

She looked at me with big eyes, "What's wrong with her? Do you think she would want to climb that tree with me?"

I suppressed a chuckle and said, "She's all right. She's just a little worried about you. I think she would *love* to play with you."

She nodded and ran over to Ada, who had just barely finished crying. "Nana!" I heard Bella call. "Do you want to come and play with me? Wren and I are seeing who can climb higher." Then she said disappointedly, "He keeps winning, though…"

Ada laughed, wiping away the last few tears, and said, "I would love to play with you, sweetie," she gave her hand to Bella, who started to pull the woman over to the tree.

Over her shoulder, I saw Ada mouth the words, "Thank you."

Bonneville came over now to check on what had happened, though she didn't get a chance to speak.

"That is one stubborn old woman, but I've never seen someone stronger than her," said one of the men by me.

"You've definitely got that right. Where did she learn to shoot like that?" I asked.

"Her father was a royal guard for Queen Alysia," the other man answered. Bonneville tensed at the mention of her grandmother. Then she quietly walked away from the group. "When she was born, he wanted to teach her how to protect herself. He always said there were too many damsels that he had to save. He didn't want her to be one of them."

When the men started speaking with each other, Malia and I went back to meet with the group. Finnon, Roscoe,

Kriv, Bonneville, Zook, Malia, and I stepped aside from the group so we could talk.

Bonneville said. "Now that we know where we are going, the trip shouldn't take us more than a day, but it's getting dark, and with the injured, I don't think we will make it in time. I say we stay here for the night, let them get some rest," she gestured to the group, "and make an early start tomorrow." The seven of us agreed unanimously. I turned to the rescued villagers and informed them of the decision.

"Everyone! I know that you're hungry and you want to get back to town to your homes and families, but it's too late for us to leave now. We are going to stay here for the night, but don't worry, one of us," I gestured to myself and the other six behind me, "will be up all night should something happen. So, you can all rest easy. If any of you are still in pain, you can see either Roscoe or Malia." I pointed at each of them so everyone else knew who they were. "If you need to talk about anything, you can go to either Bonneville," I gestured at her, "or myself.

"If you hear anything," I continued, "please find one of us and let us know. We will take care of it. Please do *not* leave the camp for *any* reason. Unfortunately, we are out of food and water, but Roscoe and Malia may be able to identify edible plants around us. If some of you can, go with them to help gather. Do we have any hunters? You can meet with Bonneville, and plan a short hunt. There was a stream around that way," I pointed to my left, " Some of you will need to go with Finnon and Kriv to refill the water skins. Zook and I will be staying here to protect anyone who stays behind. Other than that, please stay safe. We will have you all home as soon as possible."

As soon as I finished speaking, the crowd began to disperse. I watched as several of the men—and Ada—went to join Bonneville in planning the hunt. A few of the women, and a younger man, went with Malia and Roscoe. Then, a few adults and Bella finally joined Kriv and Finnon on their trip to fill the flasks.

Kriv and Finnon quickly passed out the skins, and the group headed to the stream. Roscoe and Malia's group received a quick briefing on which berries and plants were safe to consume and which to avoid. They then headed out to forage for food. Finally, Bonneville's group left. I was relieved to see that one of the prisoners had grabbed Ada's crossbow before coming up the rope. Between her sharp shooting and Bon-Bon's hunting skills, I was sure we would have all the meat we would need.

Only a few of the children remained with us, including Wren. I chuckled when I saw him perched on a tree branch, leaning down and swinging a young boy back and forth. The child was laughing while the other kids were calling for it to be their turn. This went on for a while longer when finally the children—exhausted from the chaotic day—fell asleep at the base of the tree. After checking to make sure they were all safe and asleep, Wren came over and stood beside me.

"So, I heard you talking about this Lily organization." He looked up at me expectantly.

"Oh, you, uh, heard that did you?" If the Lily knew how much I had spoken about them, I would be kicked out faster than I could imagine. I couldn't even think what else they would do to make sure I didn't blab about it anymore. "I'm not technically supposed to speak about that. So, I need you to forget about it, and please, don't tell *anyone* else." I looked down at him. His stare was a stern one.

"I want in," he said matter-of-factly, as if there was no doubt in his mind. I began to open my mouth, but he could tell I was going to say no, so he cut me off. "You said it yourself, you could have never hit that lizard from so far away, and I haven't even had any training. Imagine what I could do with some help." I attempted to speak again. "Don't say anything, but I want you to know, one way or another, I *will* be joining your group." He stared at me without blinking.

I smiled and patted him on the back, "You've sure got some spirit. We'll talk about it when we get back to Brownstead. But *nothing* happens without your father's permission." I wished I could tell him no. I felt he was too young to risk his life as I do, but then I remembered that I was even younger—much younger—than he was when I left home. And only a year or so older when I joined the Lily. I hadn't even been eighteen at the time.

He smiled as if he had won the conversation and walked back to the group of children. One of the girls had begun to shake in her sleep, clearly having a nightmare, but he slowly brushed her forehead, and she fell back into a restful slumber. Wren, however, kept staring at me with a defiant stare.

CHAPTER THIRTY

The Hunting Party

The groups came back quickly. The water flasks had effectively been filled, and Roscoe said a prayer over them to cleanse the liquid. Roscoe and Malia's group had armfuls of foliage and berries, more than we could ever need. Finally, I saw the hunters come back. Two of the men had a stag over their shoulders, and Bonneville and Ada were carrying a boar. Bonneville told me they had to travel quite far, given that it seemed the animals avoided this area. We quickly got to preparing the food while Wren watched over the sleeping children.

The meat was seared in a fire that Malia set up, and the berries and leaves were cleaned using a flask of water. Once the food was prepared, Wren woke up the children, who were ecstatic to find such a delicious meal in front of them. The meat was quickly devoured.

We then passed out the fruit as a sort of dessert. I don't know if it was the exhaustion or the starvation, but the meal tasted phenomenal.

Slowly the villagers began to fall asleep, along with some of my team. Eventually, the only ones left awake were Malia, Bonneville, Wren, and myself. Wren was sitting on a low branch in a tree, carving a stick with my dagger. Bonneville was seated near the fire, clearly looking and listening for danger. Together Malia and I walked out just to the edge of the firelight, and we sat down, looking at the stars.

"It reminds me of the old times," I said quietly.

"Yeah, it does," Malia replied, "I remember the time my father found us watching the stars that one night. He was furious. If he didn't have such high hopes for you, I'm sure he would have shipped you off to the ogre lands." We laughed, and it felt as if everything was right in the world again. She shimmied her way over to me, resting her head on my shoulder. I wrapped my arm around her, tilting my head so it was against the top of hers. We stayed there for what felt like hours. After a while, I could tell she had fallen asleep.

I stayed there, watching the stars until Bonneville ran over to us.

"Clef!" She whispered, loud enough to get my attention. "Wren is gone." I stood up quickly, accidentally making Malia fall back. Her head, unfortunately, hit the ground, and she woke up.

"Where did he go?" I asked.

"I don't know, I heard a rustle in the bushes, and when I looked over, he was gone."

"Who's gone?" Malia asked through a yawn.

"Wren." As Bonneville said this, she helped Malia to her feet. We quickly rushed over to the tree where Wren had been previously and looked around. We could easily see the footprints of the children that Wren had been entertaining. In the midst of them was a set of larger ones—clearly his. They went directly into the bushes.

"Bon-Bon, you stay here and keep guard. We are going to look for Wren." Bon-Bon agreed. Malia and I started going after the tracks. We had followed them several yards when we heard a cry. It didn't sound human. I was horrified when I realized it was a goblin—too close to camp for comfort. And I thought we had destroyed all the exits…

Malia and I ran towards the sounds in time to see Wren surrounded by four goblins, each holding a large sword. We were still several yards away when I saw one of them charge Wren. The boy slashed out with his dagger and managed to parry the large blade away, then quickly stabbed the goblin in the chest, who fell to the ground.

The goblin behind Wren charged, and as he was nearly to the boy, Wren ducked, and the creature rolled over his back. The goblin was then launched off the nearby cliff when Wren straightened his legs. There were only two goblins left, and they both looked hesitant. Wren chose the weaker-looking of the two and charged him. The goblin pulled back his sword, but from the weight of it, he was too slow. Wren leaned back and kicked it in the chest during the swing, and the creature followed his comrade off the cliff.

Finally, the last goblin looked at Wren, then ran off, unknowingly towards Malia and me. We were nearly to Wren at this point. I drew my rapier and pierced the goblin through the stomach, watching him collapse to the ground. Wren was looking around to see if there were any other goblins waiting in the shadows when Malia and I got to him.

"That was very foolish of you," Malia scolded him.

At the same time. I said, "That was amazing." Malia looked at me sternly, and I corrected myself. Saying, "*Extremely* foolish, but amazing." Malia looked at me with pursed lips. I changed the subject, "Why did you go off alone like that?" I grabbed his arm and started guiding him back to camp.

"I was coming to get you but didn't want to seem weak or foolish if it turned out just to be a deer or something. So I followed the sound. I realized it was a goblin, clearly a scout. I think they were part of a hunting party still out here when you cut off the entrances. It seemed they couldn't find a way back in." I was relieved to know we hadn't missed an exit.

"I was about to come and tell you, Clef, but it was too late. Suddenly there were goblins all around me. There were eight in total. Only one of them got me." I looked down and saw now there was a deep gash on his left shoulder, clearly from a blade.

We got back to camp, and when Bonneville saw the boy was alive, she was clearly relieved. Malia asked for bandages. I directed her to Roscoe's pack. She found in it a roll of fabric along with a small bottle of a tincture. Malia applied the liquid to the wound. Wren winced in pain. She quickly wrapped the gash and told him to get some sleep.

Wren reluctantly went over to the large tree, laid down, and fell asleep. Bonneville took her post by the fire once more.

While she had healing in mind, Malia looked at my rat bite and arrow wound. After rummaging around in Roscoe's pack, she grabbed various leaves, flowers, and herbs. Pounding them into a paste and mixing it with water, she poured it into a vial and handed it to me.

I drank it, and instantly felt a stabbing pain in each of my wounds. They began to throb, and then suddenly—nothing. All pain and soreness was gone, both topical and below the surface. I looked down and saw flawless flesh where there had previously been ripped skin. Even my broken nose from the door was healed and straight once more.

"It feels good having a whole arsenal of herbs," Malia said, still looking in Roscoe's pack, "I've been working with only what I could find. There are *so* many potions I could make with these."

I managed to pull Malia away from the pack, and we sat back down to look at the stars like we had so many years ago. Malia quickly fell back into a deep sleep. I couldn't sleep—well, really—I didn't want to. I wanted nothing more than to savor this moment in time with her. I lay there for several hours until I finally saw the first sign of the sun rising. I gently woke Malia, and we walked back to the rest of the group. Bonneville had fallen asleep at the fire, her sword in her hand.

The party woke up quickly as I said to them, "It's a long trek back to town, but we can make it in one day if we move quickly. With the little ones, make sure to carry them when they tire out. We can't make any stops. We have some meat left from last night, so we can eat that on the trail." When I saw them nodding in agreement, I began to lead the way back to town. Malia stayed near my side, and Zook walked near her. I looked back and saw that Bonneville was carrying Bella, with Ada doing her best to keep up, talking with the two of them along the way.

Finnon and Roscoe were fighting over something, and Kriv was in the far back, making sure no one fell behind. Several of the adults were carrying the young children. Wren was keeping pace just a bit behind me with the dagger tucked in his belt.

The trip back to town was, fortunately, uneventful. The relief of going home seemed to give everyone a new sense of urgency, and we made the trip faster than we could have hoped. We got back to Brownstead just before dusk, and the villagers quickly ran to their homes.

I smiled as I saw a middle-aged woman run up the path from her home into the arms of Ada and Bella. Clearly Bella's mother and Ada's daughter. They all laughed and cried and wouldn't let go of their embrace. Men ran out and scooped up their wives. Mothers and fathers held their children. Grown men wept and turned to us, with their children and wives in their arms shouting, "Thank you!" through the tears of joy.

Malia, Zook, Wren, the team, and I walked back to the tavern to reunite Wren with his father. As we walked through the door, the barkeep didn't even look up, he just continued his cleaning and grunted, " We're closed."

When we didn't leave, he looked up to see who had ignored him. He choked on his words, "My boy, you're home." He ran over to Wren and embraced him so tightly that Wren had to fight away to breathe. "Thank you, there is no way I could ever repay you, but I'll try. There are a few rooms upstairs that are empty. Take them for as long as you need," he said to me as he was crying, still holding Wren's shoulder.

My group climbed the stairs to find that there were two rooms available. Malia and Bonneville shared one. Leaving Kriv, Zook, Finnon, Roscoe, and myself the other. There were only two beds. One of which was taken immediately by Roscoe and Finnon. Each with their heads at opposite ends of the bed. I took the other while Kriv and Zook slept on opposite ends of the room on the floor. It seemed like Kriv was angry at Zook, and Zook was afraid of Kriv.

Roscoe and Finnon had, once more, started their cacophony of snores, but I didn't care. I had found Malia, and I already knew what would happen tomorrow.

I fell into a deep and, luckily, dreamless sleep.

CHAPTER THIRTY-ONE

The Proposals

I awoke to find that the rest of the group was already downstairs. I headed down, and before I hit the bottom stair, I could already hear the group speaking. I could smell a fantastic meal awaiting me. As I entered the room, I saw Bonneville and Malia laughing with each other at a table. Finnon and Roscoe were at another table, bickering over who knows what. Kriv and Zook were each at a table alone. Every plate was piled high with bread, meat, and vegetables. As I came in, Wren's father brought me a plate with just as much food heaped on it. When I tried to pay for it, he refused the gold. The barkeep just looked at Wren, who was sitting on a stool behind the counter.

I walked over to Malia and Bonneville's table, which prompted Bon-Bon to stand up abruptly, saying, "It's so nice out today, just the perfect weather for a run. I'll be back in a bit," she then winked at me, not very subtly, and Malia laughed. Bonneville started to walk away towards the door.

Before she took more than two steps, I stopped her, putting my hand on her shoulder. "You might want to wait a minute."

I turned to Malia. "Malia, these last several years have been the worst in my life, and I've had some pretty terrible years. Being without you is like… well, it's worse than being without air. It felt as if a part of my soul had been taken from me, and I never want to feel that way again." She quickly reached up to brush a tear away from her cheek. "I may have just found you, but I never want to find you again."

Her face scrunched up. I could see that she went from happy, to angry in a heartbeat, "You never want to find me again! I thought we had something Clef, but clearly I was wrong." She pushed back from the table, about to storm away, but I grabbed her arm, laughing.

"Malia, wait, no, no. That's not what I meant. It came out wrong. You know I've never been one with words when I'm around you." I guess it wasn't just my teenage self that was awkward around her. "I never want to *need* to find you again, because I never want to *lose* you again. What I'm trying to say is," I got down on one knee, "I may not have a ring, but my love could be no greater. I asked you this years ago, and I ask you once again." She knew the words that were coming next, but she was still on the edge of her seat, anticipating them. "Malia, will you marry me?"

She said nothing, but she nodded her head furiously. She leaned down, grabbed the sides of my face, and kissed me. I could feel tears of joy on my cheeks. I couldn't tell if they were hers, or mine. I had a feeling it was a mixture of the two. She leaned back from me just enough to speak and said, "I love you, Clef."

"I love you too, Malia."

I looked over to the group and could see that everyone was watching us. Even Wren and his father were watching with smiles on their faces. Bonneville had tears streaking down her face, with a huge grin. Then, for the first time, I thought I saw a smile on Kriv's face.

"I could perform the ceremony," Roscoe offered.

"Thank you, Roscoe. I know just the place." I looked at Malia, and I could see that she slightly nodded her head. It seemed that we had the same idea.

We quickly finished our breakfasts and gathered the few items we had unpacked, getting ready to leave. We were just walking out the door of the inn when Wren's father stopped us. "These came for you last night. They were sitting on the bar with this," he held up five leather pouches and a single white lily, "I assumed that they were for you." He tossed me one of the bags, and it was heavier than I expected. I peeked inside and it was filled with gold coins. From the weight and feel of it, there were at least a thousand of them in each bag.

I put mine into my pack, and Bonneville put her hand on my shoulder and pulled me aside, out of earshot of the others. She handed me her bag, saying, "I want you to take this, get Malia a ring…" she glanced back at my bride-to-be, "…an emerald, I think. It would set off her eyes." I tried to refuse the bag, but she insisted. "Just think of it as a wedding gift. And let's get her some new clothes. She shouldn't have to wear that sack any longer than she needs to." Malia was still wearing the clothes Arkra had given her.

I slipped the second bag of gold into my pack, hoping that Malia wouldn't see. "Well, I expect your help picking the ring out." She laughed, agreeing.

Before rejoining the group, I took the lily from Wren's father, handing it to Malia with a slight bow. She laughed, accepting the flower.

We tried leaving once more but were again stopped, this time by Wren. I had almost hoped he had given up on trying to join the Lily, but he hadn't.

"Clef, I don't break promises," I looked back at him, "and I'm going to keep the one I made. I *will* be joining your group."

"I'm sure you will," I replied with total sincerity while ruffling his hair.

Our third attempt to leave was successful.

Before we left Brownstead, we stopped at the local tailor to buy Malia more suitable clothes to wear. She picked out several lovely gowns and a tunic with trousers that she could wear when foraging for plants and herbs.

I stopped to collect Andante from the stable I had left him at. I was pleased to find him in excellent health. He even took an instant liking to Malia. We all agreed Malia should ride Andante for our travels. While she may have the sparkle back in her eye, she was still very thin and had a healing journey ahead of her. The group was grateful to have Andante carry their packs as well. We were all a bit worn out from this adventure.

The trip we had to make was a long one, but it was worthwhile. It was nearly a week's journey. We were able to stop at a town each night, allowing us a real bed. We would always take three rooms, one for Malia and Bonneville, one for Finnon, Roscoe, and Kriv, and a final one for Zook and me. I decided it was best to keep Zook and Kriv apart from each other. Zook couldn't seem to relax or sleep in front of my blue-scaled comrade. And Finnon and Roscoe still didn't seem entirely comfortable with an Ascabolate in their presence.

Our journey was peaceful, a time of friendly conversation and laughter. One night Bonneville and I snuck out to the local jeweler. We were, coincidentally, in the town of her jeweler friend, Frederick, who she'd mentioned to me back in the Ascabolate prison. He was pleased to see her, and gave me a significant discount. I purchased Malia a beautiful silver wedding ring, which had a large round emerald. Lining the band were small diamonds. While I was making my decision, the jeweler was in the back, fixing my necklace.

When I took it back, I quickly placed it around my neck, and as the cold blue gemstone touched my skin, I felt a warmth grow within me. It felt like everything was right again. Before heading back, we made one more stop at a florist. I bought a large bouquet of white roses mixed with pink orchids, and white snowdrops. I suppose Rose's suggestion to the panicked man at the flower shop had stuck with me.

We snuck back into the inn we were staying at, and—to our luck—no one had realized we were gone.

The following day, Malia woke up to find the flowers at the foot of her bed, with the ring tied to them with a satin ribbon.

When she came out of her room, she hugged me and held up her hand with the new ring on it, saying, "I love it, Clef."

"And I love *you,* Malia." Every day she began looking more and more like her usual self, thanks to Roscoe's stock of herbs. Malia had been brewing a few tonics each day from them, which helped her recover quicker.

Her eyes were less sunken in, and the vivid greenness of them came back. Her cheeks began to have their usual fullness, and her hair began to shine again as it once had.

Our trip came to an end the next day.

We were finally there.

I was staring at a small cottage with a rose-lined path leading to the door. Behind the building was an orchard of apple trees.

"Home." Malia and I said it at the same time. We were standing at the entrance to Athelstan's home. Our home.

"We'll just wait here, you two," Bonneville said gently, "give the new family some time together."

My fiancée and I nodded appreciatively. We looked back to the house, preparing ourselves. We walked up the rose-lined pathway, and a million thoughts were running through my mind. What should I say? What would *he* say? After all, I hadn't shown up for years, and then I come to his door—out of the blue—saying that I was marrying his daughter. I hadn't even asked his permission. He knew some advanced spells. I couldn't—and didn't want to—imagine what he could do to me.

I couldn't even begin to imagine what Malia was thinking.

We reached the door, and at the same time, Malia and I knocked. A heartbeat later, the door opened, and I saw Athelstan. He didn't seem to have aged at all. His usually brown hair may have had a few streaks of white, but other than that, he looked the same.

He seemed confused for a moment as if he couldn't believe that he was looking at us. Finally, he choked out the words, "Malia! Clef! What are you two doing here? I thought you were off seeking your fortunes."

I tried to find the words to say, but Malia beat me to it with a simple gesture. She slowly held up her left hand, pointing to her new ring, while looking down at the ground.

I was expecting the worst, a bolt of lightning from the sky. A wave of fire rushing over me. But what happened instead hurt even worse, and at the same time, it was the best feeling in the world.

Athelstan stepped forward and hugged the two of us together. He was crushing our ribs with his tight embrace as he said, "Oh, I always hoped that you two would work out." I began to fight away from the hug so that I could take a breath when Athelstan suddenly released the hug and pushed past Malia and me. I looked back and saw that the rest of the group was walking up the path.

"Bonnie?" Athelstan called as he passed us, nearly knocking us over. I looked back and saw him holding Bonneville around the waist.

"Stan!" she replied. He picked her up and spun in a circle.

I was too stunned to say anything, but Malia managed to croak out the word, "What?"

Athelstan put Bonneville back down and said, "Bonnie! What are you doing here? How did you know where I lived?" He seemed utterly infatuated with her, like there was nothing else in the world that mattered.

"I didn't, Stan. I was coming with them," she gestured to Malia and me, "I never thought I would see you again."

He looked at us and said, "Thank you, this is the best gift you could have ever given me."

I was finally able to speak again, and I said, "You called her Bonnie? What does that mean? Do you two know each other?" My voice showed my confusion.

They both chuckled nervously. Athelstan looked at Bonneville. Grabbing her hand, she nodded for him to speak, and he did. "Well, before your mother, Malia… Bonnie and I were… well," he coughed, "old sweethearts." My mind erupted. "Unfortunately, time drew us apart, and we each lived our separate lives. I moved here with your mother, Malia, and we had you. After your mother died and you two left, I thought I would never know what love was again. But this… this…" he turned back to speak to Bonneville. "This is fate, Bonnie. I knew we were meant to meet again."

She laughed and looked at me, saying, "When you mentioned your old tutor's name was Athelstan, I never thought it would have been my Stan," she looked down into his eyes endearingly, for she was a good six inches taller than him.

"Bonnie, do you know what fortune this is? I don't want to leave this to chance again." He turned to face her directly. "Bonnie, I don't want to live without you." I saw a look in his eyes that I found familiar. He knelt down and said, "I know this may feel sudden, but Bonneville, will you marry me?"

Her eyes went wide, and she giggled, dragging the toe of one of her boots along the ground. She nodded her head, "Yes, Stan, I will," and she giggled again. She sounded like a teenage girl in love.

After a long kiss between the two of them, Athelstan led us into his cottage. Walking through that heavy wooden door hit me with a wave of emotions.

It was just the way I remembered it. We walked into an expansive room that seemed too large to fit in the small cottage.

Athelstan had explained to me once that the door led into a seemingly vast space that could take any shape it needed, meaning the cottage's interior could be as large or as small as required. This was why Athelstan was the master and I was merely the apprentice.

In the main room were plush padded chairs covered in golden fabric. Against one wall was an oversized stone fireplace. No matter the weather, there was a fire roaring in it. Though magically, when it was hot outside, the fire let off cold blasts of air, and when it was cold out, the fire nicely warmed the room.

Above the fireplace were three taxidermy animal heads. Well… I guess I should say *mythical* taxidermy animal heads. In the center was a unicorn with a long silver horn. To its right was an elk head, though rather than the hair an elk usually has, there were multicolored feathers, like that of a parrot. To the left of the unicorn was a dragon. Though if these unique animals' heads weren't enough for you, they could also speak to people. It was quite enjoyable to have a conversation with them, though the elk is quite judgmental, and the dragon is a bit of a hothead.

When I had first come to live with Athelstan, I partook in a long conversation with the unicorn about its home field, with all the daisies he could eat. It seemed the animals didn't realize they were mounted on a wall, and they seemed to be both on the wall and in their homelands—just more of Athelstan's impressive magic.

Off of this magical room, there was a long hallway that I knew led to four rooms—the study chambers, Athelstan's room, Malia's old room, and mine. When I walked to the hall, I discovered there were a few more doors, probably part of the magical house accompanying the new guests. But I didn't care about those doors. I only cared about one specific door. My door.

I mindlessly walked to the door, remembering to lift up on the handle to prevent squeaking. When the door opened, I was hit with a wave of memories from my past. And unlike my time with my aunt or living on the street, these ones were all pleasant.

CHAPTER THIRTY-TWO

The Lily

Looking into the room, I found that everything was exactly how I had left it. There were still piles of sheet music scattered on the bed. The wardrobe was still filled with old tunics and cloaks. On a shelf next to the cabinet was my lute. Not the one that Athelstan had made for me, but rather the one I had bought while living on the street.

I carefully picked it up and blew off a layer of dust that had collected on it. I began to strum a tune on it. There was no magic in the song, but it felt nice to play on the old lute again. This was the instrument I had learned with. Without this lute, I would not be the bard I am today.

I had to take longer than usual tuning it, as the enchanted lute Athelstan gave me never went out of tune, so I was a little bit out of practice. However, I eventually got it in tune and was nearly halfway done with the song when I heard a knock on the door.

"Hey Clef, you mind if I come in?" It was Athelstan. Of course, I had no problem with him coming in, and I told him so. He opened the door and walked in. He was smiling nearly ear to ear when he came in.

"Where are Malia and Bonneville?" I realized I hadn't seen either of them since we came into the house.

"Oh, they're getting ready for the wedding. I think Bonnie's trying to find a dress to wear." He replied. "I can't even explain to you how glad I am to have you and Malia back home. And this bizarre chance that Bonnie was with you. It makes me so overjoyed. If you don't mind me asking, though, how did you and Bonneville meet? And what brought you and Malia back together?"

I paused for a moment, debating whether I should tell him about the Lily or not. I had already shared more than I should have in the last several days with Wren, Malia, and Zook. But I decided that I had known Athelstan so long, and he had done so much for me, that I owed him the truth.

I told him about joining the Lily and working my way up the teams. I explained to him that Bonneville and I had been on the same team since the beginning and that she had been like a mother to me. Next, I told him about going to Brownstead and the sunken fortress. Finally, he heard about me reuniting with Malia as we fled the Ascabolates.

He didn't seem as shocked as I expected about the Lily. When I finished speaking, he asked, "Did you say you are a part of the Lily?" I nodded slowly, and he laughed his rolling laugh and clapped me on the back. "Good job, my boy. I knew you would do great things." He could see the confusion on my face, so he explained. "I once was an agent for the Lily myself, well actually, more than just any old agent, I was one of the original four founding members."

I stood there slack-jawed and stared at him. He laughed again and simply said, "Follow me."

He led me out of my room and towards the study chambers. As we walked down the hall, I saw Bonneville come out of one of the new rooms in a long silver dress and then dash into Malia's before Athelstan could see her.

I followed Athelstan into the study chamber as he silently walked to one of the chests in a corner and pulled out a small wooden box from within it. I could see on the top of it a painted yellow lily. Its age showed as it was now starting to crack and peel. He set it on the desk but, before opening it, began to speak.

"Years ago, this kingdom was in utter chaos. Chimera and ogres were running wild. You couldn't walk over a bridge without encountering a troll. So, a few friends and I decided something had to be done to restore order. We formed an elite operation, which you now know as the Lily. That name took some time to come upon. We all agreed upon it because they are a symbol of purity and rebirth, exactly what the kingdom needed. "

At this point, he started opening the small lily-emblazoned chest to pull out a piece of parchment. On it was an intricately drawn portrait of four people: three of them men and the final one a woman. I instantly recognized one of them as a younger—*much* younger—Athelstan.

As he showed me the image, I gasped when I saw one of the other men blink and look down at the young Athelstan. The woman then proceeded to put her hand on the last man's shoulder and say something which made him laugh, although I couldn't hear anything.

Athelstan laughed again and said, "Just another simple charm, really," and handed the parchment to me. "These are the four founding members of the Lily. Obviously, you know me," and he pointed to his younger self. "The others were Venecous…" he pointed to the man who blinked. He was wearing long navy-blue robes and a pointed hat. "He was a wizard like you have never met. Then there was Sylvain…" he showed me the man who had laughed. When the figure turned his head, I could see that he had tall pointed ears, "a fighter that no one could rival. Finally, there was Rose, a great sorceress." I looked at the woman and realized she looked familiar.

"Wait, Rose was one of the original Lily members?" I cried out.

Now it was Athelstan's turn to look surprised. He seemed at a loss for words. "Have you met her?" was all he could say.

"Yes. She was the one who recruited me to the Lily, and she was our contact for this last assignment." I looked up at him, and I could see a mixture of surprise and pride on his face.

"She must find you and your team very important. Very rarely would one of us risk showing our faces or revealing our identity. We preferred to work in more subtle ways." He put the charmed drawing back in the chest while continuing the history lesson. "Anyway, the four of us founded the Lily, and we each selected our chosen champions. I chose those who were skilled in charms and incantations, particularly those with musical talents. Venecous, well, he chose the magicians that preferred more abrupt forms of magic, primarily evocation. Sylvain selected the men and women who were the best fighters that would never run frightened from a battle. Finally, Rose. Well, she chose the people who would use physical violence as a last resort."

I thought about my team and what each of the original Lily members would think of us. I was sure Venecous would take a liking to Finnon and Roscoe. Sylvain would surely also like Roscoe. Bonneville would likely gain the favor of

Rose and Sylvain. I didn't quite know where Kriv would fall in.

"So, are you still active in the Lily?" I asked Athelstan.

Once again, he laughed and said, "Oh, no, no, no. To be honest, I didn't know that the Lily was still active. Only a few years after the Lily formed, Sylvain left suddenly. I don't quite know all the details, but we all slowly went our separate ways after that. It wasn't long after that when I met Bonnie, but we, sadly, slowly drifted apart. Then I met Malia's mother, and several years after that, I met you. And—well—you know the rest." He started to close up the box when he looked at something at the bottom. He smiled slowly and pulled it out. He looked at me and smiled.

"As you know, each member of the Lily must have their emblem. Well, in the beginning, each member received a pin that matched their skills, and this… was mine." He opened his palm, and I saw in it a lily brooch, much like mine, however, music notes seemed to be frozen in a dance around the stem and leaves of it. "Now that you have followed in my footsteps, I want you to have this." He reached up and pinned the brooch onto my vest, and I smiled as he did.

"Thank you, Athelstan." I paused for a moment and said quietly, "I'm sorry that I never came back. You quite literally saved my life, and I couldn't even find the time to visit you."

He chuckled, "Don't you even think about that. You were busy with such a grand and adventurous life. But now, onto more personal matters." He rifled through a pile on the desk and pulled out of it a large grommet. He held it up to me, saying, "Do you think Bonneville will like this?"

"Oh, uh, well, as a ring?" I asked. When he nodded, I didn't know what to say. It wasn't much for a wedding ring. Although I didn't see Bonneville as one to wear jewelry, I still thought she would be insulted by this. "It's, um, well… round," I answered with a grimace.

He smiled and said, "Ha! As if I actually thought this was a wedding ring." He now waved his other hand in front of the grommet, and when it passed, there was now a beautiful silver band with a sizeable glittering opal on top. "Even I can crack a joke once in a while."

I couldn't help but laugh and say, "She'll love it."

"Well, then we have a wedding to get to."

CHAPTER THIRTY-THREE

The Wedding

That night, we had a small, intimate wedding in Athelstan's orchard. I had found a white tunic, a pair of black trousers, and black boots left in my wardrobe so that I didn't have to wear the dirty clothes I had taken from Zedgrar and were ruined from my adventure. The trousers and sleeves were slightly too short. However—with another of Athelstan's charms—they magically grew to the perfect length. Athelstan was wearing a black tunic and vest, along with black trousers.

Malia was wearing a long green silk dress that I remember from when we were younger. Bonneville was wearing another of Malia's dresses that I believe her mother had given her. It was a long gold one that was embroidered with flowers. It was strange seeing Bonneville in a dress, but somehow, it didn't seem wrong. On her hand was the ring I had watched Athelstan make, and as I had guessed, it seemed perfectly at home on her hand.

She and Malia both had their hair pulled up, and they had woven some of the bouquet I got Malia into their braids. They had split the rest of the flowers into two bundles, and they were each holding one. Athelstan had taken a rose, and I took an orchid and pinned them to our lapels.

An old string from one of Athelstan's spare instruments was woven into two simple silver rings with one of his spells. One band for himself and the other for me as our wedding bands. He said it could be temporary, but it seemed right, so I decided I would keep it, and he made the same decision.

Malia and I were looking into one another's eyes, and on the other side of Roscoe, Bonneville and Athelstan were facing each other. In a few chairs in the field were Zook,

Finnon, and Kriv. It was nearly twilight, and the trees behind them were only visible as a silhouette against the pink sky.

"Let us begin," Roscoe said. He went through the wedding monologue, but I was lost in Malia's beautiful eyes, and barely heard him.

Finally, I was brought back to reality when Roscoe said, "Do you, Athelstan Mylls, take…" he snickered, "*Bonnie* Arroway to be your wife?"

"Yes," he replied in a gruff voice.

"Do you," another snicker, "Bonnie Arroway, take Athelstan Mylls to be your husband?"

"Yes," she answered with a giggle.

"Clef Cantatio, do you take Malia Mylls as your wife."

"Of course, I do," this was the moment I had been waiting for since I had met Malia.

"Malia Mylls, do you ta—"

"With all my heart," Malia said through tears of joy.

"Then," Roscoe finished. "I pronounce you husband and wife," he looked at Bonneville and Athelstan. "And husband and wife," he said, looking at Malia and me.

He paused for a moment dramatically and then cried out, "Now, kiss already!" And we did.

CHAPTER THIRTY-FOUR

The First Dance

After the wedding, we had a vivacious party in the field. The chairs had been moved aside. Malia and I, along with Bonneville and Athelstan, were having our first dance. Athelstan had performed another charm, this time on the instruments. My two lutes, his lyre, and a harp were floating in the air, playing themselves.

"I have been waiting for this day since I met you, Malia."

"I remember that day," she replied with a smirk, "I thought you didn't like me. You didn't say a word to me for weeks."

"It was because you were so beautiful that I couldn't even remember how to speak when I was around you," I replied, realizing I still often felt that way around her.

She laughed and said, "Well, you are not bad-looking yourself."

"Malia," I said, "I love you."

"I love you too, Clef," she replied and laid her head down on my shoulder.

I will say I am more of a musician than a dancer, so I am not light on my feet. I felt that when I was supposed to lead right, I went left instead, and I was constantly trying not to step on Malia's toes. Fortunately, after a few painful moments and several nearly crushed toes, Malia took the lead, and I found it much more manageable.

We danced slowly for a few more beautiful moments when Athelstan came over and tapped on my shoulder.

"May I?" he asked, and he promptly whisked Malia away, and they began to dance. I couldn't hear what they were saying, but I saw Malia reach up and wipe a tear off her cheek as she smiled. I was about to walk to a chair and sit when a hand grabbed my wrist and pulled me back to the dance floor. I turned and saw it was Bonneville.

We began to dance, and I was grateful she immediately began to lead. She had clearly seen Malia and me dancing.

"So, *Bonnie*? Huh." I said with a smirk.

"Yeah…" she said, embarrassed, "Athelstan's the only person who calls me that."

"It seems to work for you," I replied.

She smiled and reached up to tuck a loose piece of hair behind her ear. "So, I guess I'm your mother now, aren't I?"

"Well, you've already done better than the one that abandoned me," I said with a sad laugh. "Now, what should I call you?"

"Well, mom doesn't exactly sound right, and mother sounds too formal. Let's just stick with Bonneville for now if that's alright with you," she said.

"Bonneville sounds great… Bonnie." I answered with a laugh. She punched me on the shoulder and smiled, giving off another infectious laugh. "So now that you're married, are you going to leave the Lily?" I hoped that the answer would be no. It wouldn't be the same working without her.

"Oh, definitely not. I told Athelstan all about it. Did you know he was one of the founding members?" she asked. From her tone of voice, I could tell that she was just as surprised as I had been to find out.

"Not until today, he just told me," I replied.

"Shocking, right? When we met, he told me he used to be a sort of adventurer, but I never imagined him a fighter like that. Anyway, he said as long as being in the Lily was what I wanted to do, he would support that. And there is no *way* I would give up fighting for a living."

"That's good," I replied. "It wouldn't be the same without you."

She smiled and said, "I *will* have to stop working with that family back home. Well, I should say my *old* home. It feels strange changing plans so suddenly. But that's fine. That job was supposed to be temporary, and this is much better." She looked over her shoulder at Athelstan and grinned. He didn't see her, though. He was still talking with my wife.

Bonneville looked back at me, and we kept dancing. I was starting to get the hang of it and even managed to take back the lead by the end. Eventually, the song ended, and we all headed back to the chairs before a loud and energizing tune started to play.

As the song started, Kriv, Zook, Roscoe, and Finnon walked out to dance. Kriv and Zook began some sort of archaic-looking jig that I doubt I would ever be able to perform. Roscoe and Finnon were dancing together, though not in the way you would imagine. It seemed almost like a fight dance. I saw several times Finnon kicked Roscoe, and a few other times Roscoe hit Finnon. So, in addition to not playing card games with them, I also need to remember not to dance with them.

The strange archaic dancing and the fight dancing lasted for the rest of the song, and then it slowed down.

Roscoe came our way and led Bon-Bon away to begin dancing with her. To everyone's surprise, Roscoe led her in a serene waltz. Well, mostly. Given that he only came to Bonneville's waist, it was hard for her to dance with him, but she tried her best.

Zook led Malia over to the dance floor, and I could just barely overhear them talking about their newfound freedom and what Zook planned to do now. Athelstan and I walked over to the floating instruments and seamlessly grabbed them, continuing the song from where it was. Whenever we changed melodies, the other instruments followed along with us.

We continued the celebration for many more hours until the sun just barely began to rise above the misty horizon. At this point, we decided it would be best for Malia and me to spend a few days at Athelstan and Bonneville's house before heading back to the *Brazen Unicorn*. It was a perfect break from such a chaotic last few days. I was able to just spend time with family and have no other worries.

Andante was happy to be able to roam free in the large orchard and graze on all the apples he could eat. Kriv enjoyed speaking in a guttural language with the mounted dragon head, and Zook tried to keep his distance from Kriv.

Roscoe spent most of his time reading over the priest's journal, with Finnon reading carefully over his shoulder.

After a day or two, Zook, Kriv, Roscoe, and Finnon all went their separate ways, and when they did, their rooms magically disappeared from the hallway. Now there were only three rooms: one led to Bonneville and Athelstan's, one led to the study chamber, and the final one was Malia's and mine. The house seemed to know about the weddings, as

Athelstan's room had grown, and the wall between Malia's old room and mine had disappeared that same day, and the two small rooms had become one large one.

Eventually, we did have to leave for the *Brazen Unicorn.* Athelstan and Bonneville tried to convince us to stay with them, but I knew I needed to help Brand. I just had to hope Brand had kept the tavern open while I was gone.

EPILOGUE

It has been nearly a year since the wedding, and I am glad to report that there have not been any missions from the Lily. Malia and I are living at the *Brazen Unicorn* now. Brand had just barely managed to keep it operational. I still have my job as a performer. Malia has been helping Tillie with serving and cleaning, though she refused to allow Brand to pay her. Tillie started looking up to Malia as a sort of maternal figure, and Malia was happy to fill that role.

Brand was no longer having financial troubles due to a donation from an anonymous donor.

A few nights after Malia and I came back from Athelstan's, Brand found that the till box had over a thousand gold coins in it. When he asked if I knew where they came from, I told him I had no idea. From his smirk and nod of his head, I knew he saw through my lie, but he didn't press. Magically, a few days after that, my old lumpy bed had been replaced with a larger soft-down one. However, the most precious addition to the room was Malia's crystal flower, which lived in a pot in the window. It made me grin when I looked at it and saw images from our wedding—our first kiss as a married couple, our first dance, her in that beautiful gown.

The women of the tavern seemed disappointed to learn that I was now married, but it only *slightly* discouraged their blatant flirting.

Bonneville and Athelstan now lived nearby, less than a ten-minute walk. After the wedding, they insisted on living close to their son and daughter. Malia and I could not have been more pleased. I don't know how Athelstan managed to do it, but the entire cottage, orchard, rose-lined path, all of it, was transplanted outside of town. I didn't ask any questions, and I certainly didn't mind. Andante was also clearly glad to be able to continue roaming the orchard. The other people living in Evenglade were surprised at the sudden addition, but quickly forgot about the cottage's seemingly magic appearance.

Kriv hasn't been heard from in a while by anyone, and I don't know if that is a good or a bad thing. He never explained why he didn't use his wings or fire more often, but Kriv is the type of person that you still don't get answers even when you ask questions. And being honest, I was too scared to ask the questions. I still didn't know what else he could do. Maybe he could turn into a full-fledged dragon.

Zook is now leading an army of soldiers against the few remaining Ascabolates, and with his spear skills, I have no doubt he will succeed.

I have spoken to Roscoe a few times, and it turns out that we really were, in fact, in the Fortress of Elpis. That priest's journal Bonneville found confirmed everything. From his discovery, he was now a very respected name in both the religious and historic communities. I don't know if he was looking for fame and fortune, but that was assuredly what he found.

Finnon has resumed his duties as a professor. He received several promotions and is now honored as a traveling lecturer to schools around the kingdom. While he wasn't the one to discover the Fortress of Elpis, he has been able to ride Roscoe's coattails, being his half-brother and all.

I hadn't heard anything from Wren or his father, and I hoped he had finally given up on joining the Lily. Unfortunately, I soon found out that my assumptions were wrong.

It was the end of the day now, and I had just finished performing. Malia and Tillie were wiping down the tables, and Brand was counting the gold from the day. All the patrons had already left, though there was a man passed out drunk just outside the tavern stoop.

Despite the closed sign, the tavern door flew open with a resounding thud. Malia, Tillie, Brand, and I each turned to look. Standing in the opening was a defiant-looking Wren. He looked older and healthier, but there was no doubt it was him.

He was several inches taller, his forehead being at my chin. His bony body had now filled out to where I could see muscles under his shirt and vest. His dark hair was cut short, and his brown eyes glowed with pride.

Around his waist was a thick leather belt, and hanging from it were eight shining daggers, each different from the one beside it. I saw that it even included the one I had given him.

"I told you I would keep my promise, and I have." He was staring directly at me, smiling, when he said this. He lifted his left hand and pointed at his chest. I looked down, and my eyes locked on the lapel of his vest. A white silk lily was pinned there.

"Come on," he said without waiting for a response, and he walked to one of the tables. Unrolling a large parchment, he started reading out loud. It seemed we had work to do…

The End of Book One

The Bard's Ballad

Keep an eye out for the second book

The Royal's Requiem

King Richard and Queen Rowena's lives are on the line,

and it seems the only way to ensure their future… is to visit

Bonneville's past.

ACKNOWLEDGMENTS

There are so many people that I want to thank, but that would be a whole other book. However, I can thank some of them.

First off, to God, for giving me the abilities and talents to do this.

Now, I want to thank my mom. Truly, you have inspired me more than you could know. You have always helped me strive to be the best that I can be. You are the reason that I try so hard in life, and I couldn't be more thankful. I love you, and you are my guidepost to everything.

Next, I want to thank Ed. There is no step in your dad. Since the day that you saved me from the golf course troll, I have wanted to be as strong and brave as you.

My Auntie Candy, for encouraging me to work harder and move forward in my education. You are a role model for me, and I love you for that.

Uncle Justin for always being there to help with math and video games.

To little Emery, who showed me that miracles can happen.

To my Grandma, for always encouraging and supporting me in any endeavor I could dream of.

To Gunpa and Grannie Pixie for giving me the Mad Money to make this book possible.

To Dad and Lindsey, thank you for all the movie nights, and Treat Yo' Self days.

To all of my honorary aunts: Aunt Katie Hull, Aunt Katie Broadwell, and A.A. Moe LeCompte. You have all brought so much laughter and magic to my life, and I love you all for it.

To my honorary uncle, Uncle Jeeves Hatcher. For encouraging me and helping me walk in faith.

To Mr. Layman, I mean… Mr. James… I mean James… I love you, man. Thanks for all the support.

To Melinda Haugh, Lisa Wallace, and Antoniette Saunders. For always seeing the magic in me and telling me that I can do so much.

To Gloria Williamson, for covering our family in prayer.

To Curtis Anderson, thanks for always reminding me, "Don't screw it up."

To René Anderson, for always being such a kind and encouraging person and for being the best professional aunt.

To Aaron Anzalone, for always knowing the most insightful and meaningful thing to say.

To Georgia Lloyd, for being someone to talk to even in the wildest of times.

To Dr. Judy Belk, thank you for always being on my team.

To Dylan Jordan, my Bro-Bro, my brother. There's no one else I'd want to sneak out of camp with.

To Shaun T, for helping me to be the best version of myself that I can be and live.

To Josh Gawel, for keeping music alive in my life.

I would also like to thank Matt "Weasley" Troxell for allowing me to join him on his amusing campaign and inspiring my imagination.

A big thanks to Grant McBride and Jamison Dobbs for game nights and inspiration at the clubhouse.

All my teachers who have encouraged me and told me I could do great things: Mrs. Maria Doyle, Mrs. Jennifer Batts, Mrs. Susie Christensen, Mr. Seth Parsloe, Mr. Jon Escott, Mr. Tyler Robbins, Mrs. Eugenie Farrow, Mrs. Camille Nielsen, and Ms. Arlana Nielsen. I would not be where I am in school if not for you.

To Cali Ramos, you are my favorite heathen in all the land. Thank you for putting up with all my jokes and random moments of singing.

To Maddie Ballard, forever the Megan to my Chad, and the Lucille to my Ray-Bud. Thank you for being there.

To the All Saints Squad: Ainsley Albano, Ajanna Dizon, Amy Bosch, Annika Hennington, Clara Carpenter, Connor Reagan, and Isabella Amador-Navarrete. For sticking with me all these years.

To all my other friends through the years: Maddy, Morgan, and the whole Diaz family, Ryan Lint, Katie Hunton, Alexis Garcia, Noah Vavra, the Beers, the Kirkseys, Richard and Mary Jo Woods, and the Elses.

To my dogs and cats for keeping my feet warm on cold nights.

Everyone else that I haven't mentioned by name. I am so appreciative for all that you have done.

To all the authors out there that have made me into the reader I am today. J.K. Rowling, for showing me the world of wizardry. Fellow Eagle Scout Ridley Pearson, for showing me my favorite park after hours and the certificate of congratulations when I became an Eagle Scout as well. Dave Berry, for making me rethink fairytales. And all the other authors that have inspired me.

Finally, to Walt Disney, for creating a world of true magic that helped me to become the creative and cheerful person I am today. You are now, and will always be, my role model.

C.T. CAREY loves all things literature, and can most days be found with his nose stuck in a book. He obtained dual bachelor's degrees in Business Administration and Anthropology and is currently a graduate student of Classical Studies. C.T.'s debut novel, *The Bard's Ballad* was released in 2021, followed by *Model Number Unknown*, a dystopian murder mystery. He is also the author of the children's series, *A Jack B. Nymble Mystery*, which introduces the mystery genre to young readers through the use of familiar and beloved fairytale characters. He lives in the Pacific Northwest with his family.